ALSO BY JONELLEN HECKLER

Safekeeping
A Fragile Peace

WHITE LIES

JONELLEN HECKLER

G. P. PUTNAM'S SONS

NEW YORK

G. P. Putnam's Sons
Publishers Since 1838
200 Madison Avenue
New York, NY 10016

Copyright © 1989 by Jonellen Heckler
Published simultaneously in Canada

Grateful acknowledgment is made to Dr. Mary Catherine Bateson for permission
to use the quote from Margaret Mead.

The quote from Dr. Martin Luther King is copyright © by Martin Luther
King, Jr., and the Estate of Martin Luther King, Jr. Used by permission
of Joan Daves.

The poem "Treasures, Treasures" is by Steven L. Heckler

Library of Congress Cataloging in Publication Data

Heckler, Jonellen.
White lies / by Jonellen Heckler. — 1st American ed.
p.   cm.
I. Title.
PS3558.E315W4   1989
813'.54—dc20   89-3890 CIP
ISBN 0-399-13472-7

Book Design and Composition by The Sarabande Press

Printed in the United States of America
1   2   3   4   5   6   7   8   9   10

For
Lou Heckler
my husband, my friend

No matter how many communes anybody invents,
the family always creeps back.
—Margaret Mead

WHITE LIES

Richard and Diana Morrow
announce with pleasure
the birth of their daughter
Sterling Beth
June 30, 1941
at 6:32 p.m.
Weight 7 lbs 2 oz
Length 19 1/2"
Allegheny General Hospital
Pittsburgh, Pennsylvania

Richard and Diana Morrow
announce with pleasure
the birth of their daughter
Rosalind Lowry
August 6, 1943
at 5:51 a.m.
Weight 6 lbs 5 oz
Length 18"
Allegheny General Hospital
Pittsburgh, Pennsylvania

Richard and Diana Morrow
announce with pleasure
the birth of their daughter
Quinn Suzanne
September 24, 1945
at 12:11 p.m.
Weight 8 lbs 8 oz
Length 20"
Allegheny General Hospital
Pittsburgh, Pennsylvania

1 9 6 3

Rosalind

Dr. and Mrs. Richard Grey Morrow
request the honour of your presence
at the marriage of their daughter
Sterling Beth
to
Dr. Randolph Carter Hamilton III
on Saturday, the twenty-fifth of May
nineteen hundred and sixty-three
at half after six o'clock
Heinz Chapel
Pittsburgh, Pennsylvania

Dinner reception
immediately following
the ceremony
Webster Hall
Fifth Avenue

May 10, 1963

Roz—

I wish you were here. Mom's in a twit about the wedding. She doesn't like Randy much and thinks Sterling's gown is way overblown. It's got pounds of lace and beads and ribbons on it. The ones we're supposed to wear have mantilla headpieces—combs & all. Ouch. I just lay low & say nothing. Can't you get here sooner than the 24th?

Love,
Quinn

P. S. Hope your finals aren't too hard.

❑

May 10, 1963

Dear Rozzy,

Things are going beautifully! Everyone exclaims over my gown. It is magnificent and cost a fortune, but then you only get married once. It's frost white with a scoop neckline and poof sleeves caught by satin bows. The headpiece is a pearl tiara in a cloud of imported Spanish lace. The dress is the same lace, gathered in tiers and decorated with bows and pearl clusters. I'll carry three dozen white roses in a jeweled basket.

To tell you the truth, I look like Cinderella at the Ball. That's why I went for it, I guess. I've always loved that story. Wow.

The seven attendants will be in floor-length lace, too, with mantilla head-pieces. Each dress is a different pastel. You, as maid of honor, will wear pale creme. Then: pale yellow, pale pink, pale blue, pale green, pale lavender and pale purple. Quinn's got the yellow. Each girl will hold one white long-stemmed rose. The ring bearer and flower girl will be in frost white. Wait til you see the outfits. You'll flip.

Randy's here a lot of the time and just fits with this family. Mother and Dad treat him like a son. He mows the lawn and everything.

I'm enclosing a piece of your dress fabric so you can have satin shoes dyed to match.

Love and XXX
Sterling

❑

May 10, 1963

Dearest Rosalind,

We are counting the days until you'll be home. Good luck, dear, on all your exams.

Plans for the wedding are progressing well but . . . Please keep this confidential: I don't think Sterling really loves Randy. I know this is an odd thing to say, but mothers know. Sterling thinks it's time to get married. All her friends are doing it. One can only stand so many kitchen showers. Randy's a nice man but dull. Forgive me for being so frank. I guess the reason I'm sharing this with you is in the hope that you can talk some reason into Sterling. You girls have always been so close.

Could you, perhaps, call Sterling? She shouldn't be doing this — it's too hard to untie a marriage knot. She has lots of time but she thinks if she waits any longer she'll be an old maid.

Dad and I send our deep love.

Mother

❏

STUDENT HEALTH SERVICE
UNIVERSITY OF MARYLAND
COLLEGE PARK, MARYLAND 20742

Rosalind L. Morrow   5/14/63
1107 Castle Drive
Sewickley, PA 15143
Valium 5mg   XXX
Sig: I tid

L. J. Pounds M.D.

NR   DEA #AP6432108

❏

5/15

Gosh, Rozzy, what did you say to Sterling? She cried and cried. I can't stand it
here right now and you're not helping any! I'm having finals, too! You're not the
only one! Senior year of high school is <u>hard.</u> Can't you fix whatever you upset?
Try!

Q.

❑

May 15, 1963

Dear Rozzy,

It is so shocking that you could know my innermost heart. I have been crying
since your phone call. You always knew me best. What can I do with the
wedding ten days away? Randy's a good man and I can learn to love him. It's
just time to make babies, that's all.

I know you won't really understand this til you're my age and see all your
senior class girlfriends screaming with joy because of those big diamond
engagement rings. You feel so unwanted and left out if you don't have someone
to love you. The biological clock is ticking and all the great men are being
sucked up by the system. They're <u>all</u> getting married. For life! God. You can't
picture these fraternity parties at Pitt, everybody sizing everybody else up.
Jump! Don't be a leftover! Don't <u>get</u> a leftover! How did you ever stay out of the
Greek system? You're the supreme independent. I envy you.

At least I found Randy at the dental fraternity. He's got a future other than in
insurance or a steel mill. It was awful at those parties—creepy guys coming at
you because they're the only ones loose. The good ones are always, <u>always</u>
taken. Don't you see? Randy had just broken up with a nursing student. I
grabbed, believe me!

It was glorious at the sorority house after I got Randy's pin. You keep it a
secret and hide it on the top of your slip, under your blouse, at the next sorority
meeting. There's this ceremony where all the lights are out and they pass a
candle around. It goes around once for pinning, twice for engagement and
three times for marriage. You blow it out according to what your news is. I blew
it out and the girls just yelled, and tore my blouse open to see that gold and opal
dent pin. They were dying. I have never been so happy as I was that night.

Listen, there's another thing: I don't want to teach. I think I made a big

22

mistake on that. The guidance counselor sort of talked me into it because there's a teacher shortage and I'd always be able to get a job. Elementary Ed was the rage: Kiddie Lit, clarinet, etc. It was fun. But I don't want to teach! I don't know what else to do.

Randy comes from a nice family. He'll take care of me. Don't worry. All the marriages in a lot of cultures are arranged and they work out better in the long run.

Tear this up.

Sterling

❏

May 20, 1963

Dear Sterling,

I am begging you not to do this. Life doesn't end with graduation. You won't be a leftover!

Since you told me your feelings (as usual), I'm telling you mine (as usual): STOP.

STOP! STOP! STOP!

XO
Ros

❏

5/25/63

Annie—

She did it. I'm writing this to you late at night after the wedding. I am sad clear through.

It was weird—it was a Dress marrying an Occupation. Her face was so little in all that white stuff—she has that straw blond hair and creamy skin and grey-blue eyes. Very delicate. Anything can outshadow her. The face seemed like just another ornament on the dress, like the dress was gliding down the aisle by itself.

I think halfway into the ceremony, she got scared and realized what she was doing. During the vows, she would open her mouth and no sound would come out. It was a dreary night, rain blowing every which way, roaring at the stained glass windows. Uncanny: when she couldn't speak, thunder would pound at the church like the voice of God saying, "You've got this man at the altar, don't make a fool of him." So then she would whisper, "I will" or "I do" in a frightened way.

Randy seemed to notice nothing but Sterling. I kept thinking of how deeply hurt he'd be if he realized why she said yes. (Imagine, a lifetime of reaching into another person's mouth and drilling and watching them spit. Yikes. And the only reason he's doing it is for Her.)

I miss college and you and, most of all, seeing Glenn on some weekends. He's in an Army training exercise for six weeks. Under wraps. Wonder what that's all about. My problem's the opposite of Sterling's. I want the man but not his occupation.

Mother and Dad are great but I don't belong here anymore. And it's all breaking up anyway with Sterling going and Quinn about to enter Merrill University.

I didn't mean to get so negative and melancholy. Write me a letter. How's summer school? Details, please.

Love,
Ros

❑

July 9, 1963
Dear Rosalind,
I've landed in Oz. Everything in Charlotte, North Carolina, is just too cute. At first I was busy unpacking boxes and didn't notice anything but the Southern accents. Then I wormed my way out into the sunlight and this is a different world. Two-story Colonial brick houses with Priscilla curtains on all the windows. It's eerie. I don't think I've seen a single window without tie-backs.

I should have known when I went into my in-laws' house for the first time (they live about 2 mi. away). I almost cuted to death. Herb bags covered in calico and hanging from the ceiling in the kitchen, teeny print flowers on the wallpaper, a hearth broom tied round with silk flowers, cross-stitch pieces on walls and pillows and even the toilet seat! Oh, yes, and one of those miniature ladies' hats to cover the extra roll of paper on the commode tank. Etcetera!

Randy's settled into dent practice with his dad and I have too much time alone. He doesn't know it, but Fridays at noon I go to a reader on the West Side.

She's a Negro and wears robes like a preacher. Other women are there to hear her, too. We sit on the front porch and her husband passes a hat. In it, you put $2 and 2 questions all folded up. Then, you write your initials on the outside of the questions. She comes out and holds our folded notes one at a time to her forehead and reads for us. I don't see how she can guess the questions because her husband gives her the hat at the very last minute and I've been looking straight at him the whole time. So she's a real one. I always ask about a baby but she says the time isn't right.

How are you doing?

Love,
Sterling

❏

August 3, 1963

Hi, Roz—

Glad you're having a good summer at home, resting and reading. Can't believe you're half done with college already.

In answer to your questions: listen, I can't work. Randy doesn't want me to. I don't really mind because it's easier to conceive a baby if you're not too active. And, yes, I guess there are some clubs around to belong to. You sound as though you think the loneliness is my fault. Everyone else was here first—I'm the outsider. A Yankee. Sometimes I don't even know what I'm looking at in a grocery store or cafeteria line. They've got stuff like okra and kale and turnip greens. (I've tried that last one and it's bitter.) They don't have grammar. They say things like, "I might could show you around the city" and "I Swanee," which means "I swear." One lady said to Randy and me "Y'all favah" which, I found out later, means that Randy and I look alike!

Every month I have dreams about the baby and every month I'm so disappointed. Maybe I should go to a fertility doctor. But Randy gets up-tight when I spend. It's hard to get a practice going, even if he is with his dad.

What day do you go back to school? Is it Southern like this in Maryland? Hi to Quinn and M & D. When does Quinn leave?

You Know Who

❏

16 August 1963

Sweet Ros — Would you believe I'm not allowed to say where I am? The censors will snip it out if I do. Please forgive me for not telling you I was going. I didn't even know it until 24 hours before we left and I was barred from contacting anyone. That's what I get for being a West Point grad, I guess. Hope this assignment will be short. I adore you and treasure every little memory of you. Mornings when I wake up I believe that when I open my eyes I'll be looking at you. So far, it hasn't happened! More bad news: you can't write to me. As soon as you can, I'll send you the address. Reading back over this letter, I see how impersonal it is but I'm not used to having my mail scanned. I am thinking all kinds of personal things, though, and you know what they are.

Love always,
Glenn

❏

21 August 1963

Ros, At least we had that special time together right before I left. That's what's keeping me glued. This place is the pits. I would describe it but I can't. CENSORED. Could be that any day I won't be able to write — we'll be on the move.

The memory I keep playing is seeing you the first time — under the boardwalk. Hot, hot and I was watching that dirty, wiggly couple play guitars. Quite a crowd. BAM, the guy in front of us falls straight back like a tree, dead faint, eyes open, then gets back up and watches again. You gave that big snorting laugh. It's the snort that did it: love at first snort. You are beautiful.

Still can't write to me but stay by me, will you? I need you.

Love and lust,
Glenn

❏

9/5/63

Dear Roz,

I am making Mom a cross-stitch pillow for Christmas. It says, "Wishing you butterfly mornings and wildflower afternoons." It is so pretty with the black-eyed Susans and butterfly. I saw it in the Cross-Stitch Cabin. I bought a couple of books with patterns and some fabric, floss, hoop, etc. Also, am learning needlepoint at the same time from Sue Hensley, my neighbor across the street. She has her own work throughout her house and it is amazing. And I'm borrowing her book of patterns for Christmas ornaments. I can make them as gifts. One says, "The warmth of Christmas is friendship." I can work pretty fast. I start in the morning, after Randy leaves. Next time I look at the clock, it's nearly suppertime!

Still no baby. It's been three months plus. Maybe one of us is infertile. The reader (Mrs. Shevach) insists it's not time yet. It's almost like she's standing in the way of it. I have read everything on fertility and am doing it all. Randy isn't concerned and it infuriates me.

How is school this year? What's happening? Thanks for your letters. I live for them.

Hugs from Sterling

❏

9 September 1963

Darling Ros, You can write to me at the FPO San Francisco address on the envelope. We did move but it's still a secret. I feel like I don't exist. If a tree falls in the forest (or under a boardwalk) when there's no one around to hear, does it make a sound? If a man lives among strangers where no one he loves can reach him, is he still a person?

I know. Self pity stinks.

It's a sunny day, very warm, humid. That's all the hints you get. I brushed my teeth this morning with canteen water. Get out your map and see if you can guess.

Ros, I love you endlessly. If this letter sounds like game playing it's because I haven't slept in a couple of nights. Hurry and write to me. I can't think of anything else to say.

Glenn

❏

Sept. 17, 1963

Dear Glenn,

I am so frightened to tell you this. I am pregnant. What can we possibly <u>do?</u>

Nobody knows but Annie. I am scared about what's going to happen with you so far away and we can't get married. I am afraid of your answer. Please don't tell me to get an abortion. Please, could you come home? Somehow! I love our baby and I love you. I miss you every second of my life. I hope you are in a safe place and well.

Ros

❑

9-18-63

Hi, Ros!

Haven't heard from you in a while but I know how busy college can be. So I'll keep you company by letter — OK? Wish you could come to Charlotte and visit Randy and me.

You were right in telling me to take charge of my life — that we control our own destinies. I have stopped going to the reader. All she ever did was tell me the time wasn't right! With her out of the way, I just know I can conceive. I think what happened is that I believed her, you see? It put a mental block on me.

Last night I had this dream that I was walking outside and lots of babies were hanging by their umbilical cords from a tree — like fruit! I just had to shake it to get one. But I was afraid all of them would fall at once and I couldn't catch them and they'd get hurt.

Yes, I'm obsessed!

Write and tell me how your classes are, especially Visions of Women in Lit. That sounded interesting. Are you sure you want to major in English? Don't look now but that might be unsalable in the job market.

X's from
      Sterling

❑

23 September 1963

Ros, Take good care of our baby. I want both of you. I'm trying like everything to get compassionate leave so we can marry. Our CO has already put in for it

but our location is the problem. I'll call and let you know when I'll be arriving.
You are precious to me.   Glenn

❑

October 4, 1963

Oh, Goodie Roz!!! I have skipped a period!!! This could be the magic moment.
Get out your knitting needles. Do you want a niece or a nephew?

Somebody told me to take my temperature every morning before I got out of
bed. Your temp rises at the middle of your cycle, after you ovulate. After a few
months of keeping a chart, you can pretty well figure out when you're fertile. I
had Randy coming home for lunch on the right days! It was hilarious—such
orchestration. Disrupted his schedule and he's so compulsively organized. I
think he's glad it's all over!

I bought an antique crib at a flea market last Saturday. Randy had a fit
because it was filthy, but it cleaned up to reveal beautiful cherry wood and I am
having it professionally refinished. I am looking at wallpaper with fabric to
match for the nursery. The one I like has colored hearts on a white background. This doctor is making me wait until I skip two! periods before he tests
me. I had no idea it was such a long time. Doesn't make sense. Wouldn't it be
neat if there were a test you could do yourself?

How are you? Your letters are nonexistent. I have called the dorm a few
times. Did you get the messages? It's okay. Junior year is rough.

Love,
    Sterling—soon to be "Mom"

❑

October 5, 1963
Dear Rosalind,

I am writing because I know that you are a special friend of my son Glenn. It
pains me to tell you that he was killed by enemy fire in Southeast Asia on the
25th of September. This is all I know. I don't even know why.

We are having a small memorial service for him at our church in Arlington,
Vermont, on November 2nd. The Army assures me his body will arrive by then

for burial. If you will come, please let me know and I will send you directions. We would welcome you to stay in our home.

Yours,

Ethel Brawley

❑

God, that's awful, Roz. I can't stand it. Your angel Glenn. What is life anyway? How could this happen? I feel shocked and cheated, heartsick like you do. I cry for you, my friend.   Annie

❑

October 10, 1963

Oh, Sweetheart—I am so sad about your Glenn! Won't you please come home so that we can comfort you? What a fine person he was—Dad and I admired him very much and grieve for you and for his family.

What can we do to help you? Would you like us to drive to school and take you away to the shore for the weekend? Just tell us your needs. We are here for you.   Mother

❑

October 10, 1963

Dear Rosalind,

I wanted to write you a separate note. This is just between us. I know there will be some extra expenses at this time. Here's a few dollars to help—how you use it is your business. Your mother doesn't know about this. Tell me what else you need and I'll get it for you.

Loving you,

Dad

❑

Roz,

Look, if you want this, I don't think you should wait any longer. It's too dangerous. All you have to do is get to Miami. I talked to my brother. Believe me, he's a well-respected gyn—he wouldn't hurt you. Shall I go with you? I will!

Annie

❑

October 20, 1963

Rosalind Dear—

I guess your roommate told you Dad and I were there on Friday afternoon. She said you had gone away with Annie for the weekend. We had it in mind to do the same thing. Dad made reservations at the coast for the three of us. We should have let you know we were coming but we wanted to whisk you away!

I hope you are okay, Honey. Could you give us a quick call so we don't worry?

All my love,
Mother

❑

October 28, 1963

Dearest Sterling,

Rosalind has been so reserved since Glenn died. I don't hear from her much, do you? Does she call you? I dread to think of the funeral this Saturday. Please, will you give her a lot of attention? She'll respond to you. You girls have always been close.

Roz wants to attend the funeral by herself. Dad and I will honor that.

Hope your pregnancy is progressing well. Dad and I send love to all three of you.

Mother

❑

Nov. 6

Roz, Why won't you answer my phone calls? I spoke with Mom tonight and she said she had just finished talking with you. Your silence toward me is baffling. Have I done something to offend you? I love you.   Sterling

❑

Nov. 13th

Rozzie—
    Please call me back. You are making me upset. <u>What's going on?</u> Where are you?
                              Sterling

❑

November 17, 1963

Dear Sterling,
    I am here. Just give me some time to get myself together. I don't feel like talking.
    I know you care and I thank you for that.
                              Love,
                              Ros

❑

November 21, 1963

Oh, it was wonderful to hear from you, Roz! I perfectly understand your reluctance to write. Take all the time you need. Meanwhile, I'll be faithful with my letters.
    My little tummy is poking out and I spend hours in the maternity stores looking at (and buying!) clothes. I wouldn't wear them yet—but soon.
    I feel life, like a flutter-flutter-flutter of excitement. It tickles. It's the most special thing in the world.
    A friend of mine, Sarah Greene, has just had natural childbirth with a new system called Lamaze. You don't feel any pain because you have prepared your

body through weeks of exercise and you are concentrating so deeply. Her husband was her coach in the delivery room. I am going to ask my doctor about it.

Randy is fine.

Love to You from Me

❑

God, can you believe it, Roz? We are in the day room watching it on TV. Come on down. There's a prayer service for Kennedy today at 5. We're all going. Who the hell shot him?

Jean

❑

December 3, 1963

Dearest Rosalind,

Dad and I truly sympathize with you, but it doesn't make sense to drop out of college so close to the end! Couldn't you try to slide through with passing grades for now? It's no disgrace to give up being a top student when you've had such a tough blow. But to quit!?

Please consider that the President's assassination has further colored your thinking. We were all devastated by what happened to Glenn and then to witness such a shocking event. Television is so powerful—you feel as though you were actually there. Your future must look bleak, to say the least. Honey, we cannot understand why these things occur, but life is worth living and I know that yours in particular will be a wonderful life because you are a wonderful woman. We see so much strength and talent and beauty in you. Be strong and life will turn around. Believe me. We will never be the same but we will smile again. Hold fast.

We love you.

Mother

❑

20 December 1963

Dear Rosalind:

You said you would be receptive to a letter, so here it is. I just wanted to keep in touch. My brother is still alive for me when I commune with others who loved him.

Boston is sleet and slush this Christmas. I thought I'd see Glenn everywhere but grief is even trickier. No one looks like him. No one.

Can you share your feelings with me? Or have I crossed the invisible line into your privacy?

I am grinding away at my doctorate, waiting for enthusiasm to return. Do we lose it forever in cases like this? It's the first time for me.

Thom

❑

Annie—I can't talk about this, can only write it. This haunts me, the dead baby. I did it. When I try to sleep I see pieces of my baby being pulled off of him: arm fragments, bloody legs, the little heart still beating being torn from him and existing on its own for minutes, maybe beating inside the plastic trash bag or wherever they put it. My baby. My son. Did he feel pain? He had to! I am sick and will never be well. The minute he was gone from me, I knew it. I wanted him to be put back inside me, but it was too late for that. He was all ripped. A human. And I let that happen. I let strangers murder him. Annie, how can I live? Please don't speak about this to me. I can't stand it. Please just help me in whatever way you can think of.

R.

❑

December 30th, 1963

Dear Roz,

I really wish we could have come home at Christmas. I miss you and Quinn and M & D terribly.

The spotting has stopped but the doctor's not likely to let me go anywhere. I think I'm stuck here for the duration.

34

Thank you for the gorgeous baby quilt you sent—it's absolutely exquisite, the best I've ever seen. It's obvious that much love went into selecting it.

XXX's from

Sterling

❑

1 9 6 4

<hr>

Quinn

January 20, 1964

Dear Mom and Dad,

I am amazed that Rozzy quit, and even more amazed that she is living with Glenn's brother in Boston! How did all this come about? She sure looked bad at Christmas time—so quiet and listless. I wish Sterling had been able to get home. That might have helped. What should I do?

Finished semester finals and am enjoying Break. Freshman courses are lackluster. A lot of them are taught by graduate students who basically do it for the money. They'd rather be working on their own degrees. And so many foreign instructors! I can't understand their speech patterns. My Soc. course had lectures on Mondays and Wednesdays by a German prof—unintelligible. I knew the recitation section on Fridays was taught by a grad student and figured I could catch up there, but he turned out to be an East Indian—unintelligible. So, I just read the book and hoped for the best. Can't wait to get into journalism. I'll have News Writing next semester.

Dad, thank you for the Christmas check. You'll be glad to know I have taken my first step into entrepreneuring: I raffled it off, doubling it. Only $1.00 a chance, to win $100! 300+ students bought in. The girl that won it was ecstatic. She had left all her books on the plane at Christmas and never got them back. She was able to get new ones. Guess I helped somebody in the bargain.

Love to both of you,
Quinn

❑

Jan. 23, 1964

Dear Quinn,

How can we convince Roz to come home? She must be under enormous emotional stress. It's so out of character for her to move in with a man—especially a man she'd only met <u>once</u>! Does she write to you? Mom and Dad and I seem to be getting the silent treatment. Well, not silent exactly, but she doesn't respond to our comments on The Key Issue. She's become strange. She should have stayed in college. What can she do without a degree? I feel sorry for her and isolated from her.

I had a fitful night last night but woke up with a fabulous idea. It just appeared in my brain, like a gift. I'm going to take a photograph of the baby every single day! I don't know anyone who's done it but what a perfect record it will be of a child's progress. I'll be able to relive his (or her) growing up years anytime I want to. And it will make a great present for high school graduation.

Congratulations on your 3.8 first semester. Beats my record. I'm proud of you.

> Love and hugs,
> Sterling (feeling fine
> but fat, fat)

❑

1/27/64

Dear Roz,

My God, you must feel that you're in the trenches! I've never seen such fireworks in this family. But I say: stick by your convictions. If you want to stay there with Thom, do it. It's all cultural anyway, this notion that you have to be married to a man before you live with him. He must be a good person or you wouldn't have picked him.

I miss you. Don't cut me out of your will. I'm on your side.

> Love,
> Quinn

❑

Saturday, Feb. 1
Dear Quinn,

You never subscribed to traps and roles. Your letter sounded just like you: open. I am much better. I'm still not working but, with Thom's help, I will be soon. He has been generous to me. I don't need anyone's approval in order to approve of him. I hope that someday soon you'll meet him and see for yourself.

He's big and bearded. Looks like a mountain man. He wears size 13 shoes and lots of seedy flannel shirts. Oh, yes, and suspenders. No kidding. He's got medium coloring and millions of perfect teeth. He laughs a lot, a low laugh that keeps going down and ends up in the basement. Except that he's clean, you'd judge him to be a coal miner: he always appears surprised and curious, like he's emerged from a dark hole into the sunlight. His hair won't comb; it points to various places on the wall. His shirt doesn't tuck. Objects slide onto the floor when he walks by.

We're in a rented furnished bungalow. It's pleasantly battered. The tables, chairs, dishes, rugs, give off auras of previous tenants. It's like being surrounded by friends you've known all your life. He makes the sour piano sound sweet. Classical only. That's Thom. He wants to spend his life making movies and is completing his Ph.D. in film (May). Haven't decided whether I'll go to the West Coast with him. This feels right for now.   ROZ

❏

Journalism 107
News Writing
Dr. Charles Deviney

Assignment #2: Write a news article of less than 500 words concerning an on-campus problem that has not yet been resolved.

Due: February 28, 1964

❏

Quinn Morrow
Journalism 107
Assignment #2
February 28, 1964

PARKING SCAM UNCOVERED

A group of students who printed and sold illegal staff parking stickers are facing suspension from the University. Jed Gibson, Lettie Harmon, Seth Hopkins, Russell Kopf, Thomas Martz, Carla Schwilm and Drew Stevens, all seniors, say they created the scheme when constantly frustrated by the lack of adequate parking on the Lake Forest campus.

"Having a legal student parking sticker meant nothing," said Stevens, who published the illegal stickers last summer in his father's print shop in Cleveland. "We just got tired of fooling with it." The group later sold two dozen stickers to students for $50 each.

Suspicion was aroused when staff and faculty members, whose stickers bear a special red "M" emblem, began having difficulty finding parking spots. Complaints from faculty and staff had been circulating since November. A member of Dr. Charles Deviney's news writing class compiled a list of staff and faculty license numbers and surveyed restricted parking areas for three weeks, finding 28 license plates which did not match the list. Close inspection of the cars revealed discrepancies between their illegal parking stickers and the authorized ones. Findings were turned over to campus police.

❑

Miss Morrow—

An excellent start. Your grade: A —. You have the gift of curiosity essential for a journalist. The minus is for creating part of the news your story rests on. We're only here to observe and report.

C. Dev

❑

March 4, 1964

Dear Quinn,

Thank you for providing us with the scoop on the parking scam. We have had much reaction to your article.

Dr. Deviney has recommended you as a University newspaper staffer. If you have interest in this, please call for an interview.

Yours,
Bob Sherman
Editor

❑

March 9, 1964

Dearest Quinn,

Here is a check so that you can replace your clothes. I can't believe no one in the dorm saw anything. Do you think whoever did it threw your belongings out the window? It is possible, since you're only on the second floor. I can't imagine what you thought when you came in and realized every last item you owned was missing.

Dad and I agree that the incident was probably a result of your uncovering the parking ring. I hope you don't get into that type of story anymore. It seems to us a prank rather than grounds for expulsion from the University. These are just kids, after all. Be careful not to be a crusader in your work. (I can just hear you saying, "Mother!")

Your reaction to the robbery in your room alarmed us. Expecting trouble and wearing defiance like a sign will tempt future incidents. I tell you with all love and concern that I can remember you as a little girl taunting bullies, riding your wagon or scooter or sled faster than anyone else down awesome hills and bringing your wounds home like trophies. It was as though bleeding made you happy, made you feel fulfilled. I have never been able to figure it out but I can, at least, point it out.

We adore you.

Mother

❑

March 13, 1964

Dear Dr. Deviney,

Thank you for recommending me to Bob Sherman. He has given me a job as reporter and I am anxious to begin. I appreciate your interest in me and will not disappoint you or Bob.

Sincerely,
Quinn Morrow

❑

Mrs. Deviney and I are having a small gathering of students at our home Friday evening, March 20, at 8. I hope you will be able to attend.

CSD

❏

March 24, 1964

Dear Dr. and Mrs. Deviney,

Thank you for your hospitality Friday night. I enjoyed being with you in your home and was fascinated by your collection of objects and art from around the world.

I appreciate your friendship.

Sincerely,
Quinn Morrow

❏

FORMER INSTRUCTOR ALLEGES
UNIVERSITY GRANTS "ATHLETIC B"

Marion Gillis Malone, 28, a former instructor in the French Department has told The Merrill Record that she was coerced into granting a grade of B to each of her students who was attending on an athletic scholarship. She said a list of names and grades was hand-delivered to her in her office near the end of the three semesters she was employed by the University. All three deliveries were made by Alan Boyce Spearman, French Department chairman, Miss Malone alleges.

Miss Malone, who says she was released by the University in January when she failed to grant B grades to athletic scholarship students in the third semester of her employ, later learned from an Admissions Office clerk that the grades mailed to her athletic scholarship students were all B's.

Miss Malone plans to file charges against the University and is seeking other instructors and former instructors to join with her in a class action suit.

She said she decided to speak up about the coercion when a student in her first semester French I class discovered that athletic scholarship students in the class failed exams and then were granted B's on their term grade slips. She contacted Miss Malone who, by then, had left the University and was teaching in a Chicago high school.

❑

Sherm— I disagree totally. Use it or I'll turn it over to another paper. It's honest. Are you?

Q.

❑

Q. M.—

You have balls. You are attacking a sacred cow here. We'll run the story since Malone is going to sue, but you stirred this one up like you stirred up the parking deal. You'll be dragged into this since you are the anonymous student. Is this what you want? Don't get me wrong, I'm impressed.

Sherman

❑

Miss Morrow,

I applaud you for your story on the Athletic B—and for your courage. You have my support.

CSDeviney

❑

April 16, 1964

Dear Quinn,

Your article on Malone is a mind-bender. Thanks for sending it. You be careful. I don't like the fact that you've had anonymous threatening phone calls. Did you report them to the police?

I got a job this week with a small public relations agency in Boston. They book authors for interviews with papers, TV and radio stations. Since I have a background in English, I write news releases. We don't just book for Boston, we book nationally. Publishers send authors on tours and we arrange it. I contact the authors and write them up.

Thom has had some feelers from major motion picture studios. Nothing definite. Don't know if I'll go or stay. You will understand this: we love but are not "in love."

Hugs from   Ros

❏

She's here!
Early!

Amanda Melissa
born
May 11, 1964
6:36 a.m.
Presbyterian Hospital
Charlotte, North Carolina

Proud Parents
Randy and Sterling Hamilton

May 16, 1964

Dear Family—

I am going to duplicate this letter and send it to all of you because my childbirth was such a marvelous experience that I want to share it. I know that none of you have actually seen a baby born since when we girls were born they wouldn't let fathers in the delivery room and mother was put under total anesthesia with each one of us.

I was so proud of Randy. He really did well. He coached me all night long, then sat in back of my head in the delivery room and coached some more. The doctor was funny. He came in wearing a shower cap with camouflage coloring on it. We could see everything in the mirror. What a lot of hair on Mindy's head. We just couldn't believe it. The doctor pushed her back in a little and expertly stepped in front of the mirror to do the episiotomy. She was coming so fast, he didn't have time to do a local. But I hardly felt it. When he stepped away, I was bleeding. Then, he maneuvered her out and said, "We have a little girl!" What a thrill! Everyone was so excited that no one looked at the clock. A couple minutes later, we were all saying, "What time was she born, did anyone see the clock?" We guessed, because we didn't know for sure. It will always bother me that I'm not sure. She'll never be able to have her astrological chart done accurately. The umbilical cord was thick and gray and rolling with a clear jelly. The baby looked disgusted to be covered with all that junk. Her expression was humorous. Then, in a few minutes, the placenta came out. It was as big as the baby and pinky gray. Heavy. I could tell by the way the doctor lifted it. He said they save it and ship it somewhere where they make gamma globulin to inject into sick people. I couldn't sleep all day. Just kept thinking of my little girl! They put her in an incubator for 24 hours. Standard procedure, they said. One of the nurses told me that an uneducated woman who had given birth last year in that hospital named her child Female. She had seen a sign on her baby's crib in the nursery. It said: FEMÁLE JONES. The lady thought the hospital had already named her baby!

People ask me about the pain but I honestly don't remember. It was difficult but it all faded away as soon as I saw her. She is an angel.

Thanks for all your flowers and calls and cards. We got home yesterday and Mom is here to help me. I'll hand her her copy of this. We are trying to get organized but it's wild with a new baby in the house. Fun, though.

Love,
Sterling

❏

Ms. Morrow—

Your final grade: A. It has been a real pleasure having you in my class. You have much promise. Enjoy your summer. See you in the fall.

C. S. Deviney

❑

June 11, 1964

Dear Quinn,

Thanks for your visit! As I told you, no one else has come to see us (or would consider it, I'm sure). We were pleased to have you. Thom was full of praise and compliments for you. I'm glad you two had a chance to get to know each other. You're a dear heart.

This will surprise you: Thom has decided to go to L.A. and I've decided to stay here, at least for now. Nuff said.

Work has cranked up since a lot of books are due out in the fall. Alexis (the boss—remember?) is teaching me how to call and get interviews. I spend a lot of the day on the phone. Enjoyable, exciting.

She seems to freak out when we're extra busy. She's always kind of desperately chipper anyway—talks double time in a high voice and delivers both good and bad news with a smile (more like a grimace). I find myself steadying her and am gradually steadying myself in the process.

God bless.

Roz

❑

6/15/64

Sherm—

My grades arrived and I am stunned. I KNOW I did better than this! I'm being punished for exposing the athletic B. Shit. Only makes me more determined not to let them win. When the Malone hearings come up, let me cover them.

How's your internship going? I envy your opportunity. My summer's moving slowly.

Best,
Quinn

❏

June 28, Sun.

Dear Quinn,

Sorry you couldn't find a job that suited your interests. I know you're restless at home this summer, but Mother and Dad are glad to have you there. It's a generous thing Dad does, letting us laze around between school years if we want to. I don't know any other kids that have had that advantage. You can go back to school refreshed. It's a gift. A wonderful gift.

I have seven weeks worth of photographs and you should see Mindy grow! This is an awesome experiment. She is beautiful. But it's hard to catch her without her mouth open. She screams <u>all</u> the time. I am worn out and Randy sleeps in the guest room with the door closed so that he can go to work the next day without being too tired. I am exhausted. After Mother left, it was terrible. I have had Mindy to the doctor but he says she's fine. "Babies cry," he says. I feed her, change her, love her, and she still screams. She can scream four hours at a time. She only quits when she wears herself out. I don't have a minute to myself. When she's sleeping, I either sleep fast or try to get chores done: simple ones like showering or like changing the bed! I never dreamed this would be so hard. I am OWNED by another human being. I'm nursing her and so can't go very far from her or for very long. I went shopping the other day and had to come running home. It's like being on a leash. Randy (as I suspected) will change the wet diapers but not the messy ones.

How are you?

Love,
Sterling

❏

July 6, '64

Hi, Quinn,

The Sun-Times has got me galloping in nine directions. I've seen it all this

49

summer, from a Beatles concert to a helicopter that dropped through a house. Don't know which was worse.

Sorry about your grades. Appeal them. But I can't give you the Malone hearings: you're likely to be called as a witness.

Pal, you love being in hot water. I don't know what to do with you but I can't do without you on my staff. Forget impartiality, you'll never achieve it. You're not a straight news reporter, you're investigative or a columnist or? Rethink your course.

See you last week of Aug. & we'll talk.

Sherm

❑

August 17, 1964

Dear Quinn,

Thom left for L.A. this morning. As I told you on the phone, he'll be working for Paramount. It's a great opportunity, one he's waited and hoped for 3 months. But the house is so empty without him! I didn't know how much I depended on his buoyant magnetism. It's as though someone's turned off the lights and heat.

I walked him to the gate at the airport. We thought we were saying good-bye as friends, but when the time came, we clung so long they closed the plane door without him and almost wouldn't let him board.

I'll give myself a couple of months to sort it out and if I don't feel better by the New Year, I'll follow him to L.A. We agreed on that.

We helped each other through difficult months and aren't sure which parts of our relationship are real and which parts we've created from need.

Whimsey (the cat I inherited from Thom) and I send love to you.

Roz

❑

Q—WELCOME BACK

How about doing a bit on your favorite prof, Deviney? He's celebrating 30 years with the University this fall. Crank it up and we'll do a nice spread.

Sherm

❑

September 8, 1964

Dear Quinn,

Who _am_ I? My identity has been taken away. All I am is a servant to Mindy! Is this motherhood? I can't tell Mom this, she'll think I'm awful. She had 3 of us and I never heard her complain. All I do is serve, serve, serve. I serve Randy and the baby all day and night. I feel so isolated, so tired. She's a sweet little girl—she really is. I try to keep her from seeing my frustration. I can't figure out a way to manage this.

Yesterday, I had it out with Randy when he came home from work. He told me that Mike Lambros (another dentist) wanted to play golf with him Saturday. I was up to my eyebrows in dirty baby bottles and dirty diapers and I popped my cork. Golf?! When do I get the rest cure? I accused him of being lazy and not putting us first. He accused me of being self-pitying and told me to hire day help. He said he works like a dog. I said I _feel_ like a dog—on a leash. He slammed out the front door but came back in crying. That hauled me up short! Dad never cried! It was devastating. So we made up and made love. But we can't afford day help and he knows it. He's promised to feed and change her more when he's home, but he's always at work! No matter what anyone says, raising a child is all on the mother. You shouldn't have a baby unless you are willing to be the baby's slave. That's what it is.

Write to me!

Love,
Sterling

❏

9/13/64
Dear Sterling,

I am sorry you are having a rough time. It isn't easy to be a mother, I'm sure. But you are telling me more than I should know. Please—I don't want to hear personal details. Some situations shouldn't be shared. Don't stop telling me, just don't tell me so much. It isn't right.

Love,
Quinn

❏

September 14, 1964

Dear Quinn Morrow:

We have researched our files as you requested in your phone call of September 10, 1964, and can find no Charles Soule Deviney as a journalism Ph.D. recipient in 1928. There was a Charles S. Deviney listed as an M.A. degree recipient in June 1926 (Department of History) but this is the only similar name.

I hope this information fulfills your purpose.

Yours truly,
Bertrand Chan
Registrar
University of Oklahoma

❑

September 22, 1964

Dear Quinn,

I hope you will reconsider your decision to make my college education record public. After we talked, I realized I had reacted on the basis of anger and fear and had not provided you with sufficient information.

I won't bore you with a lengthy bio, but will give you the pertinent facts. I received my M.A. in history at Oklahoma in 1926, as you discovered, and went to work at the local newspaper which was run by my uncle. The degree in history was an asset as I pursued journalism. It gave me perspective. In that era—as in this—some of the best reporters were launched from college degrees other than English or journalism. I intended to go back to school for my Ph.D. when I had earned the funds but my uncle died, thrusting me into the position of editor, and then the Great Depression struck and I gave up my dreams. By the time America had recovered, I was married and had a child. Supporting them was my first duty.

Our child became gravely ill and, during those months, I was offered a teaching position at Merrill by a man who admired my work and presumed I possessed a Ph.D. A friend of mine (now deceased) in the records department at Oklahoma saw to it that the letter of inquiry was answered in the affirmative. I lied. But it was my only lie. I have spent my life trying to make up for that lie by honestly and diligently doing what I felt called to do: nurturing young people and encouraging them in the profession for which I have the highest respect.

I grew up smelling printer's ink. My mother and I lived with my uncle and his family over the shop. I loved newspapering from early childhood and, when the time came, I believed I was suited to teach it. I still believe it.

Yours,
Charles Deviney

❑

I asked you to celebrate Deviney, not crucify him! He's been here 30 years. There's a damned building named after him, for Christ's sake. If you think I'm printing this, you're crazy. The only two sentences people are going to see out of this laudatory 2000 words are the two that say he's a fake. I don't care how gently you constructed it. You're probably ending a man's career.

S.

❑

Damn you! I won't have it appear in some other paper. I'll run the fool thing and God help us.

S.

❑

7th October, 1964

Dear Miss Morrow,

I am severely disappointed in your judgment. Your story on my husband has caused him distress beyond telling. It is fortunate that the University officials have more wisdom than you and will allow him to stay, based on the devoted service he has given. He has earned at least the equivalent of a Ph.D. in his lifetime. No piece of paper needs to confirm his breadth of experience and depth of knowledge.

You are young and will learn that what is true does not necessarily equate with what is just. May you never have to pay the price for your self-righteousness.

Mrs. Charles Deviney

❑

October 26, 1964

Dear Miss Morrow:

Have been following your career at The Merrill Record and am interested in having you string for us on campus. When situations warrant it, I can send in a photographer to assist you.

I'll call in a day or two and I hope that we will be able to meet and work out a mutually beneficial arrangement.

Cordially,
Anthony Wilhelm
News Director
WCHI-TV

❑

Nov. 8, 1964

Dearest Quinn,

I am pregnant! Randy wasn't (isn't) certain this is a good idea but I can see now that what Mindy needs is a playmate. People who have their children close together say they entertain each other. That will be great for Mindy, and a big relief for me. The baby is due in June. The kids will be just 13 months apart. Perfect.

Love and kisses,
Sterling

❑

Police Officer Dies In Shoot-Out

LAKE FOREST, Ill. — A police force SWAT team member was shot to death Thanksgiving morning in a pre-dawn raid on a house in which a hostage was being held. Captain Gregory L. Cobble, 33, of the Chicago police department, was fatally wounded when a man who had held police at bay for six hours shot at him through a closed rear door of the house. The man, Dewey A. Goff, 29, of Evanston, was subdued by police and led away in handcuffs.

Cobble was preparing to enter the house in a swift assault designed to save the hostage who was being stabbed by her captor. The hostage, Marie S. Glogowski, 23, who lives with Goff, was hospitalized in fair condition suffering from multiple lacerations. Police decided to storm the house when she screamed from a side window that she was being attacked.

Police are investigating the possibility that a student reporter doing live audio updates for WCHI-TV, Chicago, inadvertently disclosed Cobble's location behind the door. Goff's television was tuned to WCHI when he was taken into custody. He had apparently been watching it to monitor the activities of the SWAT team. The reporter, Quinn Morrow, 19, became hysterical and was treated for shock at the scene.

1 9 6 5

Rosalind

1/11/65

Dear Rozzy,

You are right—I wasn't comfortable at home during Christmas. I'm glad the others didn't notice it. I feel that I can be honest with you because you have been honest with me. I had a terrible incident happen in November. I'm enclosing the clipping. Mother and Dad would be appalled and guilt-ridden, and I've had enough of both. I went to his funeral and the widow asked me to leave! I was crying my eyes out. They've got little children, too. I keep seeing his body lying behind that house, the contemptuous faces of the policemen. Sterling doesn't know. Don't tell her. She's got enough struggles without my dumping this on her. Besides, I had just told her to keep her troubles to herself. Justice?

Now that I am over the shock, I can see that his death wasn't my fault. After all, I wasn't the one who shot him. It was a freak accident. The chances of something like that happening are about the chances of being struck by lightning. The public has a right to know what's going on. I was merely reporting—doing my job.

I am kind of scraping along. WCHI didn't fire me. A real surprise. But they send me to ladies' club meetings and library book-fund presentations. I've applied for a summer internship with them. They say if you get thrown off a horse you should get right back on it or your fear will keep you from ever riding again.

Sherm brings me assignments like he's feeding a sick dog. We haven't fought in two months and this worries him.

How is Thom? What do you hear?

    XXX

    Quinn

❑

January 16, 1965

Dear Quinn,

I am so sorry! I didn't know about it, of course. It's awful, and I'm sad for you and for them. But it was an accident. You have to forgive yourself. Thank you for telling me. If you want to talk about it, I am available.

Still full steam at the office. It's OK, but I have missed Thom desperately and, now that he's established at Paramount, I'll join him. My target is Valentine's Day. He's so busy he hardly has time to write or call. It will be good to settle in together. This separation has proved to me that he is The One.

I loved it that you, Sterling, Randy, Mindy (The Flash Bulb Kid!), Mom and Dad and I could be together at Christmas. Thank you again for the scarf, hat and gloves to match. Terrific! Did Mom and Dad look a lot older to you? Perhaps it's just that it had been a whole year since I'd seen them. I like Sterling's idea of having a family party for their 25th anniversary at her house. I agree it can't be in June because she's due then. Maybe autumn or even next Christmas. We'll make it a bash!

I am thinking of you.

Luv,

Roz

❑

22nd January 1965

Dear Thom, Thank you for the glorious Christmas roses!

I miss you, I miss you, I miss you!

I've given Alexis notice and will be there on Valentine's Day. Can't wait! Mr. Bracci found another renter for the house. I'll bring Whimsey, yes? We are anxious to see you.

Work here is fine but I am (truthfully) short-timing it. Alexis has a person (Inga Sturges) lined up to take my place. She comes in two afternoons a week and I am training her.

It's really hard to get you on the phone. Could you give me a call so we can finalize plans? I understand that the motion picture business is all-day all-night, especially when you're getting started. But you're so insulated. You never answer your own phone—even at home. (Not complaining, just communicating!)

It will be fun to be in on the excitement surrounding Tropical Cavalry. Will it have a world premiere? Will we go? Ah, limousines, bright lights, tuxedos! Fame!

You're already famous with me.

Love and rapture,

Rosalind

❑

Jan. 30, 1965

My dear Rosalind,

I've been avoiding this issue for several weeks, hoping it would resolve itself. Believe me, nothing you can say to me or think of me is worse than what I'm thinking of myself. I'm not even brave enough to tell you by phone: please don't come.

Life in Southern California is backwards and upside down. It's like living on a different planet. The people don't even look the same; the girls are made-up to the max and the men are sun gods. It's a total youth cult, with plastic surgery standard for all. The Eastern U.S. traditions and sense of values are entirely absent. The Rules of Life have been erased or never existed. I don't know what to expect. What arrives is not what I envisioned.

Tropical Cavalry has become my focus, and after that it will be the next film and the next. I am a man crossing a raging stream on slippery rocks.

I need time to think, and to work—obsessively, I guess.

Also—and I hate myself for this—I am different now, too. There is a woman in my life. Kara Barber, an actress. (A cliché, isn't it?)

You are very special but I have changed. It's not your fault.

Your friend (I hope, still), Thom

❑

Dear Roz—

Attached, your last paycheck! Damn it! Don't want to lose you from my staff. When another position opens up with us, I'll get you back on board. You are a marvelous person and an exemplary employee. It's a bummer that your plans changed against your wishes & I had already hired Inga to fill your spot. I feel bad about it but can't be unfair to Inga. I know you understand!

Thank you for your devotion to me and to this company.

Alexis

❑

February 23, 1965

Dear Miss Morrow:

We have considered your application and are sorry to inform you that we have no openings on our staff at the present time. Your résumé is being placed in an active file and you will be called for an interview should an opportunity arise.

Thank you for your interest in our firm.

Cordially,
Davis N. Pierce
Personnel Manager
Kenley-Stoughton Public Relations

❑

March 1, 1965

Dear Rosalind:

It was a pleasure to meet you. You have been highly recommended by your former employer, Alexis Turgeon, and your writing samples are impressive. However, we are currently in the midst of a moratorium on hiring, based on our 5-year Financial Growth Plan. When we are again in a position to hire, we will contact you.

Rosalind, you are extremely qualified and it is with deepest regret that I write this letter.

Sincerely,
Sheila Gruber
Vice President
Creative Promotions

❑

3/12/65

Rozzy,

I didn't mean to hurt you. I don't blame you for not answering my letter. But I want you to know that I care for you and will always be glad to hear from you. I can't see closing this off forever because we are no longer lovers. I want your friendship and will feel deprived if I have to go through my life having no contact with you.

I called Alexis and she told me you are between jobs. If you want to join us in

Zanyland, I can offer you employment on the set of TC. I can use someone with brains. What say you.

Friends forever?

Thom

❏

Thom—

Go to hell.

Roz

❏

March 25, 1965

Mrs. Ungersma—

I can appreciate your situation but I am asking you please not to make me move out. I expect to have your money for you any day now and will bring it to your door rather than mailing it. I trust you will bear with me a little while longer.

Sincerely,

Rosalind Morrow

❏

March 28, 1965

Dearest Rosalind,

What are dads for? I am happy to help you out. Job hunting can be a lengthy process. Don't settle for second-best. Get something you really like. Look toward a career.

I know you say you don't want to go back to school but please consider it. I'll pay. Gladly!

Keep ole Dad informed. He sends you love.

❏

March 30, 1965

Dear Rosalind:

Thanks for filling in for Connie those two weeks she was on vacation. You are one heck of a copywriter. You bet I'll keep your name and number on my desktop and call you if there's an opening. You done good.

Excelsior!
John Howe
President
Ads and Events, Inc.

❑

Hi, Roz—Sorry we've had trouble connecting by phone. I've been doing an awful lot of running around. I have an idea for you, on starting your own business. Call me at home some night after 10?

    Alexis

❑

Rosalind Morrow
formerly Assistant Publicist
for Jomar-Strand, Inc.
announces the opening
of
On Tour
a chauffeur service
specializing in escorting visitors
to and from media interviews
1162 Dalglish Street
Boston, Massachusetts
617-555-4312

April 21, 1965

Dear Mother and Dad,

Thank you! for the money to buy a nice car! I purchased a new Chevrolet Impala—white, with white interior. Glamorous. So! I'm in business, as it says on my announcement. I consider this a loan and will repay you as quickly as possible.

I already have bookings (through Alexis) and have done my first couple of assignments. One was Corey Keane, the pitcher, who's written a book called

Windup (did you see it in the papers?) and the other was Dianne Beaman, the fading dancer, who had her memoirs ghostwritten.

I pick the clients up at their hotels, get them to interviews on time, wait with them and take them back again. It's intriguing.

I miss you.

LOVE,
Roz

❑

April 24, 1965

Dear Ros,

Now that you are going into business for yourself, it would be a good idea to consult with the intrinsic powers of nature. Much depends on timing in harmony with our sphere.

I've been taking classes in astrology for several months and have drawn up your chart as a gift. It's in a box along with some gift books on the stars and fortune—you'll get it any day now.

I know you're not inclined in this direction, but I've become convinced that we can move with our celestial flow and achieve—what would seem to others— miracles.

You were born with luck shining on you! Just observe the confines of your sign and respect its laws as you move forward. Watch and listen. Make no major moves without tapping in.

Sterling

❑

April 27th

Dear Mrs. Ungersma,

I am sorry to be late with the rent money again. I should have it to you shortly. As you know, I have started my own business and there is, necessarily, some lag time in collecting from my clients. I regret any inconvenience this is causing you and will try to make sure you don't have to wait in the future.

With appreciation,
Rosalind Morrow

❑

May 3, 1965

Dear Rosalind,

Many thanks for patiently squiring me around Bean Town. You're a pro—
you didn't seem to need clock or map to put me in the right location at the right
time. It looked effortless but I know better.

I'll be back in Boston next month. May I call you for dinner?

Sincerely,

David O'Gorman

❑

Muchas gracias, Roz! Fun to be with you and acquaint you with the classical
guitar! You made it so easy to promote my new album here, there and
everywhere. I appreciate.

Dario Laros

❑

May 11, 1965

Dear Mother,

Please don't worry. I am perfectly safe with "strangers" in my car. As I told
you, they are authors and other celebs (promoting books, records, movies,
etc.) sent to me through Alexis and other public relations agencies, publishing
houses, etc. I meet politicians, sports figures, movie stars, musicians, psychi-
atrists, artists—the gambit. It's fascinating! The other day, I chauffeured an
Arab sheik (grossly obese). The seat springs will never be the same!

Love to you and Dad,

Rosalind

❑

Rosa Linda—

Hope you enjoy these dresses. I bought them in Hawaii. When I looked at
them, I saw your personality in their cheerful colors and chains of flowers.

Te amo!

Dario

❑

5/17/65

Dear Rosalind,

Truly great to be with you. I appreciate your punctuality and savvy. When we parted, I couldn't help thinking about you over and over. I hope to see you again soon.

If this TV show flies, I'll be mobile when not filming—able to jet back and forth. As you know, Hartford is my hometown and it's just a hop to Boston.

I'll call you in a couple of weeks.

Chase Holling

❏

May 26, 1965

Dear Roz—A note of thanks. Thanks! You made Boston a breeze. Easiest whistle-stop I've had.

Now some advice: don't worry so much about money. It always shows up when you need it. I have a strong feeling some will show up in your account this week. Perhaps it's already there.

Hearts & flowers
Jack

❏

June 4, 1965

Dear Ros,

How generous of you to remember my graduation with the burnished silver friendship ring. It is exquisite and I will cherish it. (You spent too much!)

I think of you daily—have since you left—and mourn that you are not getting your diploma with us Sunday. People ask me constantly how you are and what you are doing. I tell them you are fine and living life well. Is this true? Please, let's talk and write more.

I ask myself over and over whether I gave you poor advice. It changed you profoundly—forever? Your leaving school is a burden in my heart.

Perhaps we can get together this summer. I have taken a position as (math) analyst with ITT, Annapolis. Meanwhile, I send good wishes and best love.

Annie

❏

It's a boy!

Lance Morrow Hamilton
June 21, 1965
3:49 a.m.
Presbyterian Hospital
Charlotte, North Carolina
Weight 8 lbs 3 oz
Length 21"

Euphoric Parents
Sterling and Randy Hamilton

22 June 1965

Dear R. —

When I saw you standing in the lobby, I looked around for another. Surely, this couldn't be my ride! But no, it was. Beautiful dark eyes and light beautiful skin—that dark hair wrapped around your head. And decently tall. Petite women seem like toys, unreal. I like the way your one tooth laps over the other just a tiny bit in front. I like you.   Kirk

❑

June 28, 1965

Dear Rosalind,

We were so surprised to open your letter and find the check for the car. That was so quick. Are you sure you're not shorting yourself? Dad and I don't need the money right now. Let us know if you'd like it for capital. We are proud of your initiative and success.

Sterling told us about the anniversary party you girls would like to hold for us this Christmas Eve at her house. What a thoughtful idea. We have marked our calendar with red letters! We'll be grateful to have all our family together again. Won't it be fun with the little ones? I am already sewing Mindy's gifts.

Love + Love
Mother + Dad

❑

July 1, 1965

Dear Roz,

Summer in Chicago is HOT. I like being a reporter for CHI but all I've done is cover civil rights demonstrations. We've been in turmoil here since June 10 and no end in sight. Hundreds of people have been arrested. I'm sure you see it in your papers. They even lie down in the streets and stop traffic.

The big target's the school system. Negroes are infuriated because the Bd of Ed has not moved decisively to integrate and to bring up the quality of education for them. They want Superintendent Willis OUT. In fact, they almost got rid of him in May but, at the final vote, 3 board members changed their minds. Negroes see Mayor Daley's hand in this because he had appointed the 3. Leaned on them?

I go to these things at risk. I'm not sure who's going to take a whack at me. Some Negroes welcome the coverage and some think it'll be biased because I'm white. I get trouble from whites who hate Negroes, and support from whites who believe the Negro cause is just and urgent.

In the midst of it all, I'm doing a flat, superficial job, a bird's eye view: "X number of people showed up with X number of demands."

Who's been riding in your car these days?

Love,
Quinn

❑

July 26, 1965

Dear Roz,

I'm in bed, exhausted but keyed up. Just covered the biggest civil rights demonstration Chicago's ever seen. Martin Luther King, Jr., leading 10,000 (Negroes and whites) to city hall. Incredible.

Fortunately, I'm no longer at the distance I was. Lou Fortner, a friend of my news director, has managed to wrangle me into key places. From the inside, it looks a hell of a lot different. I am angry at lack of progress for the Negro. Angry at narrow-mindedness. Angry at the damned South where Negroes are intimidated and beaten to keep them from registering to vote. (How can Sterling stand to live there?) I can't believe I grew up where I didn't have occasion to speak to a Negro til I went to college. The Civil War was 100 years ago.

Pardon my soapbox.

Quinn

❑

7/26/65

Dear Rosalind,

Joyful, joyful—being with you! You've even made me like the symphony which, prior to you, was just a bunch of whines and toots. I'm uncultured, but infatuated.

7 1

See you practically immediately.

Your beau,
David

❏

Rozzy—You're making such a big deal about the coat. It's just a dead animal, try to look at it that way! I gave you a dead animal. Whatta guy. Keep it. Wear in good health.

Samuel

❏

Aug 3
Ros:
I can't just report this anymore, like it has nothing to do with me. These latest marches are small and silent, but more touching. They take place in Bridgeport, Mayor Daley's (segregated) neighborhood. The demonstrators are peaceful, but the opposition they get is indescribable. Eggs and tomatoes, spit and spite. KKK signs and shouts of "Go back to the zoo!" Can you imagine?! I am not neutral, especially when I see the demonstrators getting arrested and the police totally ignoring the attackers. The cops take their good old time about coming to the aid of those who are being assaulted.

CHI's getting testy about my partiality. But I can't just blah-blah, "They did this, they did that," like it's a ballgame!

Lou has the inside track on all this and has made me see with new eyes. I've learned a lot from him. He's pre-law at U. of Mich. and working this summer as a gofer at a Chicago law firm that's been turning screws for civil rights. He's at every event I cover—very active and vocal for the Negro. He is admired by Negroes and whites because he is even-handed.

We wear ourselves out and I'm beginning to believe I never felt closer to anyone than I do to Lou Fortner.

Lots of love, Quinn

❏

The 12th Day of August, 1965

You make an old man feel young. Thanks, Roz, for your attentiveness. You were an excellent companion and got me everywhere on time. Boston was a bonanza for promotion of the seafood cookery book. Natch.

All best,
Arthur D.

P.S. I took the liberty of ordering you some delectables from various states . . . froz. steaks, fruit, pecans, Alaskan crab & salmon. Bon appetit.

❏

8/15/65

Rozzy—

Tying up loose ends at CHI and ready to go back to school. The other night was Act III, I'll tell you. I was sent out to a huge riot (12th Aug)—hundreds of people battling 100+ police. It was brutal. Negroes had been picketing an all-white firehouse in their neighborhood. Then, the fire truck came out with no one steering the rear wheels and killed a Negro woman. Bedlam.

When I was trying to interview witnesses, some white guy grabbed me by my hair, pulled me to my knees and slammed my head against the sidewalk. Lou was right there and they really got into it. Lou won. My partner had his camera smashed by the crowd and ran off and locked himself in the car. When Lou and I arrived, he was hiding in the back seat!

CHI says I'm a source of controversy. I'm a demonstrator in my off hours and they declare that news people have no business taking sides. That's illogical of them.

Lou's going back to Ann Arbor next week. You've probably guessed, we're dating. I can't wait for you to meet him. He's the most exciting, intelligent man I've met. Tremendous dignity. Calm (most of the time!) and assured.

More later.

Love,
Quinn

❏

August 20, 1965

Dear Rosalind,

Don't say NO until you've thought this over. I am going to Bermuda on a cruise out of NYC in three weeks. This is a rest for me. I bashed my brains out promoting <u>Stock Strategies</u> and finishing the manuscript for <u>Bond Strategies.</u> I'm whipped. I know you've been working hard, too. Come with me. No strings. Promise.

David O'G

❑

August 30, 1965

Dearest Rosalind,

You must be doing well to be able to afford a cruise already! Dad and I are proud of you. Your business sounds so interesting.

We've decided to take a junket to New York and do some shows. Could we come on up to visit? You're busy—we understand. We'll sightsee when you're working. Would late October suit?

With great love,
Mother

❑

Sept. 1

Rozzy—

I've been at this astrology junk for nearly a year and have to tell you it doesn't work. Throw away the stuff I sent you. It is useless. I've been dancing "in harmony" since last fall and am completely out of kilter. I've checked my signs before setting foot out of the house or making a call! It's baloney. In fact, it's like a practical joke: whatever I do, I should have done the reverse.

For instance, I am overwhelmed with two children. Dote on them but they're too close together. I must have been crazy to let a book tell me when to get pregnant.

Hope this hasn't caused you any problems.

Love and X's
Sterling

❑

10/8/65

Now look, I know what you're going to say but . . . Cape Cod is glorious right now. It's the best month. Help me celebrate the show's debut. Hey—I'll only be there for a weekend. Come stick your toes in the sand (official invitation & map enclosed).

Chase

❏

Dear Ros,

What a weekend! Here's a key to the beach house. <u>Yours.</u> Use when you please.

Chase

❏

November 6, 1965

Dearest Rosalind,

Thank you for a memorable four days in Boston. Dad and I were delighted to be with you and to see you doing so well. You look like a million dollars. The excitement of running your own business seems to have brought you into full bloom.

Wear your success in good health. You're our treasure.

Devotedly,
Mother

❏

Rosalind:

I want you to come to Washington to be with me at Thanksgiving. Two days with you was simply not enough. I'm enclosing your plane ticket so you can't say no.

Carl

❏

11/20/65

Dear Annie,

I could never fool you. I apologize for shouting at you. I should have asked you to stay.

I don't need to defend my lifestyle. It pleases me. That's all that's necessary. Be my friend.

Roz

❑

November 30, 1965

Dear Mrs. Ungersma:

This letter will be my notice that I'll be moving on January 15. I have purchased a home in Danvers.

I appreciate all you have done for me, especially in being so understanding about late rent payments.

Sincerely,
Rosalind M.

❑

December 1, 1965

Ros,

I can't believe you would take Quinn's part in this! Why is she insisting on bringing Lou to the anniversary party when she knows Mother and Dad would drop dead—and so would Randy and his folks.

We CAN'T call off the party—M & D have been looking forward to it all year. And we CAN'T do it without Quinn. She has to be here.

She's stubborn and selfish—I told her that. She's always liked to be opposite and this is the height of it. There are tons of men she could have picked and she did this on purpose. For myself it doesn't matter. I can accept a Negro. But he hasn't a right to be at this anniversary celebration. He's not her husband. She just wants to shock everyone.

I can't understand your attitude. You know darn well you'd never do anything as scandalous & hurtful in this family and neither would I.

Sterling

❑

1 9 6 6

Sterling

January First

Quinn,

I can't believe you would choose another person over your own parents! They were typically gracious about your absence but I believe they were deeply hurt that you did not come to the anniversary celebration. The big bouquet you sent was no substitute for you.

Why do you always choose the hardest (on everybody else) path? Don't you care what impact you are having on others?

Sterling

❑

1/6/66

Dear Sterling,

I do care what impact I am having on others. I intend to have impact. If Lou was not welcome at the anniversary celebration, I wasn't about to attend. I still feel that way. He is the man I love—a good and worthy man.

I choose what's right. If it is a hard path for others, that's their problem.

Sterling, your world has become so small I'm having trouble fitting into it. Please stretch it and make room for me again.

Love,
Quinn

❑

January 6, 1966

Dearest Sterling and Randy,

Thank you for the glorious anniversary/Christmas party at your home. I realize that it took tremendous forethought and planning. Dad and I feel honored, and blessed. We have such a special family.

Sterling, I know you were upset by Quinn's absence, but please do all you can to preserve your relationship with her. I am asking you to do this for me. There is nothing more important than keeping one's family together.

Quinn is trying to find herself. Rosalind has established a successful business and her career fulfills her. You are fulfilled as wife and mother. But

Quinn is still searching for her fulfillment. We must be patient and show her our contentment as a model. We must pray that she will turn out to be as happy as we all are.

Randy, thank you for being our son. We are lucky to have you.

Mother and Dad

❑

January 11, 1966

Dear Quinn,

My world is wide enough for me. I feel comfortable. I have a secure, interesting and (to me) exciting life. I wouldn't know what else to desire.

You are trying to justify crossing lines that shouldn't be crossed. Yes, Lou is our equal but, culturally, totally different. I fear this fact will someday close in on you and stunt your sense of adventure—your greatest strength.

Still your sister,
Sterling

❑

15 January 1966

Dear Sterling,

Just had to respond to your Christmas card! I didn't do greetings this year because I've been so busy. I got out of the Peace Corps in June. Two years in Libya and an American hamburger is a delicacy. I had diarrhea the whole time I was over there—when hungry, the Libyans would just kill and cook lambs along the road. I did acquire a taste for grape leaves, however. But the grapes in the supermarket here come without leaves. Seriously, my life is rich with the experience. I am a new person. I traveled deep into Africa and witnessed with exhilaration herds of zebras, giraffes, elephants and antelope. When they stampeded, it was like Judgment Day—crashing noise against my heart, brilliant flashes against the land, an explosion of Wonder.

Since I've been back, I've lived in the Florida Everglades with a wildlife team. People don't realize it but there are panthers here, and bears. We are working against their extinction. Florida is full of Indian burial grounds we are also marking and preserving as we explore. (The spirits are friendly.)

Did you know a gator can run 40 miles an hour and I outran one yesterday?

How vast the earth is! How lush and varied. I hope you are getting your share of it. Write and tell me what you are doing other than wifing and mothering. We've come a long way from Pitt, eh? Best, Jeannette

❑

February 2, 1966

Dear Roz

I have embarked on a new phase of my life! I felt my world had gotten so small that I wasn't comfortable in it.

Please don't tell Quinn or Mother and Dad but I have signed up to be a prison volunteer. I don't know a whole lot about it yet but I'll be starting Tuesday night visits in March with a citizens' group. The only training is OJT (on the job).

I wanted exposure to people and settings really different from mine and this is the most radical thing I can do locally, I think.

Randy had a fit when I told him but he's willing to let me go and said he'll be my babysitter.

I feel as though I'm on a launch pad.

I enjoyed hearing all about your job when we were together at Christmas. What fun you must have! I am amazed you say there's no special man in your life—you are meeting so many. Don't they ask you out sometimes? Well, romance isn't everything. Believe me.

Love ya,
Sterling

❑

February 2, 1966
Dear Jeannette,

How marvelous to hear of your adventures. Isn't it amazing how people can content themselves with staying in their own backyards when there is so much to see and do in the world?

You asked what I am into, other than wifing and mothering. I am heavily involved with prison reform. Your experiences in Libya and the Everglades give you a panorama. But imagine, for a moment, working with those doomed to inhabit—year upon year—a space as small as a walk-in closet. They do so without meaningful intervention: without psychological counseling (unless they are the worst of the worst), without useful employment, without significant job training, without consistent opportunity for higher education, without adequate protection from one another. In short, without hope. Further, most are divorced and abandoned by family and friends while they are incarcerated. The recidivism rate is 75 percent.

I am currently a volunteer teacher in the system and will shortly expand my role into that of activist and lobbyist. I look forward to an enlightened America where convicts are rehabilitated instead of caged.

Good wishes for The New Year. May peace and joy be yours.

Always,
Sterling

❏

2/18/66

Dear Sterling,

Sounds great—about the prison. Write details. I'm intrigued.

This week I chauffeured Zeb Capriotti, the expert on organized crime. He's written a book called Made in Sicily, about the inner workings of the Mafia. It includes info never before revealed. I read it at one sitting and couldn't sleep all night. While he was inside buildings having interviews, I was standing in the snow watching my car, making sure it wasn't being wired with explosives. I spent more time staring into the rear view mirror while I was driving him around than I did staring at the road.

Next week, I've got Florence Firenza the opera singer who's touring with La Traviata and Gabe Kleindorf, a mentalist. Well, she's not touring with him— you know what I mean. They say he can force people to do things using only the power of his mind.

A big hello to Randy, Mindy and Lance.

Love,
Rozzy

P.S. You said at Christmas you think Mindy will be ready for a swing set this season. When the weather breaks, I'll have one delivered to your yard. Pick a spot.

❏

March 9, 1966

Dear Roz!

My first time at the prison was Tues. night. The place is way the heck out in the middle of nowhere. When you park and walk up to it, the inmates call to you from the barred windows. I felt uneasy and embarrassed. We volunteers went in a group—men and women—so I had plenty of support. Some of the volunteers have worked with the program a doz. or more years. There are five volunteer groups—one for each night of the week.

Inside, there was a large lobby where we showed our ID cards and waited for them to raise a wall of bars so that we could pass under it. They brought the bars down again and I discovered we were in a small holding room with bars on the other side, too. A guard was staring at us from a booth, checking out each person, I guess. When he was satisfied, he pressed a button to raise the bars on the other side. We spilled out into a big room, then into a smaller meeting room beyond.

The inmates came in a few minutes later and took seats in a circle with us. They are under 30 years old, felons—which means murder, arson, rape, etc. (but the worst criminals are sent to another prison, at the coast). I couldn't get over their appearance. I expected them to be scruffy like street derelicts and they were a sharp looking bunch. The prison garb is blue work shirts and jeans. The men were super clean and slicked up. Great hair cuts—not crews. You could tell they had just showered. Fresh uniforms. Lots of aftershave. No beards or mustaches (rules) and everyone was polite, quiet. Mac (our leader) says the inmates think we have some say over whether they get paroled. But we don't.

Our job is to teach them re-entry skills—how to fill out job applications, manners, budgeting money, being interviewed for employment, methods of birth control (!), anything they want to know about being "on the outside." Supposedly, these guys are within 6 months of possible parole. We have an informal visit for an hour, then a lecture, then split into discussion groups.

The men are pretty talky. No problem getting going. We were there from 7 to 9. This commitment is for every Tuesday night. I can't wait to go back.

Thank you in advance for the swing set!

Love,
Sterling

❏

March 31, 1966

Dear Ros,

Tuesday was my fourth visit to the prison group. I know the inmates' names now (20 men) and their stories. By stories I mean their version of the crime. Interesting thing: nobody here is guilty! Not a soul! Again—they think we have some power over whether they get paroled. So they're all establishing their innocence with us. Sometimes I almost laugh out loud. A guy will say, "We just rolled up to this gas station and my friend went inside. I thought he was going to use the restroom. How was I supposed to know he was knocking over the place?" They put us on incessantly.

They've got a whole other culture here. It's a complete community in which they make do with what they have. No women, so some of the men take the roles of women (sexually) and are even referred to as "she." No money, so they pay in cigarettes (3 packs to a dollar). Each person has an occupation, according to what he was or studied on the outside—or according to his aptitude. It's a complete society with lawyers, writers, artists, doctors, insurance salesmen, etc.

Got to go feed the kids now. Oh—congrats on your new Cadillac! Ritzy!

Love, Sterling

❑

May 1, 1966

Dear Quinn,

I think I owe you an apology for having a closed mind about Lou. I am growing in new directions. No kidding. I didn't want to hear about Lou before, but I do now. Please write to me this summer. Much luck on your assignment with the Free Press.

Love,
Sterling

❑

June 9, 1966

Dear Sterling,

I appreciated your note and confession.

It is good to be near Lou and his family at last. They welcomed me with open arms. This summer will be too short. I have a room in Lou's aunt and uncle's house, down the block from where he lives with his parents. My hours at the paper are quite opposite his school hours but we do the best we can. I have a lot of time without him and I spend it getting to know his people. Some of his friends aren't sure what to make of this. Mine was the only white face at a wedding last week and there was a distinct chill.

Lou's parents treat me like a favorite child. They think I am skinny and frail and constantly put food in front of me. They are a hugging and laughing bunch, his family. There are so many of them I haven't got their names straight yet. They go in and out of his parents' house at all hours. This is not just nuclear and extended family, this is FOLKS. I think the deal is that they don't have to be related to consider themselves family. They only have to feel related.

His Aunt Marie—the one I live with—is younger than Lou is. She's married (?) to a 40ish man—Billy, who's a hospital orderly. They are trying to have kids.

Time to go to work . . .

Love to everybody,
Quinn

❏

6/21/66

Dear Sterling,

I have a new best girlfriend. Lou's sister Dagmar is a genuine original. She's all hoops & jangles. You can hear her jewelry coming before you see her. She's got nine wigs and lies upside down on a slanted ironing board 45 minutes a day to ward off facial wrinkles. She pierced my ears with safety pins. Did a decent job of it—no infection. She's a bodyguard for the wife of Willie Dodson, the boxer.

Just had to tell you!

Love,
Quinn

❏

June 23rd

Dear Ros,

Spent Tues night interviewing inmates for the new group. The cast changes every 14 weeks. Standard list of questions to ask and one of them is, "What was your conviction for?" Hearing the actual crimes gave me pause. One guy stabbed a friend to death with a paring knife (he was under the influence so it wasn't 1st degree). Another guy instigated the gang-rape of a woman at his house. I just kept my eyes on the paper and wrote the answers.

They are so charming in the group that you forget that they're really in there for A REASON. Randy would die if he knew the extent of all this. He thinks I'm just a do-gooder who needs this project. I guess he doesn't really think about it, so don't say anything to him, OK? He is such a dear conservative man.

Your turn to write.

Love,
Sterling

❑

July 19, 1966

Dear Sterling,

Very sticky here. But, then, probably not as sticky as in NC.

The Free Press is still treating me like a student. Dull assignments. Print is dull anyway. I think I belong in TV and I'm going to switch my major from journ. to broadcasting.

Lou and I have been on the fringes with each other a little. I don't see him enough? I'm not sure what's the matter.

I can't get any privacy here unless I go out of the house. There's too much going on and none of it on a real schedule. The family is delightful but I am not in pace with them. I keep viewing myself as a compulsive—I am. But . . .

They're never in a hurry, even when I am waiting for them and it's urgent. Lou good naturedly says they're all on CPT (colored people time), which runs ½ to 1½ hours behind what the clock says.

And I get bossed a lot, in a loving way. Eat! Do! Mostly by the women. That's the way of it. Matriarchal.

Lots of children and they don't seem to be assigned to caretakers—the whole family takes care of them i.e. whichever adults are handy. The children live in the happiness of constant attention.

I am devoted to the Fortners et al, esp. Lou & Dagmar, but maybe I chose to get too close too fast. Still, I doubt Lou could live with any of the Morrows either. Except me, of course.

Love,
Quinn

❏

August 8, 1966

Dear Roz,

Want to hear something pathetic? One inmate in the new group paid 9 packs of cigarettes for a photo of me that was taken one Tuesday night. He wanted me to sign the back of it to him, so I did. It made me sad. His name is Jeff Mather. I didn't even recall having my picture taken—he said it was by the inmate photographer for the prison newspaper.

Jeff hasn't got the bearing of the others. Most of the inmates have a way of tipping their heads forward and glancing up at me that I would recognize anywhere: THIS MAN IS A CONVICT. I guess it comes from keeping their heads down in the presence of guards and using only their eyes to check out their surroundings. It's like they're hiding under a rock and peering out and up.

Jeff has a straight-on style and two bachelors degrees (he says), one in philosophy and one in psychology. I almost believe him when he says he was framed. His girlfriend—who had a history of mental problems—jumped off their apartment balcony (9th floor). They had been arguing for days. He said she smiled before she did it—I guess because she knew he was going to be blamed for her death. The ultimate revenge.

Tuesdays shake up my life. The rest of the week, it's dirty diapers and cracker crumbs and who needed what gold crown or filling. I'm leading two lives. Tell me about yours.

Love,
Sterling

❏

Sterling

I need to write to you. The
weeks are so long. There is at least
a solid year between Tuesday nights. When
you leave, the silence of society overtakes
me. I am reminded of my aloneness
and how few people care or have
contact.

We who live here are on an island
of regret. When you go through
that barred room, out into freedom,
think of us. Whatever we did,
exile is not an answer. You
will come to understand this.
Three people are assigned to
simultaneously sweep hair
in a prison barbershop
20 feet by 20 feet.
Rehabilitation?

Remember us.

Jeff

❑

Jeff—
   I will say this as clearly and kindly as I can. Do not ever write to me at home
again.

Sterling

❑

Sterling

I remember roses
frozen on their stalks
at this time of year.
I have not seen a flower
since 1962
but there is a picture
of one
in the infirmary.
I have been there twice.

I have one blanket
and line my bed
with newspaper
to keep warm.
I have been asking
for another blanket
since 1962.

Remember.

Jeff

❏

I will not tolerate your writing to me and this is your last warning. You will be dismissed from the group if you continue.

SH

❏

October 1

Dear Rozzy—

I am falling apart! Lance's teething is awful! I can't get any rest. We have tried freezing the teething rings, tried gum-numbing ointment, tried everything but whiskey—which my friends say they rub on their kids' gums then give them a couple teaspoons to knock them out.

Mindy is jealous. When I try to rock the baby she screams and pulls at me. I get so impatient.

I am tired of breast feeding! I've been nursing kids for two and a half years, non-stop. I feel like a cow.

I cry and Randy is frantic to please me. He cooks for us and he'll change the messy diapers now, too. I know you'll say this upset is temporary but it has fundamentally altered both Randy and me. I don't know how to get back to where we were or even if I want to. Don't tell Mother. She thinks I'm the perfect homemaker.

Sterling

❏

Sterling

At your mailbox, you read my
letters and tear them up into
the garbage can before you
enter the house. Your husband
finds you vaguely alien,
like one born in another country
and brought here at an early age.

You speak another language.
Because.
You remember us.

Your gaze follows as I come
and go from the prescribed room, as I
sit listening to the prescribed lecture.
When we speak to others, we speak to
one another.

You move with the surprised grace
of a woman who has discovered
She is not
who She thinks she is.

J.

❏

December 10, 1966

Dear Rozzy,

Our volunteer Christmas party at the prison was this week. We baked dozens and dozens of cookies to take.

A cold night. When we arrived, the cookie boxes were sent through one channel (I guess to be inspected) and we were taken via a different route, down corridor after corridor, then outside through the prison yard. The shouting from the windows was extra loud as we walked toward the auditorium. Dark, dark above. We couldn't see the shouters.

The auditorium is a disgrace. The ceiling is caving in. No heat. A terrible musty smell. Rows of hard wooden chairs that are beat to death. Ghosts. But the guys were so happy. The musical show was their show-off time for us. A lot of talent in these poor souls. And then, they were coming toward us for cookies. (Three of the boxes we had brought disappeared enroute to the auditorium but mysteriously reappeared when the warden announced there would be no show until they arrived.) These characters wore their jackets over their shoulders—with the cuffs sewn shut! They stuffed cookies down the sleeves. It took me a while to catch on.

Quote of the evening came from the inmate who told my friend Mac—who was using his 35mm to record the festivities, "A guy gave me a camera just like that once." "Gave it to you?" Mac asked, incredulous. It's a fantastically expensive piece of equipment. "Yeah," the inmate said, "gave it to me. Of course, I had a gun on him at the time."

All set for Christmas? See you at Mom's!

Tons of love,

Sterling

❏

December 12, 1966

Dear Sterling,

It galls me to think you might have been right about something but Lou and I split. The trouble started this summer.

HE IS a fantastic person with a fantastic family. Why couldn't we make it work? Truth is, we were OK in a vacuum but there are cultural factors. I don't mean that I'm cultured and they're not. They've got as many diplomas and paintings on the wall as the next family. But I found myself in an impossible situation, a square peg in a round hole.

Lou wants us to continue. I even got a call from his mother asking if she could apologize for anything. I tried to answer but all that came out of me was squeaks. I don't want them to think I am judging them!

You see, this makes it more complicated. A white couple would simply break up. But because we are of two skin colors there's imagined innuendo and tremendously hurt feelings. If I reject Lou, I'm rejecting a race. I feel like a hypocrite. Am I?

Crossing lines is dangerous to one's mental health. You heard it here first.

Always your sister,
QUINN

❏

Sterling

This letter, the only one
in your secret post office box
rented just for me,
is to its cubicle
as I am to my cell.

Looking up, I see a cartoon:
the third grade Christmas pageant
and me as Joseph!
I see angels, too.
For a while
I stopped believing.
Until I heard wings.

Jeff

❏

1 9 6 7

Sterling

Friday, January 6

Dear Jeff,

I don't know what to write. I don't know why I did this. I just couldn't imagine not communicating with you once your time in the group was finished, and I knew my husband wouldn't understand my getting letters from you. I don't want you to think there is a romantic interest on my part. That has to be clear from the outset.

I wonder what you'd like to hear. I look around and see so many things you can't see. Should I describe them? There was a hole in winter today so I got out our red wagon and took the sides off, then rode down our street over and over with Mindy in front of me. We were screaming with laughter! It took forever to walk up the hill each time because she is so little. (I left the baby with a neighbor while we did it.) I'll always remember this day. I don't play enough, I guess that's why I felt such joy. I'm too purposeful and directed—and bogged down with details. I have choices you don't have, but yet choose to keep my world narrow. Your situation makes me consider this.

Bye, Sterling

❏

January 7, 1967

Dearest Sterling,

What a perfect Christmas! The only thing missing was Rosalind, but we understand how hard she has to work to sustain her own business.

You looked gorgeous—absolutely. You looked like—well, like you have a magnificent secret inside of you. Are you pregnant again?

Dad and I were amazed and intrigued to receive the article from you about your involvement in the North Carolina prison system. You had said nothing about it when we were together. Our first reaction was of pride in your devotion to those less fortunate. But then parental caution crept in and we became concerned for your safety. We don't mean to meddle in your affairs but have you considered: these men go into society once they have paid their debt, but not all will be cured of their errant ways. Surely you aren't planning to use your home as a "gathering place and source of strength" like Mr. and Mrs. Harleyson who were quoted in the article. What about Mindy and Lance? Please think this over carefully. We would be interested to know Randy's feelings.

Nevertheless, we want to support your efforts and we agree that prison reform is long overdue. The enclosed check for the Citizens' Action Group is our statement of faith and is the first of three we will send this year.

Much love,
Mother

❏

1/14/67

Dear Mother and Dad,

Thank you for the check! No, I'm not pregnant. And, don't worry. The citizens' group has had enormous success in relationships with inmates. It isn't right to befriend them in prison and drop them when they get out. They need for people to trust them and to include them—to open their homes. Most were raised in such poor (emotionally) backgrounds that they must have access to normal families in order to learn new ways. Gwen and John Harleyson epitomize the citizen-volunteer couple. They give of themselves totally. The ex-cons "police each other," according to Gwen, and her home and children are even better protected than if the men weren't there. I believe prison reform begins with each person's attitude.

Best love,
Sterling

P. S. Randy is in your category:
      still making up his mind.

❏

Sterling

Your beauty
opens doors
opens ceilings
opens flowers
opens me.

Your beauty
opens clouds.
I fly away

You open days.
I can examine
their hearts
beating under my fingers.
Inside each heart
is a house;
inside each house,
latched slumber
and a dream.

In the dream
you are combing
the waterfall
of your hair.
Slowly. Smiling.

Jeff

❏

February 1, 1967

Dear Sterling,

Just got back from a week's visit with Roz and let me tell you she looks great. Happy, polished, sophisticated. She has this gingerbready old house with big high rooms. The wind comes through the walls but she doesn't seem to notice. She's got the whole thing decked out in her favorite colors: white and gray. A splash of summer green here and there.

She's hired an answering service but has her office at home—keeps her own books. The phone rings constantly. She goes tooling off in that white Cadillac, confident as you please. She's chauffeuring senators and dukes. I didn't see any of them.

I almost went dizzy when I glimpsed her at the airport. She had on a white fox jacket and hat. STUNNING. Her face was framed by all that fur and those dark eyes and curls were such a contrast.

She says she's satisfied with her life and she told me she's gotten into investing (stock market). An author she met had written a couple of books on it and got her started. She discovered she has phenomenal luck—senses whether a stock's about to go up or down. It's a game.

She's still Roz. Brought me breakfast in bed with tulips on the tray. She was always hugging me. The only time I saw her depressed was when we went to see Tropical Cavalry (the one Thom Brawley directed). She clutched my hand through the interminable 2 + hours and kept whispering, "It's a bomb." And it was. So forgettable. An embarrassment, really. I think she's glad she didn't go to LA with him. She has her own life now.

I heard from Mom and Dad that you are a volunteer at a prison. How come you didn't tell me? I'd be interested.

I'm on a job search. I've applied to several large TV stations and all three networks, but no answers yet. Keep your fingers crossed.

Luv,

Quinn

❏

February 9, 1967

Dear Roz,

My life at the prison seems much more real than my life at home. I wake up when I go there. It's an eyeful and earful. These characters have a unique communications system. They figured out that when you flush the toilets in each cell block, the water swirls around in one central pipe juncture. They flush long strings, simultaneously. The strings meet and tangle together. Then, one inmate can lower a note or whatever on the end of the string and another inmate can pull it up through his commode. The things people can invent if they have unlimited time to think!

Quinn said she had a super visit with you. I missed you at Christmas. Come to Charlotte.

Love,

Sterling

❏

Feb. 13, 1967

Dear Jeff,

I keep looking around for stuff you'd like to see. I want to be your eyes in the world. But I am housebound a lot and my car goes over the same paths: to the grocery store, to the nursery school, to the pediatrician's office.

At home, my usual view is from the kitchen window. There's the backyard, then woods, then—way beyond—a railroad. The tracks are hidden from the house by shrubbery, but the train—when it barrels by—is huge and loud. The children jump! I know the whistles now and can hear the odd ones coming. Once I saw an old steam engine with a bell on the front. And yesterday, the circus train. I grabbed Mindy & ran to stand by it. The performers and animals had their heads out the windows like a picture of Noah's ark. The people waved with grand enthusiasm and shook red satin handkerchiefs at us. They were exotic: swarthy and draped in jewelry, caps, headscarves. When the train rattled away, the animal smells and dander engulfed us, billowing up as if in an explosion and raining down in tiny, stinging hairs.

Til next time,
SH

❑

Sterling

Through your eyes
I see
oceans,
galaxies, wagons,
circuses. You
pleasure me.
You see?

Through my eyes,
travel. Be
me.
Count the sameness
of spoons,
of shower stalls,
of shirts.
Measure time in
shaves,
in sheets
delivered twice a week.
See.

See me
seeing you,
seeing through
your eyes,
your pretty, pretty eyes.

Jeff

❑

Honey

I need to write this down. I care for you. I don't want to lose you. Do I see you
drifting away? We've been under pressure from the kids and from work for a
long time but I hope it won't take us from each other. Please talk to me. I
remember beginning to desire you. Did you realize when? That crazy frat
party. I was with Patty, nearly engaged. You were with Richard Solomon.
(Why?) We had hired the hypnotist and she wasn't putting anyone to sleep — we
were hysterical because she couldn't do it. She was mad and frustrated. Here
you come, clear from the back of the room, floating like a sleepwalker, eyes
glazed. The crowd grew quiet where you moved. I doubted you were hypno-
tized but she had you lie down across three chairs and took away two. Your
exquisite body didn't bend at all. Talk to me, Sweetheart.

❑

March 18, 1967
Dear Sterling,

I had a couple of dillies in my car this week. One was Coulter Lubin the
restaurant critic. He wore a tux but all he ate was junk food! He insisted that we
stop for lunch at a drive-in hamburger place and he stuffed himself with greasy
fare (licked his thumbs). On the road, ate Mallow Cups and Clark Bars he had
brought in a paper bag. Put the wrappers carefully in his pockets to save for
premiums. But I did get to hear what constitutes a first class restaurant.

Rayton Fields, the actress, was here. She travels with a parrot, Emerald.
That bird left copious deposits running down the seat backs.

The most interesting client: Poe Edgar (that's right), a retired 32-year-old who wrote <u>Why Work?</u> It's about real-estate investing using bank capital. I read it and might try it.

XXX
Rozzie

❏

April 3, 1967

Jeff—

   If only you could see our yard. The man who lived here before us worked for a bulb company and planted hundreds. Spring is a symphony of blossoms: yellow daffodils, narcissus, red and yellow tulips, orange tiger lilies, purple iris, white amaryllis. Hundreds, grouped for show. Beneath the pine trees in the woods, mammoth azalea bushes spread their glory: pink, white, red, purple. To right and left, we can see through the yards of neighbors and— against Wedgwood blue sky—the landscape is ablaze, dotted with white, graceful dogwood.

Sterling

❏

Sterling

Your letters,
apples,
ripe,
I take and eat,
think of Eve,
the child in her apple
belly,
think of Snow White
contemplating
her sphere,
think of seed.
Cut across an apple,
find in its wet
whiteness

a star.
Never judge
by the firm, cool
exterior
what
an apple
or a woman
holds shimmering,
silent
in her belly.

Jeff

❏

Jeff—
   The sensuality of your poem astonished me. I felt offended by it until I was truthful. I have never experienced my own passion—it is like blooms beyond the window glass. I have wondered for weeks why I dared to write to you. Now, I admit why.

S.

❏

2 tickets for my Angel. My folks will keep the kids. We're off to Chicago for your sister's graduation and a whole lot of hanky-panky, shows & late dinners. Happy 4th anniversary to the One I Adore.

❏

May 29, 1967

Dear Sterling and Randy,
   Thank you for attending my graduation! You and Roz—and, of course M&D—are the best friends I have. I couldn't believe you ALL came!
   Thank you, too, for the mantel clock. It is elegant.

I hope I won't be in Pittsburgh with Mom and Dad very long. I have applications in to so many TV stations that something is bound to turn up soon. Love to you, Mindy and Lance.

Quinn

❏

Sterling

Who is he?
I wonder.
How did he
make her love him,
make her long to see
children in his image.

Who is she?
I wonder.
How did she
make him love her,
make him long to see
children in her image?

The marriage mirror:
a piece of glass
reflecting the couple
and yet no other.
Outsiders gaze into it, curious,
anxious, tilt it,
find it blind, blank.
But the marriage partners
can stare at the mirror
from both sides
viewing each other fully through it,
as if it were a window.

Jeff

❏

Jeff—

Please don't comment on my marriage. It makes me uncomfortable.

Can't you write to me in plain paragraphs? I don't want to have to read between the lines.

Let's start over, okay?

Sterling

❑

June 12th, 1967

Dear Mother,

Please don't show this letter to Dad. I need to know something from you: what is marriage? Does it change? Is it supposed to? Has Dad seemed like a series of different people over the years?

I married one man but now he seems like another. Better.

What happens over 25 years? Do you fall in and out of love? I hope you don't think these questions are silly.

Sterling

❑

June 18, 1967

Dearest Sterling,

I understand the questions—they are the same ones I had. Yes, the marriage changes shape and a single partner can seem like a series of partners. This is because he is growing and changing. So are you—he feels this way, too. I've been privileged to have a wonderful marriage—which is not to say that every single day has been ideal. We ride the human cycles but . . . when we married we made the decision to hold the marriage above life's events and to place each other first. Even when we don't feel like it! This has worked. For, when dismaying situations right themselves (as they always do), we find that we have kept our marriage as a sacred thing apart and that it is still there, untarnished, untouched by disappointments, waiting for us to resume our joy.

The discovery of each other on ever deepening levels is one of the great rewards of a long marriage.

Love forever,
Mother

❑

25 June 1967

Dear Sterling,

Diana said that I could read neither your last letter nor her reply. I want you to know that your close relationship with your mother makes me very happy. She is the light of my life and I hoped you would cherish her as I do.

Here's our second check for the Citizens' Action Group. Hope all's going as you envisioned.

Love,
Dad

❏

July 7, 1967

Dear Roz,

Don't—for God's sake—tell anyone, but this prison business is messing me up. It's bonkers there.

Examples:

1. If an inmate who regularly attends our group is ill or has something else he has to go to one Tuesday night, a "rotator" will come in. This is a man who has previously been in a group. This week we got a guy Mac knew but thought was "on the street": Frank McQuade. Turns out that Frank (a hothead) had been released, gone to South Carolina to find his wife, thrown her against several walls and broke her neck (she had been cheating on him). Then, knowing he would be arrested by S.C. police, drove over the line into N.C. and robbed a gas station so he could come back to <u>this</u> prison where he feels at home! (A law-breaker is usually incarcerated in the state where he committed the most recent offense.)

2. Our discussion this week was on the consequences of theft, TO THE VICTIM. They just couldn't get it through their heads that it wasn't "OK because insurance pays for the stuff and they can get it replaced."

Ouch.

Love,
Sterling

❏

Sterling

Summoned.
Fearful.
Corridor.
Office.
Warden.

Papers.
Handshake.
Parole.
August.
Speechless.
Cigarette.

Corridor.
Cell.
Alone.

Parole.
Marvel.
You.
Me.
Marvel.
We.
Adrift.

Jeff

❑

July 24th

Dear Jeff,

Congratulations on being granted parole. But I have to tell you right now that I can't be with you. I shouldn't have written so candidly to you. Things have changed a lot this year. I want to be with my family. I acted foolishly.

I'll be closing the post office box and I'm asking you not to get in touch with me. Please.

I wish you luck, health and success. You are a good person.

All best,
Sterling

❑

Sterling

Nothing ever
leaves the universe,
it simply
changes form.

I do not leave
you
ever.

I am night.
I am rain.
I am wind
in the trees.
I am the streetlamp
shining onto the bed
where man and wife
sleep.

You are the universe
I do not leave.
I am rain under the door.
Wind, through the keyhole.
Feel it?
On your face?

Jeff

❑

August 2, 1967

Dear Jeff,

I was puzzled by your poem. You can't mean that you are going to "shadow" me. That's what I got out of it anyway. It felt to me like a threat.

I have closed the post office box and am asking you not to contact me. You have many talents that will do well for you as you begin your new life. I admire what you can become now that you have a chance. But I want to remain with my husband and I don't want to be constantly looking over my shoulder.

Please be reasonable and let me off the hook. My attempts to help you were colored by my temporary boredom with homemaking. I am different now, satisfied.

Let me go. I am sorry.

Sterling

❏

August 15, 1967

Dear Sterling,

In all, I've had 16 rejections. This beats the odds and I know the school and WCHI are giving me bad references. I'm depressed! I can't keep living here with Mom and Dad.

I've tried everybody. I've even offered to be a correspondent in Vietnam. I can't stand the idea of Podunk but I'm going to have to apply to much smaller stations, I guess. I feel like my life is over and I haven't even started. I envy your security. No one can rock your boat.

Write to me.

QUINN

❏

8/20/67

Dear Quinn,

It's terrible that this is happening to you. In my fantasies, I have clout, can get you what you want. I guess that can never come true but perhaps it will make you feel better to know I wish it.

Love,
Sterling

❏

August 29, 1967

Dear Mother,

Did you have a moment in your marriage when you started loving Dad so much that you were afraid of losing him? Or afraid of inadvertently hurting him?

We had a second honeymoon in Chicago after the graduation. Now I sort of feel stricken. Do you know what I mean?

Tell me the answer. I hope it's yes. What did you do?

Sterling

❏

Dearest Sterling,

The high times in a marriage are very much like the low times in that you wonder if it all can last. Don't be afraid. You're simply entering a new stage. Enjoy your husband's love.

Mother

❏

Sterling—

I am dying. It's September and I don't have a job. These dumb little stations continue to have the nerve to turn me down. Is there legal action I can take against the people who are blackballing me? Maybe I should go to grad school next semester or switch from broadcasting to print. I could try the big newspapers. But I want to be on TV. That's what I like. I am disgusted and ready to strangle somebody. If only I knew who!

Q.

❏

September 19, 1967

Dear Sterling,

John said you called. I appreciate your concern. We are fine. We dropped out of the group because we got burned out. Too tired and disillusioned to continue. God willing, our strength will return and we will pursue helping the men again.

There were some ex-cons who succeeded. We were able to find them jobs which they took seriously and built, from that, a second chance. But the others took a tremendous toll on our personal and professional lives (especially personal).

You realize, having been in the program for over a year, what an uphill fight it is. You are bucking their background, which is deeply ingrained. I thought I could change their ideas but now I know that if I can—once in a long while— change a tiny piece of an idea, I'm doing well.

They gradually stripped our house and stripped our spiritual resources. There was a lot of lying and dishonesty in other ways, which—I'm sorry to say—seems to be part of their culture.

We leave it to you and to others who are bright with energy and we hope someday to resume our task.

Wishing you God's blessings,
Gwen Harleyson

❏

Sterling

There he was,
washing the car.
I asked him for
directions.
He replied kindly.
Blond, tall.
Half of one eyebrow
gray.

The irises of his green eyes
have yellow specks
like splinters.
The hint of a scar
divides his chin.
I breathed his breath.
I was him
for seconds on end.
His flesh stayed peaceful
as he spoke.
I could have touched him.
Easily.

Jeff

❏

How dare you come near my husband? How dare you write to me at home? I am going to get a court injunction against you if you don't keep away from us.

❏

October 2, 1967

Dear Sterling and Randy,

I finally got a job. I'm going to be a reporter for WMTN-TV in Memphis. To tell you the truth, I'm not too excited about it but it's an offer. I leave Thursday, start Monday. I don't think there's anything too thrilling in Memphis except Elvis. I'll be apartment-hunting this weekend and will send you my address.

Love,
Quinn

❏

October 11, 1967

Dear Mrs. Hamilton,

Jeff Mather asked me to write. You may or may not be aware that he left prison in early August. Your letter was forwarded to me as his parole officer. I don't open his mail, but I see that he gets it.

Jeff has asked for privacy in order to begin his life again. Therefore, I will continue distributing his mail and am not at liberty to give out his address.

Yours,

K. G. Malaschak

❑

Sterling

Does he know?
Does he know?
Does he know?

Does he know?
Does he know?
Does he know?
Does he know?
Does he know?

Does he know?
Does he know?

Does he know?
Does he know?
Does he know?
Does he know?

Do you want him
to?

Jeff

❑

November 5, 1967
Dear Sterling and Randy,
    We were delighted to get the phone call and to learn that you are expecting!

It's impossible to imagine another child as dear as Mindy and Lance, but we know Baby #3 will be every bit as precious.

We love you.

Mother and Dad

❏

November 17, 1967

Sterling, my dear—

Here's our third and last check of the year, made out to: Citizens' Action Group. You have proved to us—by your devotion to it—that this is an excellent project and we are proud of your involvement.

Love always,

Dad

❏

Sterling

Beyond tree fire,
she held him by the hand.
O, their faces!
How long since I'd seen children?
He began to run in circles
around her.
She turned and turned,
watching him
until she staggered,
giggling,
and fell.
He plopped
across her stomach
and they laughed.
The only other sounds

were bird song,
a train
in the distance,
and
the scratch
of your rake
against dead leaves.

Jeff

❏

Jeff: What do you <u>want</u>?

❏

Dear Ros,
   I need $2500 cash, no questions asked. I'm in a jam. I don't think I can pay
it back. I don't know what else to do. If you will, bring it at Christmas. Don't let
anyone see.

Sterling

❏

Dear Roz,
   THANK YOU! You are a <u>true friend</u>. I got it taken care of and I'm sure that's
the end of the problem. Please, let's just forget about it. All is well! I'll pay you
back if I ever can. I don't know when that would be. Thank you, thank you,
thank you.

Love,
Sterling

❏

1 9 6 8

Quinn

Hey girl—Whatcha doing in Memphis? Don't you know that's some bad country. What am I going to do with this brother of mine who's stomping his own heart? Don't feel any pressure, of course. You got to go where you go. But I miss dressing you up like a baby doll. You looked sassy in that blond curly wig. I got tired of not writing to you and pretending I never heard of Quinn Suzanne Who? You're still on my list. Now how about a letter.

Dagmar (Fortner in case you forgot)

❏

1/16/68

Dagmar Who?

I started smiling as soon as I saw your handwriting on the envelope. You nailed me, kid. I'm yours. Tell Lou to stop stomping his heart. Makes me feel guilty. And send me that blond wig. I've never looked as good since.

Yes I'm in bad country, working 3 to midnight (TV news). A good schedule for lazy people. I sleep til 10 or 11, go to the station at 2:30, mingle til everyone else goes home at 5. I've got an assignment editor (Ken Rankin), plus a photographer (Tee Frazer) who goes out on stories w/ me in a news car. Just the 3 of us at nite. They're good company.

News is gruesome. It's always an accident or? Cops think we're ghouls. They're right. Our mentality is: "I've got to get to that wreck before the ambulance takes the victims away! I've got to get to that fire while there are still flames to shoot!" Duh.

Send me the red wig, too. Makes me look like Juliet Prowse.

Quinn

❏

Quinn

Go out and talk to the dad of that missing girl. I'll tell you what I think: he did it himself. No one could have gotten into the house at night with the parents there and no evidence of forced entry. We'll find her in a ditch. Bet you.

Rankin

❏

After talking with him, I agree with you. The interview gave me the creeps. This guy has blood on his hands. If only they could find a body.

Q.

❑

January 28, 1968

Dearest Quinn,

How we miss you since we didn't get to see you at Christmas! But we perfectly understand that you are a new employee and have to work holidays.

It was good to talk with you on the phone and hear about the fun you're having. The news business must be exciting. We especially loved your description of fighting with the film splicing machine and how it spits glue at you. I'm glad your life has leveled out, Sweetheart. Those college years were rough.

Dad and I had the Morrisons over for dinner last night and they asked about you. I made chicken breasts with mushroom soup and seasonings, cheese potatoes sprinkled with bread crumbs, peas and onions, banana muffins and frozen lemonade pie. Deelish!

God bless you.

Love,
Mother

P. S. Your apartment sounds tiny
but cozy. Anything you need for it?

❑

To: Kip Donovan
From: Quinn Morrow
Date: February 1, 1968

Enclosed is another application for an auto loan through the credit union. As you will see, I still have no assets or collateral but my boss, Ted LaSalle, insists that I own a car in order to hold this job. I can take the bus to work; however, big news stories frequently occur in my off-hours and Ted has to send someone to get me. Please could you deduct my monthly payments directly from my salary? Thank you for considering this again.

❑

2/15/68

Dagmar!

Thank you for the wigs! I was just kidding but I do look divine in them. Audacious!

You know, I feel closer to you than I do to my own sisters. They are super but we are growing apart. I don't know why. They seem to lead such uncomplicated lives and mine seems so complicated.

Anyway, I appreciate you.

Uh-huh!
Quinn

P.S. Bought my first car yesterday.

❏

St. Patrick's Day

Dear Quinn,

Blimp time again. I never get into my regular clothes! They go out of style before I wear them out. This baby is not a kicker but a turner. Does somersaults sideways. If I'm standing up, I have to hold onto something to keep my balance. A gymnast?

I resigned from the Citizens' Action Group since I am pregnant. I was waning in my enthusiasm anyway. The men are incorrigible.

Am taking classes in Modern Health and Nutrition. Go through your kitchen and see what you're really eating. A lot of chemicals, no doubt. You can't change over all at once, of course, but don't buy any more junk. I'm enclosing instructions on how to stock your pantry and your body with food it can use effectively. For example, preservatives in food are bad for you. (Did you know it takes a dead body 48 hours longer to begin to decay in 1968 than it did in 1900?) Don't eat sugar either, use RAW honey for sweetner. Etc! Since I began to wake up to the dangers of non-food, I can hardly eat in a restaurant or at a friend's house. If you have questions, I'll be glad to answer them.

Love,
Sterling

❏

Body found 6 p.m. Couldn't raise you on the radio. Get a statement from & film of (if possible) family. I'm at Ho-Jo for a quick bite.

Ken

❏

Still bet we're right but they'll never get him unless he confesses. She'd been in the creek too long. What a world.

Ken

❏

Dag—My God. Tee and I were in the news car. Had just picked up K Fried Chicken & a call comes over the 2-way. "Police radio says man shot on balcony of Lorraine motel." Tee knows the area. Mulberry St. Very near us. We go like hell & meet a million police cars. Who? I know before I see. He has blood-soaked towels on his head as they take him to the ambulance. I get sick into a trash can & all over my sleeves. Tee grinds away, lights on, elbowing cops who poke him with sticks. We chase the ambulance to St. Joe's where we're shut out. Rankin screams at us on the radio because we didn't stay at the scene. Sniper fired from across the street in a rooming house & got away. We go back. Police have cordon around the area and won't let us in. Most are white, their eyes amused at my devastation. "He died," one tells me, searching for a reaction. I give him coldness but cry as I edit Tee's film and as I read my script on the air. At home, Lou calls me and we weep without speaking for minutes over the open line. I hate life.

Q.

❏

April 7, 1968

Dearest Quinn,

A national tragedy and in the midst of it we see you, giving a report on TV. We couldn't believe it. Tried and tried to call you but your line was either busy or rang and rang. Spoke with the station switchboard operator who checked and told us you had gone to Atlanta for the funeral.

How does that work: you are on the air in Memphis but we see you in

Pittsburgh? You looked broken, on the edge of tears. It upset us almost as much as the assassination. We've only started to settle down.

You did a good job. We are proud of you. I hope this has not affected you too much. We worry about you. Take care of yourself, Sweetheart.

Love and hugs,
Mother & Dad

❑

Quinn—

It was still wonderful to be with you under terrible circumstances. Our time in Atlanta was bittersweet. When are you going to stop pretending we don't love each other? You make me crazy.

Lou

❑

Lou—

My King story was picked up for network and I got a call from some LA TV muckety-muck who saw it. I thought he was blowing smoke but turns out he has a job for me. Still in news but it's a much better salary. I am moving May 15. New address on envelope. I feel like a beast profiting from this event. I'm ashamed, but I have to keep breathing. You make me crazy too.

❑

May 14th

Dear Quinn,

Something thrilling is happening! Our baby is going to be born at home! After two hospital births, I have ceased to believe that is the right way. It's impersonal. I've arranged for a midwife to come in since Randy doesn't want the responsibility of delivering the baby, but he will coach me same as always.

To tell you the truth, he doesn't like the idea of home birth but wants to please me. I point out to him that until this century all babies were born at home. I know I will win him over when he sees how emotionally fruitful the experience can be.

Our major hassle right now is that I want Mindy and Lance to be present for the birth so that the whole family can bond together. Randy won't hear of it, but I'm sure that when I go into labor he won't be able to say no.

When you write, please convince him.

Love,
Sterling

P.S. Enclosed is a photo of darling Mindy on her 4th birthday. I have over 1400 pictures of her now. Isn't she cute?

❑

May 23, 1968

Dear Quinn,

I am writing in the midst of bedlam. I'm having the back parlor remodeled and they are knocking out the south wall. Ah, the sound of bricks being split and crushed! When finished, this room will be sunny. They're installing a long bay window to overlook the side yard. The neighbors squawked because I had two old elms removed but I think they'll love the 70 rose bushes to be planted instead. Now, I'm working on selecting white overstuffed furniture and white wicker (pink accents) to surround the window. Plenty of plants & a gray slate floor. Oh, joy!

What's new with you? How do you like LA?

Rozzy
XXX

❑

5/31/68

Dear Mother and Dad,

Los Angeles is awesome. Huge! I have a swell apartment on a hillside in Hollywood. It's very rustic and has big rooms. The neighbors are nice. Don't worry.

I appreciated your calling me before I left Memphis. I miss you a lot. Come see me.

Love and more love,
Quinn

❑

5/31/68

Dear Dagmar,

Los Angeles is weird. I live on the side of a mountain in West Hollywood. You have to park the car below and take an ancient outdoor tower elevator up to a steep path and frame cottages. I've got a furnished living room and bedroom, separated by a kitchen & bath. Cockeyed arrangement. Unglamorous. Sparse. Ok—it's a dump. I confess. I can see the famous hillside HOLLYWOOD sign from my front door. My 23-year-old neighbor says Christ appeared to him in the elevator. He (the neighbor) made me promise to walk always in the grass and leave the path clear for the Lord.

Ho hum
Quinn

❏

Dag,

I was asleep and the phone rang. "Kennedy's been shot! Get down there!" Time warp. This is 1968. Isn't it? I couldn't figure it out. "Kennedy's been shot at the Ambassador!" Ridiculous. Kennedy was shot in Dallas. I hung up on the nut and took the phone off the hook. Three minutes later, I jumped into my closet and started throwing clothes on. I slipped in the mud and slid the last eight feet to the elevator.

When I got to the Amb, K had been taken to a hospital but every reporter in town was there including 4 or 5 of our own plus news dir. "Get a sidebar," he said to me. A sidebar? But I am well trained. I don't analyze, I just act. Campaign workers were milling around, stricken. I wandered from group to group, eavesdropping. Waiters were talking in a hallway about one of the K children who had watched it on TV in the hotel room. That's how I got that clip you saw on network. It concerns me how calm I was this time. The place behind my eyes feels like leather that's been wet & dried many times. I wept for hours afterwards but I don't think I ever will again. Q.

❏

Did we really talk 2½ hours on the phone? Seemed like 2½ minutes. Got my diploma today. I'm an attorney now. Treat me with the proper respect, please.

That includes marrying me when I ask you. How many times do I have to cry with you over the phone before you say yes?

Louis G. Fortner, Esquire

❏

Quinn—I saw you on TV. That was an incredible piece, horrifying. I had to watch the television all day as they brought Kennedy's body back on the train, so that I could grasp reality. My emotions are glazed from the violence we have endured. Massachusetts is in heavy mourning. I can't believe you are at one end of the country and I'm at the other. I want to be with you, soon.

Rozzy

❏

Randy, Sterling, Mindy and Lance
announce the birth of
their daughter and sister
Sovereign Carter Hamilton

on

June 7, 1968

at 8:44 a.m.

Weight 7 lbs.

Length 20"

Presbyterian Hospital

Charlotte, North Carolina

June 17, 1968

Dear Quinn,

I'm not writing this to everyone because Mother would have a heart attack and Roz would probably laugh and it's not funny to me. Nothing went as planned. The baby took a long, long time and the midwife got scared. I was making a lot of noise and the children (Randy had consented to have them there) started getting wild. In the middle of the whole thing, Randy scooped me up and put me in the back seat of the car. I was sputtering but in no position to argue. We made it to the hosp parking lot and the attendants delivered the baby in the car! People were hanging out of their room windows shouting encouragement.

Isn't Sovereign the prettiest name you ever heard?

Sterling

❏

July 10, 1968

Dear Quinn,

Mom & Dad's visit over the long 4th of July weekend was terrific. We did the touristy things like the parade, the North Church, Paul Revere's house, etc. They seemed healthy and happy, as usual. It's beautiful to watch, year after year, isn't it? We should be so lucky! Or is it luck? Perhaps it's a decision.

I had a small get-together for them. We ate dinner and danced.

Back to work this week and guess who rode with me! Steve McQueen. Should have mentioned that first, right? He's a little guy. You'd be amazed. They make him look big on screen. He didn't say much, so no juicy gossip for you.

Sah-ree!

Roz

❏

July 15, 1968

Dearest Quinn,

You have always been close to Rosalind so I want to ask you to call her more frequently. Dad and I think she is lonely. When we were there for Independence Day, we had a distinct feeling of emptiness in her life. The first couple of days we were fooled by her activity and smiles. She is a wheeler-dealer.

Somehow she's got hold of a lot of money. I know it's because she treats money wisely. She's been like that since the beginning.

She threw a huge champagne party for us. An Event. Two or three hundred candles flickering in glass chimneys throughout the house and yard. Many stylish people showed up: brokers, poets, politicians, the works. She was charming and gracious with them. But, on quiet nights, she would be reflective, sitting, looking out at the dark garden as if waiting for someone. She's 25 and no person outside the family has been extra special to her except the two who went away. She has substituted great numbers for these losses. She lives in abundance: $, clothes, friends, jobs, flowers. But she breaks our hearts with her heart's silence. Please help us take care of her.

Love,
Mother

❏

You did a heck of a job on that Disney chopper crash yesterday. You've refined your approach immensely since May. I see a professional who does not let sentiment get in the way of a thorough story. Keep it up.

Harlan

❏

---

*We, Quinn and Lou Fortner, announce
the beginning of our life together.*

Welcome, Good Friends

*94 Tyrone Lane, West Hollywood
August 18, 1968*

Rozzy!
Only you would air-express 15 dozen roses on ice from your garden. How
generous. We are living in heaven.

Quinn & Lou

❏

September 4, 1968

Dear Mother and Dad,

I'm sorry you are sad but I don't believe I am responsible. I honestly believe
I have the right to the type of wedding I desire. We wanted to be married by a
justice of the peace—there was no reception. I didn't imagine you or Sterling
or Roz would like to come all the way to California under those circumstances.
Also, when we made the decision, we couldn't see waiting. We <u>did</u> call our
families the night before.

Please come out here for Christmas. We'd be glad to host you. I won't be able
to get Christmas off this year because I am new at the station. Lou is looking
forward to meeting you.

Love always.
Quinn

❏

September 5th, 1968
Dear Quinn and Lou,

You sure surprised us! We are delighted for you and wish you All Good
Things. Lou, we hope we'll have the chance to meet you soon.

Congratulations, you two! May you have many glorious years together.

Love,
Sterling and Randy

❏

Quinn—

I am writing to you at work because I had to speak my piece. You are acting
totally selfish and self-centered! How could you not invite Dad and Mom to your
wedding? I know they have really been hurt by it. To get married on the spur of
the moment was thoughtless. You owe them an apology.

I don't understand you anymore. Is it because you have this important job now that you think we're unimportant?

Rozzy and I might have liked to attend, also! When I think back on my wedding and how meaningful a time it was to me, I'm glad my family was there to share my joy.

Sterling

❏

Dear Sterling,

No, I don't think you're unimportant. But neither do I feel compelled to explain myself. I have the right to choose my own course unhampered by traditions and the expectations of others.

Quinn

❏

September 11, 1968

Dearest Quinn,

The reason Dad and I felt as we did was because we know that families who start to skip rituals and leave members out of important events are heading in the wrong direction. A family can too easily come apart. We want ours to remain close. It's our highest wish that you three girls and your families share life fully (even though distance may separate you) and constantly contribute to each other's happiness.

We love you,
Mother

❏

Your story on the funeral for the 19-year-old killed in Vietnam was a masterpiece. Without stating it directly, you made him a symbol of a lost generation of young people. War is an abomination, you are a rare talent. I'm glad I hired you.

Harlan

❏

10/2/68

Dear Dagmar,

We have a new address. Against our will. I thought Lou could just move in with me. In fact, I didn't think about it at all. I didn't realize the landlady was a bigot. She's Southern (what else?) and peered, amazed, at Lou the first time she saw him. "Is that a Nigrah?" she gasped. Lou glanced behind him to see who she was talking about. Out we went. Then, Lou had his furniture shipped from Ann Arbor and we moved it into a duplex. Before we could bring our clothes & stuff over from my place, we got a letter cancelling our lease. It was obvious why. I had rented it alone & some neighbor saw us carrying the furniture in. I tell Lou to bring suit but he's a gentle soul. Maybe I can get permiss. to do an investigative on this.

Our new house is in a predominantly black area of West LA. Older but pretty. Mature shrubbery and trees. Lou got a job in a giant law firm. Nine names in the title!

QUINN

❑

October 5, 1968

Dear Dad and Mom,

Thank you for the lamp! It is beautiful and brightens our living room. A perfect selection.

I know you have had some reservations about how accepted a bi-racial couple will be but don't worry. LA is full of interesting people, of every description and persuasion. There aren't the pressures here that we might get in other locations.

Lou sends his best.

Lots of love,
Quinn

❑

11/3/68

Dagmar, mah dear.

People are so damned rude. Lou and I were in a (white) restaurant for lunch today and we could hardly eat for the staring. That's stupid. People comment on us in those loud-hushed tones. They want us to hear. Then, when we went to the cash register and the man handed Lou his change, I received a "you got shit for brains" frown. Happens all the time. Pardon, but I need to talk about it. Lou refuses to discuss and, as you can guess, we don't have many folks gravitating to us.

Love,
Quinn

❑

H. —
There have been 32 (!) underground nuclear tests in Nevada this year. I'm listing the dates on the back of this sheet. The Dec 19 explosion caused a violent earthquake. Ask not for whom the bell tolls. Give me this story. I have a statement to make.

Q

❑

Dear Quinn and Lou,

Christmas in California was great. I thought the walls of your house would blow out, we had so much fun. Dagmar is a scream.

Quinn, sorry you had to spend Christmas Eve & Day in S. Diego covering the return of Pueblo but I was well taken care of: fattened and toasted to contentment by L. & D.

I appreciate all you 3 did to make me feel welcome. I talked with Sterling last night and she said M&D's visit to them worked out fine. The kids were thrilled to have Grandma and Grandpa around. I know you were disappointed they didn't come to see you. Perhaps they will shortly. I think they wanted to see Sovereign on her first Christmas. Tough choices.

Kisses
Ros

❑

Quinn

Schaefer got his sentence commuted. Guess you're out of luck. You're an enigma. I hired you for the soft job you did on the King assassination and now you're volunteering to be a witness at an execution. Maybe next year . . .

❑

New Year's Eve
Dear Sterling,

There is a friend of yours here: Jeff Mather. He said he met you in an adult ed class. Well, he lives in LA now and saw me on TV. He remembered that your sister was a TV reporter and wondered how many Quinns could be floating around. I treated him to lunch in the company cafeteria. He's powerful. What does he do? He was kind of mysterious about his occupation. Undercover government? Lou came in to see me at work and the two of them hit it off. Both like to sail so they spent Sat. at S. Monica on a Catamaran.

Hugs for the kidz,
Quinn

❑

1 9 6 9

Rosalind

New Year's Day
1969

Dearest Rosalind,

How sweet of you to visit Quinn and Lou. I know they appreciated it. I only wish we could have all been together. Dad and I missed you three so much! I feel concerned about the fact that one or the other person is missing from the group each Christmas and, this Christmas, we were two distinct groups! Not good. Dad and I will try to think of a way to rectify it.

Sterling is one busy gal. The children are 100 percent beautiful, but there is no peace right now. Please, will you call or write to her and Randy more often? We noticed a lot of tension between them — which is normal, given their overwhelming responsibilities. I'm asking Quinn to do the same.

We give thanks every day that our daughters are living such meaningful, dignified lives and achieving success in their relationships.

Much love,
Mother

P.S. If Annie's still there when you get this letter, give her a big HELLO from us.

❑

1/18/69

Dear Annie,

You are making too much of this. It's my life, after all. Why does it matter to you what I do? We can still be friends, can't we?

I was glad to have you as a houseguest and I hope you'll come back soon. You are my favorite non-relative!

Your agitation forced me to think over my motives. Truthfully, it's simple. When I remember the effort I spent defending my virginity and, later, devoting myself wholely to Glenn, then Thom, it seems a monumental waste of time. One should be centered, not pulled off balance by this person and that, this cause and that.

I love to be loved. It's very uncomplex. I like the attention and I am never lonely, no matter who stays or goes.

Remember the pleasure of hearing an instrumental piece of music for the first time? You delighted in it immediately and a great part of the excitement was in its strangeness to you—in not knowing what notes were next. This is the way I feel.

I don't want to be caged. Can't you accept me as I am?

Roz

❏

Dear Ros,

Of course, I accept you the way you are. But your letter shook me up because, underneath the words, I could read your pain. If you never get close to any of these men, you never have to be hurt again. I still have the letter you wrote the night Sterling married Randy. I see similarities to the life you have chosen. You are settling for the only thing you think you can get, or worse, that you think you deserve. I hope this honesty doesn't break our friendship. I stand by you no matter what. Keep telling me the truth.   Annie

❏

with her as an "In." She said he sounded like a leech. But you know Sterling. Can you follow this. Sorry I'm popping up to the top of the page but I'm out of paper. Lou sends his love. Quinn   Feb. 2

Dear Rozzy

Lou and I have been totally involved with our work and suddenly realized we are out of touch with the world. It is our fault. We haven't cultivated friend-ships. In fact, at this point, we've only got one pal outside the office. He's a guy who used to live in NC. Sterling knows him, I guess. He said he was in an adult ed class with her but she doesn't remember. Anyway, he's a lot of fun. Was a mystery man for a couple of weeks but then confessed that he's a bartender. Didn't think we'd be too intrigued with his occupation. He's poor as a church mouse. A friend gave him the money to get to the West Coast but now he's living in a boarding house, with mainly homosexuals who steal his socks. I don't know why. They steal his socks, that is. Does this letter make sense? I've been nipping a little. (Not a habit, don't get excited.) He eats raw potatoes and lettuce sandwiches. Poverty. Lou bought him some clothes. We like him because he's humorous, intelligent, creative. Sterling was bitchy about him for no particular reason so don't tell her we've continued the relationship. She said what were we doing picking up with someone who used a passing acquaintance

❏

Damn it all I am pregnant again. I haven't even told Randy. He's going to be boiling. These babies keep us so tired! We are multiplying like rabbits. At our educational level you'd think we could PREVENT this. I wish I could do something to stop my pregnancy, flush it away. Don't ask me how this happened. I don't know. Rozzy, send me some energy. I don't want to have another baby. I asked my doctor about you know what and he looked at me like I was rotten to the core. "It's illegal, for one thing," he said, concentrating on my file. The bastard. Why don't they help us when we need it? Men!

❑

February 9, 1969

Dear Annie,

Thanks for your call. Wonderful. Here's something I was thinking: if you were married, we'd lose this privacy. We wouldn't be as close anymore. Every call and letter would be overheard or shared. That's what's happened with my sisters.

I got an upsetting letter from Sterling this week but couldn't answer it because she didn't want Randy to know what she wrote. I decided to phone her during the day, while he was at work, so we got to talk frankly. That helped, but I don't like the idea that I only have access to her true feelings on certain days and times.

Good luck on your interview. Let me know how it turns out.

Love!

Roz

❑

Dear Roz,

What is wrong with Sterling? If anyone knows, you do. Please call me at the office, collect. I am getting gray hairs.

Randy

❑

2/14/69

Ruth:

Put aside your predictions. I have my own. I'll take the responsibility and not blame you for loss—guaranteed. Run a check on the following companies: Avon, Burroughs, Eastman Kodak, General Motors, Ingersoll-Rand, Polaroid, Xerox. Up to the minute.

Rosalind

❑

2-19-69

Dear Ros,

I was wrong to try to involve you. You were right in stonewalling. Forgive me. She told me about the baby and I am delighted. I feel bad that she's so upset. I'm going to get her some day help and we'll work it out.

Sorry I bothered you. A breech of trust, going behind her back like I did. You're a great friend to both of us.

Randy

❑

Made the buys. I should know better than to argue with your track record.

Ruth

❑

February 25, 1969

Dear Annie,

The strangest thing happened. I was driving along the interstate, approaching a tunnel, when traffic slowed and stopped. I was anxious to get home because a big snow storm was predicted. I had just finished an assignment. It was about 4:00 in the afternoon, snow-dark, ominous. All the lanes were full of cars, waiting. Time crept on. It started to snow in giant, wet flakes. I kept the wipers going, but eventually they couldn't clean the windshield. I noticed I was low on fuel. Decided there must be an accident in the tunnel and that I'd better turn off the car. I did and within minutes I was freezing! Traffic still wasn't moving. Weird how the snow blanketed the car, like I was being entombed.

I saw a hand. Someone was clearing my windshield with a scraper. It was a man. I realized he had gotten out of the jeep next to me to do this. He smiled and I thought I recognized him.

He cleared my windshield every 10 minutes for half an hour. Finally, I unlocked the door and he got into the car with a thermos of coffee, which we drank. I had a box of Nabs, etc. that I always keep in the car. We ate, and talked. He said he was a professor of political science at Yale. He looked to be in his early 30's, with thinning blond hair and blue eyes. Very gentle, unassuming. Slender. We tried a few, "Do I know you from . . ." sentences but decided we had never met, as far as we knew. He's engaged to Elizabeth, a high school Latin teacher.

When the engines started all around us, an hour and twenty minutes after we had first stopped at the tunnel, we realized that a special communication had passed between us. He is different, Annie. Really different. I don't know where this will lead. His name is Paul Cordner. I gave him my card.

We could hardly get the cars going for the tremendous snow that had fallen. I found myself worrying about him on the way home. When I got there, the phone was ringing. It was Paul.

I don't want to feel this way. It's against my philosophy.

Ros

❏

Dear Rosalind,

You will be my inspiration for the Spring 1970 line. I see you as the most slender, white crescent of midnight moon. The collection will reflect primal femininity, delicate but enduring. Til later—

Arch DeV.

❏

10th March

Dear Ros,

I should have listened to you before the wedding. This isn't the right marriage for me and here I am trapped inside my body, with child again! I have a new vision, but it's too late. I was cutting vegetables for the salad last night and I stopped and looked at them. Do you know how dreary a carrot is, with those little hairs on it and that one straggly end and that green hard top?

My life is mundane and I chose it! I am the invisible wife of a dentist. I'll be

peeling and chopping carrots forever. How smart you were to gear your life to
your own needs and wishes. You don't have to depend on a man for every piece
of bread that goes into your mouth.

We were at Randy's folks' house the other night. She loves home making.
She can wax poetic about cleaning out a closet. His dad showed home movies.
They think big time fun is running them backwards: babies in highchairs
spitting food back onto a spoon which goes into a dish, kids riding wagons
uphill, people jumping out of pools up onto diving boards.

I am miserable.

Sterling

❑

March 26, 1969

Dear Annie,

What's happening to me doesn't make sense. I don't believe in marriage but
I am fantasizing homey things about Paul. He builds a shelf in the living room.
He sits by the fire with his shoes off, studying a fat book. He is in the grocery
store with me, picking out steak. All in my mind. I haven't seen him since the
day in the snow, but he calls me. We hardly know what to say. It's casual.
Elizabeth has selected her wedding gown, he says by way of sealing off further
emotion between us. He is busy, but wonders how I am.

I look in the mirror and talk to myself. I have better things to do than think
about floor wax, ironing, hanging around with a husband, for Pete's sake. This
is a trick my mind plays: wants me to believe I am missing special times with
single partner. Wants me to believe monogamy is better. You came close to
naming it: it's a function of my guilt.

Rozzy

❑

4-28-69

Dear Ros:

Got your card. You always comment when you see me on TV. And with
praise! Thanks. I hoped that skunk would get his just desserts. I've been in the
courtroom so much I have every hair on Sirhan's head memorized. Did you
realize I've been at this from January 7 til they announced the guilty verdict

April 17? Gas chamber, they say, but I doubt it. Death penalty's rare right now because of Supreme Court rulings. If he does go, I'll witness.

In other news, Lou and I have been playing Pygmalion with the bartender. Wants to be an actor and we are intrigued by it. We three sat around last Sunday and thought up a stage name for him: Jett Maeder. Isn't that masculine? Lou gave him money for acting lessons and fixing his teeth. Daft? But my work is so damned serious and so is Lou's. Jett makes us laugh. He's a buoyant personality. It's a two-way street. He's been doing our yard and he cooks. We gave him a key and come home to rack of lamb, baked Alaska, salad niçoise. Don't you dare tell Sterling. She criticizes me enough as it is.

Luv, QUINN

❑

May 5

Angel, Ros—

So now you know all about antiques and how to buy them. You also know all about <u>this</u> antique. (Say I'm spry for 57.)

A matchless experience, being with you. Can't wait until future books put me back in your path. You were a great companion.

You know the hand-wrought silver bowl (19th C.) you admired? It's in your china cupboard now—go see.

William

❑

Annie—

I have no heart for this anymore. I feel as though I'm committing adultery. He still calls me. He broke his engagement to Elizabeth. That would be his style, not to see me again until he was free. He's too straight-arrow. Even naive. No doubt I'll end up hurting him. I'll try to keep him out of Boston. He doesn't belong here and I am afraid.

Ros

❑

Look At The Birdie!

ON DISPLAY THIS MONTH in the lobby of the Wachovia Bank Building in downtown Charlotte is a collection of amateur but crisp color photographs depicting the first five years of a child's life. What makes this sequence unusual is that the photos were taken at the rate of one a day since the girl's birth on May 11, 1964.

Amanda Melissa, daughter of Charlotte dentist Randolph C. Hamilton and his wife Sterling, has literally been the focus of their attention since she was delivered at Presbyterian Hospital.

"The nurses didn't want to let me take her picture those first couple of days, I guess because of the flash, but I was determined," Mrs. Hamilton said. She laughingly admitted to conceiving the idea and to being the principal photographer.

For the bank exhibition, the Hamiltons selected 300 of their 1800-plus pictures of "Mindy" and asked Wercom Studios of Monroe to mat them in eight-by-ten format. The result makes interesting and poignant viewing as a baby grows before your eyes. The baby, who blew out five candles on a bank-provided five-tier birthday cake the first day of the exhibition, smiled shyly when asked to comment.

ROZZY—THE PAPER WENT BANANAS—A DOUBLE PAGE SPREAD! YOU CAN KEEP THIS COPY.

❑

June 18, 1969

Dear Annie,

Well, they sure took their time about hiring you. Congratulations on your new position. It's intriguing that they will be training you to work with computers. It hardly seems likely that people in every walk of life, every occupation, will someday use computers the way we use pencil and paper or typewriter. Your description of that when we talked stuck with me.

Don't know how to spring this on you: I'm in love. Met Paul in New Hampshire for a long weekend at an inn. It was the oddest situation. We had seen each other only once before then: in the snow. I wasn't sure I'd recognize him. When I drove up the hill, he was playing with a dog on the grounds. I sat in the car and kept staring until I was sure, then walked over to him and said hi. He was formal, kind of embarrassed. He kissed me on the cheek. I was secretly amused that he had reserved separate rooms. I did stay in (and pay for!) mine the whole time! He has a keen sense of propriety but he's not weak or fussy. No! We slept together the last two of the three nights we were there. I was careful to follow his lead in how the relationship should progress.

Where is this going? How could I extract myself from my old identity and just be with him — even if I wanted to? I would have to simply disappear from Boston without a trace and turn up in New Haven. Otherwise, my past would follow me.

He hasn't called since New Hampshire — ten days — so I may be worrying for nothing. He may have decided I'm not for him.

You're a great listener.

Love,
Roz

❑

July 11, 1969

Rozzy,

This is the most important letter I have ever written to you. Try to understand. A couple of months ago, I was asked by a neighbor to join a women's group she was in. She said it was concerned with "consciousness raising." I went and thought her friends were totally deranged. For one, they were all angry. The first time I came away from there, I thought, "Blah, blah, blah."

So now I find out they are angry but they are right. My eyes have been opened to male dominance in the world, particularly in this culture. We are spit that men polish their shoes with. We have to stop it. Examples:

1. Women don't get equal pay for equal work because "a man has to support a family." And we accept this?! Why shouldn't we be paid for the contribution we are making instead of being paid what men think we need?

2. Women are male-defined. People at parties don't say: "What do you do?" They say: "What does your husband do?" the way they used to ask, "What does your father do?" We are measured by the status of our nearest male relative.

3. Women are ignored in the English language itself. Did you know a dictionary is being written that will scrap words like chairman (now chairperson), fireman (firefighter), actress (now actor)? We are trivialized in the language (poetess, etc.). Our efforts are given cutesy terms if they are recognized at all. Why should a woman be labeled Miss or Mrs. while a man is Mr. It is our private business whether or not we are married. And to have your

own identity erased by labels such as "Mrs. Randolph Hamilton" is annihilation of the soul.

Read the literature I am enclosing. It will change your life.

S.

❏

July 21, 1969

Rozzy—

MAN ON THE MOON! How about that? Just when I was sick to death of the news business, something historic AND uplifting happens! God, we needed it. I've been wading through murder and war since I started. Excellent timing. I was hoping a biggie would upstage Kennedy at Chappaquiddick. That stuff's not worth the air time that's being spent on it.

Guess who we ran into: Thom Brawley—in a restaurant on Sunset Strip. He looks like he's been kicked. He has another film—did you see?—Glass Barrage. The critics wiped their asses with it and printed the result. My opinion: Thom has a knack for choosing pseudo actors, like Sheena Galen and Duke Farraday. He's having trouble getting backing for another film.

He asked about you and gave me his card to send to you. I couldn't be snotty with him, he was so down.

Kisses,
Quinn

❏

7/28/69

Dear Annie,

I went to New Haven and stayed with Paul, met his friends. I belong there. I belong with him. I probably haven't told you enough about him to make you believe that he is the ONE. He is.

He has a vegetable garden as large in area as his house. He likes to go rafting. He's never been married. His favorite color is tan. He's close to his parents, brothers and sister. Plays the violin. Can whistle through his teeth in perfect pitch. Knows how to milk a cow. Is bi-lingual (French). Loves me.

As I read over this paragraph, I see that it's like a jigsaw puzzle I've only given you a few of the pieces for. You can't see the picture yet.

Stand by.

Hugs,
Rozzy

❏

August 1, 1969

Dear Ros,

This is a paradox: my round stomach showing up at pro-abortion rallies. Of the many aspects of the women's movement, I find pro-abortion the most important. To have control over our own bodies is our right. Heads turn when they see this 8-mo. pregnant woman walk in.

Rozzy, you spoke to me on the phone like you think this is a fad. It isn't. This is not temporary. I will not be the same person and America will not be the same place. Things are changing forever.

I can't understand why you won't agree with me. I hear you conceding on certain points but you almost cried when we discussed abortion. Why do you say it's murder? That fetus isn't a person yet, not breathing or doing anything on its own. I have three children—you don't have any—but you want to tell me how to feel. Live inside my body once. I hate not having power over it.

I can't go back where I started from. It's not possible.

Love,
Sterling

❏

Dear Rosalind Morrow:

Thank you for your generous contribution to our organization. The work is vital and must be done quickly. Although pro-abortion efforts are scattered, the movement is gathering strength. Therefore, as unlikely as it may seem that our Supreme Court would ever sanction abortion, pro-life advocates must be diligent in preserving the rights of every future child.

We appreciate your concern and action.

With Best Wishes,
Christine Henderson

❏

8-7-69   Dear Ros,
I'm losing the battle. I've got to tell someone and my parents, of course, are
biased. You look at things squarely, tell me . . . What am I doing wrong? I see
Sterling distancing herself from me. I have been a faithful husband. I have
held a job and provided well. I have answered her requests with increased
performance: I do know how to cook now. I do play with the children and
cherish those times. I'm doing the things I think are right. I'm acting with
what—I think—is love. It's not good enough.

What do you see? Who should I be? I was raised to be a gentleman, loyal
family person, hard worker, kind—if firm—father. It's not enough. I am
somehow ruining this marriage. I don't want to do that! Do I have a fatal flaw?
Please answer. Write me at the office. Mark it Personal.

Randy

❏

12th of Aug.

Dear Randy,
I don't know the answer. You look fine to me. I mean that sincerely. Would a
counselor help? I'm not one to give advice. But I wish for things to go well.
                              Love,
                              Ros

❏

August 22, 1969

Dear Annie,
I don't think I can keep Paul out of Boston much longer and he's bound to

catch on. I am at a crossroads. He wants me to marry him. I have so many questions! Should I tell him who I really am? I believe that if I do I will lose him. He isn't the type to take it lightly. His sense of honor will be offended. Also, he will feel — and rightly so — that I misrepresented myself. He will see it as a lie that I've fed to him although I haven't told him anything untrue, I've merely omitted what I thought wouldn't please him. Should I marry and start a new life? If I do, I will exist in fear that he will someday find out. The repercussions might be worse then. Or . . . they might not be as great because, perhaps, at that point I will have proved to him that I am a worthy partner. If I marry him, how will I close off my former world? Is it possible?

I want to be his wife. I already _feel_ married to him. Do I deserve the chance to step into this dream? I can't go back and erase what I've been.

Rosalind

❏

Rozzy—

You deserve to be happy. What you should do beyond that, I can't say.

Annie
with love

❏

9/8/69

Dear Ros,

We had a party! Lou and I weren't sure anyone would come, but they did. Jett helped us make shrimp Newburg and stuffed cherry tomatoes, wild rice. We invited mainly people from the office. Don't get mad, but I asked Brawley. Roz, he's a man who's given up. Do you know what he's doing? "Consulting." i.e. Nothing. He researches what types of cars, clothes, etc. should be in a movie of a certain era. It's a waste of his talent. The party went on to 3 a.m. Lucky we have our own house and the neighbors can't knock on the walls or call the landlord.

The party helped me let off steam. The Tate murders practically put me in my own grave. I don't need to elaborate. I'm sure you've had ample details. I wonder: does the public really need that much information? You wouldn't believe what I'm told to find out for news coverage. Like what was in a victim's stomach.

Forget I said that.

Love,
Quinn

❑

Sterling and Randy Hamilton
present
their newest addition

a daughter

Laine Gloria

September 10, 1969
Charlotte
North Carolina

ROZZY, I COULDN'T SEE REPORTING
HER WEIGHT AND LENGTH LIKE
SHE'S A FISH. THAT'S THE ODDEST
CUSTOM.   S.

October 12, 1969

Dearest Rosalind,

I know this will crush you, but Sterling and Randy are separating. She called us last night to ask if she could come home with all the children! We are amazed at this development and also that she would choose this time to leave. Laine's birth weight was very low—under 5 pounds—and she hasn't been gaining much. Sterling didn't want to tell you and Quinn this for some reason so please don't mention it to Quinn—or to Sterling. We are worried about what the upheaval will do to the baby.

We haven't talked with Randy but we have much sympathy for him. He seems to have matured into a responsible, caring man. Our goal is to stay neutral and hope they can mend their marriage. We don't like to be in the middle of this but we are her parents and feel it is important to respond in a positive way. She assures us that moving in here will be a temporary step and that she will find her own living quarters and employment. I'm sure she will get around to telling you shortly. Please act surprised.

We ask you, at this difficult time, to be close with Sterling so that she will not be lost from us. This is vital.

With loving wishes,
Mother

❑

October 19, 1969

Dear Quinn and Lou,

Tried to reach you a couple of times. Want you to share my exciting news. I am getting married! His name is Paul Cordner and he is a Yale professor. I am ecstatic and pinching myself to see if it's true.

This comes at an awkward time since Sterling and Randy are divorcing. I don't think Sterling or M & D would take this well right now, so keep my secret a while, okay?

Love,
Rozzy

❑

11/2/69

Dear Roz—if you got this far

I was hoping you wouldn't toss this letter when you saw it was from me. OK.

I'm the lowest form of human life. I deserve spite from you. I deserve to be stabbed with long knives.

Now that I'm on your good side, will you listen to me? (Your sister put me up to this. I'm afraid of you.)

I am going under for the last time and I still believe I have talent. Ego! What gall! Truly. I've made mistakes but I see what they are.

I have a winning script I bought for a man I believe will emerge as box office manna. I'm enclosing a clipping about him. He has promised to work under contract to me and I need to move fast before someone else tempts him.

Roz, I'm begging you to help me. Please. I am forming a group of investors to back this new film. Can't get studio support anymore/might as well be honest. Cd you put in $10,000. Or? Anything. Please.

Please.

Thom

❏

Impressive Debut Packing Yakky's

IN YAKKY'S BACKYARD, a Hollywood theater of only 50 seats, an astounding nightly ritual is unfolding. William Inge's too-familiar "Bus Stop" becomes a many-splendored vehicle in a matter of minutes from the opening, well, lack of curtain.

The eight-person cast, led by newcomer Jett Maeder as "Bo," creates a delivery as real as it is dynamic. In the tiny house, the audience is practically perched on stage as it undergoes a life experience rather than a spectator evening. Of the 17 performances thus far, none has failed to provoke a standing ovation.

The cohesiveness of the players and the authentic texture of emotions seem to be sparked by a single actor: Maeder, who mixes uncommon energy with physical grace. Almost imperceptibly, he imposes perfect pacing on the others who breathe as a single being under his will while maintaining the contrast of character so essential to the play's spirit.

If the accolades seem overdone, see for yourself. Nightly at 8:40. Tickets $10, at the door.

—Martin Goldbloom

❏

I knelt on my prayer rug and faced Boston when I got your check. I will continue to do so 4X a day. I owe you more than money and I'll try like hell to pay you back lavishly. Watch me.

Thom

❏

November 29, 1969

Dear Annie,

I'm in a perpetual good mood, planning how to make my getaway. With each day, I think: this may be the last time I will . . . drive here, book this, etc. I have my house on the market but there's no sign out front. I plan to disappear. I've got it figured out. And I'll gradually get back in touch with two or three trusted friends like Alexis.

Paul and I will be married in New Haven. I have asked him to give me time to wind up my business transactions. I will go to Connecticut when I am ready and stay with him. We want a small wedding. I hope you'll come.

Quinn and Lou are the only ones in my family who know so far, but I'd like to have everyone there. Parents, sisters, spouses, kids.

I am glad clear through! Thom Brawley, of all people, wrote me a letter asking for money to pursue a film project and I gave it to him. Now, that's glad! Personally, I don't care for him but I'm into giving people second chances at life. That's what I'm getting.

Love & luck
Rozzy

❏

Dec. 6

Dear Annie,

I'm numb. Opened the door today and it was Paul. No suspicion on his face, nothing but affection. Said he wanted to see my surroundings before I abandoned them. He was here all afternoon. I took my phone off the hook—he didn't realize.

He told me something that knocked the chair out from under me—dropped it into the conversation with no fanfare. He has political aspirations.

I could visualize immediately the impact of that. I have the potential to assassinate his character simply by being his wife. With Quinn being in News,

I know how it works: they take nothing on appearance. They dig for background, facts.

Annie, I love him. I don't want this to happen to such a good man. It would kill him. It would kill me. Don't say "don't worry." It <u>will</u> take place. They will air my past with glee.

You are thinking: "But, he might not win an election. It's a long shot, nearly impossible." You should meet him, Annie. He IS the stuff of leaders. His family is steeped in Connecticut heritage and old money.

Seeing him in my house made me understand. I was crazy to think I could pull this off. I have to tell him I changed my mind.

R.

❏

Dear Rozzy,

I have never, NEVER heard you so distraught. No, we won't say a word to anyone. We are as sorry as we can be that it didn't work out with Paul, that he disappointed you. I'm assuming that's what it is since you were crying. Damn his hide. If I ever got the chance, I'd squash him like a bug. I'm terrible. Shouldn't say these things, but that's how I feel. Vengeful. You are the best. Always. I'll call you in a few days. LUV

Quinn

❏

1 9 7 0

Sterling

January 4, 1970

Dear Rozzy,

At last, I am my own person. Only you knew why I chose that marriage and now I am shedding it.

Mother and Dad have been good to us. I regret that you and Quinn couldn't be here for Christmas. The children were darling. Excited!

I have friends in the Movement who are helping me to make the transition. No doubt I will end up living with or near some of them. A small group of women has established a communal settlement near Deep Creek, Maryland. I am seriously considering joining it.

Thank you for the children's gifts. I hope you don't mind that I took the liberty of mixing them up a little. I gave the tea set to Lance and the truck to Mindy. As you know, I'm anxious to keep the kids from stereotypical roles and early toys make an impression. I thought I should be honest with you in case Mindy thanks you for the truck when you're talking to her on the phone! The Happy Apple and crib mobile for Sovereign and Laine were just right. The kids were delighted.

Will keep you posted.

Love,
Sterling

❑

Sterling,

I know how you feel about men supporting women financially, but please let me help you one last time. This period is bound to be fraught with unforeseen expense. The enclosed cash is a gift, never to be paid back. No matter how old you get, you're still my child. Having children of your own, you must understand.

All my love,
Dad

❑

February 7, 1970

Dear Quinn,

The minute I saw this place, I knew I was home. It's the first time in my life I've lived on acreage. Quite a different feeling.

The house itself is an old barn made over into a series of apartments. The living quarters are on two floors and surround a huge central room. You can look down into it from the second-floor balcony. There's a big kitchen. We take turns cooking.

Outside, the meadows and the lake are idyllic. The children — 14 of them — roam freely, with the older ones watching the younger. We have applied to the State of Maryland to self-educate them. There are garden patches on the grounds and we plan to supply our own food, as much as possible.

Lettie, Theda, Gretchen, Jill and I are already like family. Our set-up can accommodate two more women, with children. We believe Theda's friends Beverly and Harriet will join us.

The absence of men grants us complete openness and relaxation. In fact, men are not permitted inside the house.

We plan to work on the quality of our lives while actively pursuing national legislation to improve the quality of life for all women. Our funds will come from part-time jobs outside the Farm, our writings, speaking and gifts.

Sterling

❏

Dear Sterling,

Don't divorce me. Can't we find a way to make things work? I miss you and the children so much — I can't express how agonized I am. My life is over. No matter what you do, I will always love you. If you feel you have to be away from me a while, I'll say okay and I'll wait for you. Or I'll quit work and live with you anywhere. Please wait. Don't file for divorce now. Give time a chance to heal us.

Randy

❏

February 20, 1970

Dearest Sterling,

How we miss you and the children. We are anxious to visit you at Freedom Farm. We'll drive down for an overnight soon. It's only 3 or 4 hours from Pittsburgh, right?

Sweetheart, did we understand you to say no men are allowed in your house?

That is a strange rule. Surely, you don't include Dad in that restriction. Please write and reassure him.

I feel badly that your situation at Christmas pre-empted visits from Quinn, Lou and Rosalind. Things were disorganized. None of us could help it—that's just the way it was. But I want to ask if, perhaps, you would make a point to be here with us next Christmas. I'm going to ask your sisters the same thing. We need to be together.

God love you.

Mother

❑

February 25, 1970

Dear Roz,

I am totally happy at Freedom Farm. We are dedicated to developing one another to full potential. I have told my Sisters here things I've never told anyone. Part of our household week is an encounter group in which all adults must participate. We probe each other's minds; challenge, even anger one another in order to bring forth the interior person, the one who has been repressed by sexual stereotyping in our culture. It is akin to slapping someone awake so that you can save her life.

I no longer have complete responsibility for household chores, as I did (mostly) with Randy. Chores, including child care, rotate. And there are days off.

There is no "head of household," no member more important than another.

In short, it is ideal and I cannot imagine ever leaving. I wish you would consider encountering with women in Boston. There is much to learn. You may be surprised at your own changes in attitude. Try it.

Sterling

❑

Dear Sterling,

What a surprise to learn that I am not welcome in your house. Are you sure? This seems like throwing out the baby with the bath water.

Please don't hide behind the "house rule." People make these rules, people can change them.

Am I to be penalized because of my sex? That's exactly what you're asking the world to stop inflicting upon you.

> Dad

❑

> 18th March

Dear Sterling,

How do you like the name Zandria?

You guessed it: Lou and I are with child.

Yay!

No problem at work. I'll take 2 months off without pay and hop back on board. We've already worked it out.

Isn't that terrific?

Quinn!

❑

Yes, TERRIFIC. I am glad for you and Lou. But you shouldn't have to take time off without pay. Make them pay you. Maternity should not be punished, it should be covered by your paid leave, same as anything else that might happen to you. Raise sand.

> Sterling

❑

> April 9, 1970

Dear Family,

It's important that you know where I stand and what I'm doing. I'm under the impression that not one person in a thousand knows what the proposed Equal Rights Amendment actually says.

EQUALITY OF RIGHTS UNDER THE LAW SHALL NOT BE DENIED OR ABRIDGED BY THE UNITED STATES OR BY ANY STATE ON ACCOUNT OF SEX. THE CONGRESS SHALL HAVE THE POWER TO ENFORCE, BY APPROPRIATE LEGISLATION, THE PROVISIONS OF THE ARTICLE. THE AMENDMENT SHALL TAKE EFFECT TWO YEARS AFTER THE DATE OF RATIFICATION.

That's all it says. Nothing about bra burning or unisex restrooms. Who wouldn't be for it?

Sterling

❏

April 14, 1970
Dearest Sterling,

Great to be with you and the children! Dad and I were startled by how much they had grown in a short time. They—and you—are truly beautiful. We are glad you continue to have Laine checked frequently by a pediatrician since she is still so fragile.

Sweetheart, it was a nice idea of yours that we all go out to lunch but it didn't take the place of having Dad in your home. He was good-natured about sitting in the car while I toured your house, but we would hesitate to visit again under these circumstances. We welcome you to stay with us. We love you.

Mother

❏

April 23, 1970

Sterling:

You are a natural leader. Congratulations on your election. The Maryland Chapter is fortunate to have you.

I am pleased to serve with you.

All best,
Jayne Stanford

❏

Dear Sterling,

I don't get this at all. WHY can't I visit the children in your house? I drive a long distance to see them and then have to get to know them in motels and restaurants. God knows I'm not asking to <u>stay</u> with you.

I don't know why you were granted custody in this separation. I didn't do anything to deserve this deprivation. Why is a mother considered better than a father, more worthy to raise children?

I still care for you and want you to come home.

Randy

❏

Dear Ms. Hamilton:

We have received the three chapters and outline you sent for your non-fiction book, I Know What Is Mine. The subject of abortion is timely and you have addressed it competently in these pages.

We would be interested in seeing the entire manuscript at your earliest convenience.

Yours truly,
Rachel Gooding
Senior Editor
Nova Publishers

June 1, 1970

❏

June 11, 1970

Dear Quinn

I must tell you of the support I am receiving from my Sisters at Freedom Farm. They allow me to grow and go. They watch over my children like second mothers. I can travel when and where I like—I have been across our country several times in pursuit of women's right to abortion.

I hope your station is taking note of our progress. This would make a heck of a series. State legislatures are rapidly liberalizing abortion laws, like lights winking on all over the nation. Next month, the AMA will no doubt vote to allow doctors to perform abortion for reasons other than medical.

Here's a scoop: in a few days, WEAL will file charges of sex discrimination against the entire college and university system in California.

I will keep you informed on what's coming up so that you can be among the first to report our news.

Thanks for helping.

Sterling

❏

6/24/70

Sterling,

I have to say it: you act as though the war for women's rights is the only newsworthy activity in America.

There's still a race war. Had you noticed? Most recently two black students at Jackson State College (that's in Mississippi) died when police fired on a dormitory. I care about that.

There's still a military war. In Southeast Asia. And as of April 30, American involvement spread into Cambodia. Roz cares about that. Do you ever think about Glenn? About the death toll, which is approaching 50,000?

There's still a political war—by our government against protestors of their policy. Four students were murdered by our own National Guard at Kent State just a month ago.

There's still a crime war. I am packing my briefcase to sit in court for God-knows-how-long listening to Charlie Manson and his harem.

Your cause is only one of many. Frankly, it sounds like a lot of whining to me. "We're entitled to." "We never got." "We demand."

Look at me. I can do anything I want—I already have. I simply put one foot in front of the other. Women should do less talking about their "rights" and more measuring up in the real world. True, all of my superiors have been men but that's for lack of qualified women. Get busy on that.

Egad.

Quinn

❏

July 5, 1970

Quinn—

So far this year, NOW and/or WEAL have filed sex discrimination charges against:

1. The University of Maryland

2. Harvard
3. Florida university system
4. California university system
5. New York university system

Before the year is out, we will file class action against every medical school in the United States.

There aren't enough qualified women because women are frequently denied the education that will make them qualified.

Study your facts.

Sterling

❑

Sterling:

Fairly easy to obtain such a list. The pro-life forces are proud of their backers.

Your sister Rosalind is a heavy contributor. I'm enclosing her page from the M's.

Donna

❑

8—9—70

Dearest Sterling,

I happened across your article in the August issue of Ladies' Home Journal and understand that you feel women who spent their lives in homemaking wasted their unique talents.

I did what I wanted to do and am pleased with the expenditure of my time and the result. You were careful to say that your article was about choices, but the message was clear.

The pendulum will swing back. The world has been around a long time, and will be. Motherhood is an honorable, rewarding profession. When the first generation raised by strangers and by their own hand emerges, I will have my proof. Focus on your children.

Love from
Mother

❑

Aug. 10, 1970

Sterling,

I have an offer from the network to be a regional correspondent. I don't even have to move.

Remember that series I did on the 65 airliners that were hijacked in 1969? It was a study of security systems or lack thereof. It went onto the network feed and caught the eye of a muckety-muck in New York—Bernard Kane. You probably don't know him; he's an exec not air personality.

I'm about to be wined and dined in NYC. Details upcoming.

Love to my nieces and nephew,

QUINN

P.S. Yes, I noticed the ERA passed the House today.

I'm not brain dead.

❏

13 Aug.

Sterling—

Recognize the person in this photo? I don't think I should keep it from you any longer: your friend Jeff is ringing bells out here. I know you don't like him for some reason but Lou and I are enjoying his friendship. Nice article. Dee Maxwell's the local gossip in P.S.

Quinn

❏

Not Just Another Pretty Face

FACE HE'S GOT. Body, too. Palm Springs is agog at Jett Maeder, 32, here to film "A Mixed Bag" under the direction of Thom Brawley ("Tropical Cavalry," "The Glass Barrage"). When Maeder prowls shops and cafes on his time off, sightseers stare. What Maeder has is an innovative blend of casual strength and uncommon good looks: straight teeth, square jaw, blue eyes, copious dark hair, the works.

Brawley has kept the script for "A Mixed Bag" under wraps but the rumor mill has it the story's about a second marriage in which the partners decide to steal their nine non-custodial children and take them to Africa. Diane Kensey ("Part Earth") plays Maeder's spouse.

Maeder came out of nowhere to win the role from a foundering Brawley whose first two pictures lost mega bucks. Brawley, who discovered him at a party given by mutual friends, verified his ability by attending the opening of "Bus Stop" at Yakky's Backyard. Maeder was a show-stopper as "Bo" and Brawley knew he'd found his man.

Background on Maeder is scarce. He's a native of North Carolina and holds dual degrees in philosophy and psychology from Emory University, Atlanta. He describes himself as a "perpetual student" who "dabbled at life" until a friend loaned him $2500 to move to the West Coast. He's currently living in a tent on Brawley's Laurel Canyon estate.

—Dee Maxwell

❑

Aug. 26, 1970

Dear Sterling

You were right and I was wrong. My job with the network fell through—because I'm pregnant.

I flew to New York for the final interview. I had already filled out beaucoup papers, sent film of my best stories to committees, been screened and re-screened, taken to dinner in L.A. by top network people.

The minute Bernard Kane saw me, his gaze went to my abdomen. He spent the rest of the afternoon trying to convince me what a difficult assignment this would be. I kept reassuring him and finally asked to talk salary which, after all, was why I was there.

He shut his office door and got chummily close to me. You know that face-in-your-face pose men strike when determined to make you back down? He had the smile of a tolerant parent trying to reason with a child as a last resort before spanking.

He asked me if I'd ever heard the expression, "Render unto Caesar those things which are Caesar's." I asked him to get to the point. He advised me that I had already chosen between children and career. I advised him that I could have both, just as men do. He advised me that I was not making that call, <u>he</u> was. In the end, there was nothing I could do but get out.

The next day, I had an audience with his boss, by my request. He listened politely, then called B.K. on the carpet and made inquiry. B.K. denied my accusations. His boss stood by me so vehemently I caught a whiff of good-cop-bad-cop. I was assured my case would be reconsidered. I haven't heard a thing since I came home. Two weeks. Don't give me a lecture. I haven't got time for law suits and such nonsense. I simply want to report the news. So, I guess I'll get on with it.

QUINN

P.S. Thought seriously of joining the Nationwide Women's Strike for Equality today but I had to work. Keep indoctrinating me. Maybe you'll create a convert.

❑

9/9/70

Constance,
    Thanks for applying your expertise. I appreciate your investigating Quinn's allegation about network hiring practices—especially without her knowledge. I want to be sure before we proceed.

Sterling

❑

9/14/70

Constance:
    Your call was heartening. I knew you could tap in. Looks as though they deserve to be among the 1300 + corporations NOW has filed against for sex discrimination. Good that you have warned them and are assembling facts. As you discovered, Quinn is qualified—more qualified than the two men also in the running.

I've meditated on this quite a bit. Quinn would turn the job down if she knew why it was being offered to her again. Let's keep this confidential.

Thanks, Connie.

Sterling

❏

September 20, 1970

Dear Sterling,

Wonders never cease. Bernard Kane was transferred from news to the entertainment division. His successor liked my stuff and called to resume negotiations. We struck a deal. I start Oct. 15 and he'll pay maternity leave!

There's a chauvinist in every crowd, I guess, and I just happened to run upon him in Bernard. An unhappy exception in what has been a satisfying field thus far.

Sterling, this really proves my point. Qualified, hard-working women win in the long run.

I knew it.

Love,
Quinn

❏

Sterling—

Your lawyer called me. Are you really going through with this, then? She asked me to get a lawyer.

I don't want any part of this divorce. You can have whatever you want. I'd give you my last nickel.

Randy

❏

10/2/70

Dear Sterling,

Called your house but Jill said you were away on business.

Zandria's here early! A doll! Born in a rescue truck while I was out on assignment. S. Cal's been burning down around us. Conditions were ripe—no rain here since March 4. High winds. 100,000 acres on fire in our area by

Sept. 25. Impossible to breathe—ashes floating everywhere. I volunteered to go on to S. Diego where another 160,000 acres were burning. 100-degree heat. I gave out. It was a hard, fast labor. I crawled into a rescue vehicle which happened to be on the scene and Zandria arrived. I knew it would be a girl.

Ma Quinn

P.S. Reg. corresp. job
     postponed to Jan. 1
     Dagmar's coming to
     live with us & take
     care of Baby!!!

❑

Dear Ms. Hamilton:

Enclosed is the contract for I Know What Is Mine. I am pleased we were able to come to an agreement.

If you have questions, don't hesitate to call me.

Sincerely,
Rachel Gooding
Senior Editor
Nova Publications

October 13, 1970

❑

Dear Randy,

I apologize for hurting you, but I have to be single. Please let me go. I don't want to take anything that's yours. I won't. If I ask for money it will be child support only.

You did your best. I have no feelings of blame. I hope you don't. I just want it to be over.

S.

❑

November 13, 1970

Dearest Sterling,

Dad and I hope you will bring the children here for Christmas. Quinn, Lou, Zandria and Rosalind will be here. The Hopkins are going to be away and said we could use their house, too, for sleeping. Let us know.

We love you.

Mother

❏

Dear All,

Happy New Year!

Christmas at Freedom Farm was exquisite. Heavy snow and a sleigh. Cookies and popcorn balls. Ribbon bows on a tall tree. Carols, an open fire. Joyful children. Roast turkey.

While we missed you very much, we feel secure in the knowledge that we belong to this family of friends forever.

Our love for our family of choice does not diminish, but enhances, our love for our families of origin. May the New Year bring many opportunities for personal interaction among us all and for deepening understanding and good will.

Theda	Bart	Heddy
Jill	Mindy	Sovereign
Harriet	Garth	Ted
Beverly	Ginny	Lance
Sterling	Dawn	Laine
Lettie	Merrill	Shannon
Gretchen	Rob	Lisa
	Jason	Heather

❏

1 9 7 1

Sterling

Sterling—

What in the heck are you doing? This is nutty stuff. Those folks may be your housemates, but they're not your family. This reeks of condescension.

How do you think Mother and Dad felt? Christmas was hardly a celebration, although they tried their best.

And you didn't meet Zandria.

Q.

❑

January 3, 1971

Dearest Sterling,

How we missed you and the children. I'm beginning to wonder if we'll ever have another Christmas with the whole family together. I don't mean to be melodramatic, but I am concerned about the lack of caring I see.

Continuing love for your family isn't something that simply exists. You have to work at it. It's a decision, followed by dedication—the dedication to consistently go out of your way, to make time for your people.

I know that you increasingly feel you have nothing in common with your sisters (and, perhaps, your parents). But absence from one another and loss of steady communication feed this. Being there is all-important.

Please think about it.

We love you.

Mother

P.S. When you write to me,
would you address me as Mrs.
and not Ms.? I'm proud of
being your father's wife.

❑

1/6/71

Dear Sterling,

Christmas wasn't the same without you and the children. Baby Zandria was adorable. I'm sorry you missed her.

Christmas Eve, Randy called. When he found out you for sure weren't coming, he asked if he could. He showed up about noon the next day, having driven all night. The man looks deranged and is stricken with silence. I felt as though we were tending a hospital patient.

Are you sure you don't love him? He is suffering.

Rozzy

❏

15th Jan

Dear Sterling,

God, I missed you all at Christmas. Your family was wonderful to me. I was going to stay home but, at the last minute, had an overwhelming urge to be with them. They took me in with open arms.

I want to mention something that you might not be aware of. Rosalind is deeply depressed. I asked Quinn about it on the sly and she told me Roz had declined during the past year. She wouldn't say why, only that it was personal. I thought you would want to know this. I get the impression it's because of a failed love affair. Maybe you could give her a boost. She was gentle and kind to me.

Well . . . bye.

Randy

❏

1-16-71

Dear Rozzy,

Good of you to be sweet to Randy. I appreciate it. I realize he is in a bad way. But it's over. I could <u>never, ever,</u> in a million years, go back to him and that's that. He just has to accept it. Everybody has to accept it.

I am comfortable in our household and we are making progress in our mission.

Are you doing OK? Let me know what's going on. Keep in touch, huh? Come see us.

Love,
Sterling

❏

23 Jan

Sterling:

This separation tears my heart out. Don't divorce me. I still love you, and I'm afraid I won't get to see my kids at all.

Hey, I was in Boston for the dental convention and looked up Roz like I told you I would. She's thin and has sad eyes. I took Bobby Hughes with me. He's the party type. Thought it would cheer her and she seemed amused.

Still love you. Or did I say that?

Randy

❏

January 26, 1971

Dear Sterling,

Randy was here for a dental convention and called me in advance. He insisted that I meet him and his old college roommate, Bobby Hughes, for dinner. So I did. What a sight Randy is—skinny and morose. Bobby and I tried to console him. The wine flowed. After a while, he and Bobby were three sheets to the wind, and planning to room together again! Bobby's divorced and living on a sailboat at the Cape. I doubt it will materialize as it should look pretty nonsensical to Randy when he's sober.

Love to you and the kids.

Rozzy

❏

Randy—

Got the check. Thanks. Yes, I have been worried about Roz. I'll write her more often. It was nice of you and Bobby to take her out.

S.

❏

Rozzy—

Thanks for helping Randy along. He'll need lots of friends

as we progress through this divorce. Generous of you to take time to be with him.

Love,
Sterling

❑

2/5/71

Sterling,

You'll get a kick out of this. First thing I did when I got my new job was run a background on you. I can do that. I have access to public record info from many sources and can direct staff members to compile it!

Don't worry. It was all good news. But I didn't realize how much clout you have in the women's movement. Esp. in pro-abortion fight. A lot of articles have been in various publications about you — and even about Freedom Farm. I'll send you clips. Maybe you don't have some of them. And I didn't realize I'd have access to stuff that wasn't in the papers. I even got your credit rating and a copy of your petition for divorce.

What power! (Mine, I mean.)

A hug from
Quinn

❑

Sterling:

My life changed at a few minutes after six Tuesday morning. Jesus! You can't visualize the terror. With the ground literally moving under you, there's no place to go. We were getting up, sitting on opposite sides of the bed. The shock threw us both onto the floor. We thought it was a nuclear blast. I was quicker than Lou, crawling and staggering toward Dagmar's and Zandria's room. Dag was already lifting the baby from the crib as plaster fell onto the place where Zandria had been lying! We ran outside. For 25 minutes, additional shocks rolled through like ocean waves. After we finally thought ourselves safe and were back in the house, another big one came. About 8 o'clock. Broke everything in the china cupboard. Then, because it's my job (!), I spent the day driving into horror: freeway overpasses that had collapsed onto cars, a crumbled hospital that crushed 40 people. I don't want to stay here, I want to move back East. Mom told me you tried to call us but the lines were down for days. Thanks, though. QUINN

❑

February 19, 1971

Dear Quinn,

Your call was welcome! The quake gave me a terrible scare. I was afraid for all of you. When I heard from Dad that you were safe, it sent me into fast-forward examination of my own life.

I'm not sure I belong at the Farm anymore. It's perplexing me. I don't like close quarters. I thought this wasn't, but it is. It's big but there are more people. I look at my children and see them taking on other people's traits and values. We're all supposed to be the same here, but we're not. PLEASE keep this to yourself until I figure out what to do.

Love to each one,
Sterling

❑

20th Feb

Dear Sterling,

I have come to the point that I must make the decision to reconstruct my life. I am leaving North Carolina—and my practice—for a six month rest. I'll be living on Cape Cod, helping Bobby run his camping shop and sporting goods store. He invited me to give it a whack. A radical departure (pun) for me.

I'm sure I don't need to say again how in love I still am with you, my daughters and my son. I maintain hope that we will be together again.

Randy

❑

18th Mar

Dear Sterling,

I am getting along better than I thought I would. It is exhilarating to be out of Charlotte. I can think here. Lots of ocean air and hubs of people. Bobby's gregarious. It might be rubbing off on me.

His boat is the Windchime. We live on it. At night friends come by, board and sit while we pass the guitar around. Am I an old boy? A case of arrested development? I must not have goofed off enough when growing up. I have a lot of time to myself. Bobby stays many nights with his love, Claudia Downing, at her place. They've been together two years.

I think about you and about Mindy, Lance, Sovereign and Laine. I want to come and see you soon. I won't try to talk you into or out of anything.

Drop me a line?

Randy

❑

March 31, 1971

Dear Sterling,

I saw Randy and Bobby and Claudia (Bobby's girl) last Sunday. They were in town, staying with friends. We went to a comedy/magic show and then walked around for a while. Randy's emotions seem looser now. He's easy with a laugh. I didn't know the divorce was creeping up so soon. Are you sure you want to do this? Have you seen him lately? Maybe he never had a chance to be his true self. Maybe he was living up to his own expectations all the time.

I have sent the kids a package they can share. Hope they like it.

Love,
Rozzy

❑

4-7-71

Randy,

Please don't ask to speak to me when you call—just talk to the kids, OK? I don't want you to keep on having hope that we're going to reconcile. The divorce is going smoothly and soon we will no longer be married.

As I've told you before, I think well of you but I don't love you. It would be sensible for you to start dating others in preparation for our final split. Could you do that? Is there a woman in your life that you might start spending time with, even if she's only a friend? I don't want you to be too upset when this comes through, and it will.

Sterling

❑

Gee whiz. I didn't know your divorce was final until Randy told me! Amazing. It was over so quickly. I don't like change, I suppose. I don't like thinking in new ways. You and Randy: separate people. I can't get used to it. How are the children? What did they say?

Randy was a stranger to me before he moved to Mass. He is a special person, through and through. I've come to a fine appreciation of his character. It's a shame that it didn't work out for the two of you.

Write to me.

Love,
Roz

❑

21st May

Dear Sterling,

It was marvelous to see you and the children. It seemed strange, looking at you and realizing you are no longer my wife.

Although I'll miss my babies like crazy, I've made the decision to stay here at the Cape permanently. I don't want to resume my practice. I will visit the children as much as possible and will call and write them a lot. I will pay for them to travel and be with me when they are old enough to take trips alone.

I hope we can stay amicable. You are still my first choice of partner, for eternity.

Randy

❑

Sterling, please tell Mindy and Lance how much daddy enjoyed speaking with them on the phone. Let's stop this nonsense and get back together!

Saw Roz for lunch one day last week while on a buying trip to Boston (for Bobby's store). She's gaunt. I told Bobby and he'll jolly her along a bit, too.

Hug my babies,
Randy

❑

Randy—

I have repeatedly called Roz but she tells me nothing. Watch over her a little. She told me she likes being included in your group.

The children made these drawings for you.

S.

❑

June 14, 1971

Dear Sterling,

Randy and Bobby's crowd came to town for a baseball weekend—double header followed by merry-making. He looked great. Thought you'd want to know that. I'm part of their gang when I want to be. It's been a boon to my life. I had lots of acquaintances but not many friends until these folks. They are a pleasantly rowdy crew—equally mixed, men and women. Singles. They commemorate birthdays, fix holiday meals. Seems in lots of ways like a family. They're going to have a retreat next month, in the Berkshires. I might go.

I called a couple of times. Did they tell you?

Luv,
Roz

❑

July 17, 1971

Dearest Sterling,

What a delightful visit we had with Rosalind. She looks better than we've seen her in years. She's "smitten"—someone she's known for a long time, she says. But he didn't come around to the house while we were there. And he doesn't seem to have a name!

She's got a warm group of friends now, we understand from her. She spoke with awe and joy of the recent Berkshire retreat: bikes, hikes and tents, evenings under the stars. She's a very quiet, self-contained person. I guess all will be revealed to us when she's ready.

Best love to you 5,
Mother

❑

7/23

Dear Randy,

You seem so different. Like someone's taken the staid, meticulous you out of your body and replaced it with a slightly off-the-wall personality. I don't mean to imply that you are warped. You just have a lot of verve to you that I hadn't seen before.

The children loved your visit and the gifts. I have to tell you that it made Mindy cry and Lance has been crying too, in sympathy. Could you come back a little sooner this time?

Sterling

❑

Sterling—

Thanks for the compliments. The electricity is still there for me. No one compares with you.

You were right to divorce me. I was boring. If I'm not as boring now, it's because I'm not bored.

I didn't understand how much I hated dentistry and how trapped I was by my background. Since I moved in with Bobby, I don't wear ironed clothing. I eat, sleep and play when I want to.

Randy

❑

Sterling—Thanks for the card on my 32nd. Your sister is a beautiful human being. She gave me an incredible surprise birthday party with all the trimmings at Pappy's, a Boston pub. There were people I hadn't seen in years! Don't know how she dug them all up. I asked Bobby later who sprang for the tab and he said Roz took care of most of it in advance. He didn't have a clue how much it cost.

I've a profound respect and fondness for Rosalind. You should get to know her again. Really.

R.

❑

August 17, 1971

Dear Sterling,

I went to the Cape this weekend at the invitation of Randy and Bob. Their crowd had a dinner-fest: gauze bags full of crabs, corn on the cob, potatoes, boiling in 55-gallon drums. It was at a public park. Chilly, but the fires made a bright setting. Randy had gained back his "fighting weight" and then some. Progress. You were worried he wouldn't make it, but he seems fine.

Best love to the babes.

Ros

❏

8-18-71

Quinn,

I can't write this to Roz because she'll think I'm giving up on the Women's Movement and I'm not. I'm becoming less than enchanted with communal living, though. Ideally, it should work. In actuality, it works for some.

Example: we are self-educating our kids. Take turns teaching, spread the responsibility around. Well, here I am with a degree in Elem Ed so I get the little ones. I never wanted to teach! I can't stand it.

Yes, the kids are a lot of the problem. There are so many of them. I had responsibility for four, now I have responsibility for 16. We share the work, but this is a huge group. There is more noise, confusion and mess by far than I had at home. Have you ever scrubbed a bathroom 16 kids have used?

Not sure what I'm going to do yet.

S.

❏

Randy,

What made us do that? I am totally unstrung by it. One minute I was eating dinner with you in your hotel restaurant, the next minute we were in bed.

Don't come back for a while. I need distance.

S.

❏

Aug. 25, 1971

Dear Quinn,

I am looking forward to seeing you et al Labor Day weekend. We've got to talk. Things are go for my attendance at the NOW convention in L.A.

I'm ready for a get-away. Life at FF has increasingly rough edges. One of the biggies is our practice of encountering. This has been mandatory for adults, every week. At first, it was stimulating and thought provoking. Then, it became merely provoking. Now, I dread those sessions. We all end up furious. That's the point of the meetings: to goad each other. It's a call to action—at least that's what it's meant to be. But it's emotionally exhausted us. I've asked to stop the groups, but I'm in the minority.

Love,
Sterling

❏

Sept. 20, 1971

Dear Quinn,

It was a tremendous disappointment to me not to see you. The worst air crash in U.S. history would be on the same day I arrived. My mouth fell open when Lou told me you'd gone to Alaska.

Being away from FF crystalized my feelings. I didn't like going back to cleaning house after 2-dozen people, no matter how many of them help. I didn't like fixing meals for a mob.

I believe in the Movement but there are bizarre aspects to it. Theda is kind of a symbol of these. She and Harriet have a "relationship." Theda was waiting for me at the airport. She doesn't shave her legs or underarms. (Yes, European women don't either.) I'm trying not to get hung up on superficial aspects, but they are so evident to me now.

I think I have to get out of here.

Sterling

❏

October 19, 1971

Dear Sterling,

I have to tell you something and I can't do it on the phone. I have grown to love Randy and I believe he cares for me. For months, he has gone out of his way to be with me. Since I'm always included in his crowd of friends, we have spent countless hours together. We don't have a physical relationship—we haven't even shared our feelings about each other—but he treats me with much affection and it seems to be increasing.

Because you are divorced, this letter is probably unnecessary, but I am writing to ask your blessing.

Rozzy

❏

October 20, 1971

Dear Rozzy,

Happy to talk with you last night. A rare moment when I catch you at home. I'm looking forward to receiving the "mystery" letter you sent. What could be in it? Since you said you mailed it yesterday, I won't have long to wait.

I've got something to tell you, too. I wanted you to hear it from me first: Randy and I are getting back together! He asked me if he could tell you. I think he felt a lot of responsibility to be the one since you have been such good friends. But I thought it should come from me.

He has changed a lot—as you have observed. (You have helped him change!) His stuffiness has been replaced with a real zest for life. He doesn't want to be a dentist anymore. We are deciding where we'll live. He'll open his own camping/sporting goods store, enough states away from Bobby's not to be competition.

I felt sheepish about this change in myself. I was so definite about not wanting a man in my world—particularly Randy! But I have learned that it's okay to grow and change, to go back on old pronouncements. That makes two of us.

Rejoice!
Sterling

❏

Dearest Sterling,

I am puzzled by your plans to remarry without Rosalind present. Was this her choice or yours? Please set aside your political feud. It has no place in family life.

Let's all be together on The Big Day.

Love Always,
Mother

❏

12/30/71

Dear Sterling,

What a wedding!!! The morning snow cooperated perfectly, floating down like jewels during your vows. I had never heard of a marriage performed outdoors in December ice, but it was exquisite. M & D's yard was the ideal site.

This was the first time in ages that we could all have been together. I was upset that Roz didn't come. Why would she do that? Are you two still fighting over abortion? I tried to downplay my amazement because M & D were so angry. I couldn't get over her calling at the last minute to say she couldn't make it.

What happened with her boyfriend? Is that it? Was it Bobby? I hope she hasn't been let down again. Men! Why does it always have to happen to her? I've been trying to call her.

Q.

❏

1 9 7 2

Quinn

1/17/72

Dear Quinn,

This is like courtship all over again, with Randy in Mass. and me still at FF. Romantic! We're moving the process along as quickly as possible. Can't decide whether to go back to Charlotte or? Randy's a southerner, through and through, and would be miserable elsewhere. Other cities we are considering: Atlanta and Richmond.

Another hold-up: my book, retitled THE LOGIC OF ABORTION, will be in the stores next month and the publisher has lined up interviews. I'll have to travel.

I am sorry Roz has withdrawn from our lives. She becomes more peculiar, year by year. Really, she has some bizarre notions. Mother is having a fit over this but I can't seem to do anything about it.

Best to each,
Sterling

❏

Jan. 23

Dear Rozzy,

We missed you at the wedding.

I want to ask you not to be so hard on Sterling. She's a character, it's true, but you have to take her good-naturedly. She means well, always, and you've got to give her this: she IS involved with life. I find it rare and laudatory.

Please, Roz, whatever you have saved up against her, let it go.

Love,
QUINN

❏

January 31, 1972

Dear Mom Fortner,

I have the same concerns you do about Lou, but he has to follow his own path. He is determined that this city will respond to Judge Gitelson's ruling. Two years now, and still it's hung up in appeals court. This frustrates him terribly. San Francisco school system integrated last fall. Here, opponents have geography on their side. LA's divided by mountains—population predominantly white north of them and black south of them. Busing isn't easy to achieve.

Anyway, I notice his temperament changing, as you do. He is understandably impatient and less the pacifist than he was. And, yes, he is making enemies. But someone has to lead.

You and Dad seem to have worked out a philosophy of patience. Perhaps you could share it with us.

New fun at work. A few of my pieces have been lightly investigative. They were well-received by management, so an additional correspondent has been hired to give me more time in the investigative arena.

Love to you and Dad. I'm glad he is going to get a complete check up.

Quinn

❏

Oh, what a surprise to get your book in my mail. Congratulations! I'll read it at once. In the author photo, you exude wisdom. I expect to learn much. What a wonderful culmination of your hard work. You must be gratified that the Supreme Court has agreed to rule on abortion. I haven't had occasion to dwell on this and will be forming opinions as I read.

QUINN

❏

2-12-72

Rozzie:

I've been pondering our phone conversation. It seems strange to me that you think Sterling isn't straightforward. She's one of the most "up front" people I've known. Doesn't hide her positions—and takes a lot of flak for it. Personally, I like that. I know where I stand. We chew each other around a lot. That's okay. Can't you relax and let her be who she is?

I know it was hard for you to talk about this. I appreciate your trust in me.

Love,
Quinn

❏

February 22, 1972

Dear Quinn,

Fortners have traditionally looked to Jesus to fulfill every longing and every need. He sees our plight. We follow Him.

Beyond that, we use the words of King as our signpost: "We will match your capacity to inflict suffering with our capacity to endure suffering. We will meet your physical force with soul force. We will not hate you, but we cannot in all conscience obey your unjust laws. We will soon wear you down by our capacity to suffer. And in winning our freedom, we will so appeal to your heart and conscience that we will win you in the process."

Amen.

Mama

❑

Sterling, Talk-Show Queen of the Universe:
Here's a switch—my watching you on TV! You are cool with a hot subject. Good strategy.

I read the book and have question after question. I got permiss to do a documentary on abortion this year.

Have to tell you, Jeff Mather's movie is ready for release and he's being called "the only good thing in it except for a couple of spectacular sunsets" (LA Times). He's not a favorite of yours, but he's got guts, you have to admit.

Quinn

❑

March 24, 1972

Dear Sterling,

I feel so much heartache for Lou and Dagmar. We've been house-hunting. What a deflating mission. We only have the two bedrooms and Dag needs her own now that Zandria is older.

We know the neighborhoods we want to live in. Dag reads the want ads and makes calls because Lou and I are stuck at work. No one will tell her over the phone if a house is available. They insist on an interview. She and Zan spend hours in the car, going here and there, only to be told "a contract came in an hour ago."

I took a day off and tried it myself. I was eagerly shown every house I sought.

But when I took Lou to see possible choices, they had all been "sold an hour ago." It doesn't work any better through a realtor. Home owners have the power to sell or not. And you can't sue everyone.

This is not a temporary inconvenience. That's what's catching up with us. This is the condition we will live under our entire lives because attitudes and laws change so slowly. And now, Nixon's sent a message to Congress asking that they halt busing.

Meanwhile, Jeff brought over plans for his new house. Pool, wine cellar, 12-foot-high stereo speakers, doorbell that chimes 25 tunes. Master suite has whirlpool. When bedside telephone rings, it glides from a pocket in the wall, along with illuminated notepad which automatically opens and pencil which rises to meet the hand.

I wish I had the money to buy progress.

Honest, it's not envy I'm choking on, it's irony.

So, what's the secret?

Quinn

❏

The secret is not to let people muck around with you. For starters, male correspondents in your company are earning more than females doing the same job. I have this on privileged information. You are making less than any man of your rank. Toss it out there. Be flat-damned assertive about it.

Ster

❏

To: Winston Taylor, Corporate Offices, New York
From: Quinn Fortner, Los Angeles Bureau
Date: April 4, 1972

It has come to my attention that the salaries and benefits of men in comparable positions within this company outpace mine. This does not seem to be based on length of service or level of education/experience. Request that my compensation be adjusted accordingly, by the last day of this month.

❏

4-11

S. —

Am enclosing newspaper article on Jeff's felony record. I was shocked! Did you know him when you worked at the prison? Is that where you met him? Somebody tipped the Herald and they were off and running.

He called us right away. His main comment: "It's great publicity."

If you knew, why didn't you tell us?

Q

❑

April 16th, 1972

Dear Quinn,

This is a voice from your past. I almost fell over when I saw Sterling at the Clover Room (Richmond ice cream parlor). She looks exactly the same as she did in high school! I went right over and she recognized me, too. Our husbands thought we had flipped. They couldn't figure out what was going on. We were instantly celebrating!

I'm glad to have your address. Our 10th h.s. reunion is next year. Hope to see you there!

It is neat that Sterling and Randy are thinking of moving here. I hope they do.

She can tell you all my news. It's too long to write. But please write me yours. I didn't get any details, only that you are married, have a daughter and are a network reporter. I'll start watching for you!

Sincerely,

Joanne Fulton Sommes

❑

1. I hoped he would disappear from your life.
2. He had "paid his debt" to society.
3. You had already made up your mind to befriend him.

Sterling

❑

To: Quinn Fortner
From: Winston Taylor
Date: April 28, 1972

Salary and benefit information is confidential and cannot be obtained without
sufficient cause and credentials. It is doubtful that such figures would be in
circulation, except by hearsay. They would, regardless, have no bearing on
your compensation. You are paid commensurate with your job level, background and time with the company. We value your contributions and feel you
are an outstanding asset to the corporation. In keeping with this, your
remuneration is not only competitive but is reviewed, as you know, at six
month intervals. I hope this answers your question.

❏

To: Winston Taylor, Corporate Offices, New York
From: Quinn Fortner, Los Angeles Bureau
Date: May 10, 1972

Question not satisfactorily answered. Why is total salary package for males
outpacing those for females in comparable positions? Why do males receive
more "air time"? Why are males promoted at a faster rate than females? I have
data on each. Request immediate review of my file.

❏

May 12, 1972

Dear Mom and Dad Fortner,
    My report on housing discrimination came out better than I dreamed it
could. Weeks of work are paying off. We recorded sellers' reactions to black
and to white prospective buyers in dozens of instances. A black buyer in white
subdivisions would be told a home was unavailable, then a white buyer who
arrived thirty minutes later would be encouraged. Our "plants" also went into
rental offices in apartment complexes with the same result. The piece will air
June 11.

Dad, I'm glad you are feeling better and the medication's helping your angina. Take care.

Short note because I'm writing this at work.

Love,
Quinn

❏

To: Winston Taylor, Corporate Offices, New York
From: Quinn Fortner
Date: May 21, 1972

Still waiting for reply to my memo of May 10.

❏

6/3/72

Quinn:

Super to get your message! Sorry I was out when it came. Beverly said you sounded astonished that your raise simply "showed up" in your paycheck. You shouldn't be.

To tell you the truth, I didn't have first-hand knowledge that you were being underpaid, but I suspected it. I figured it wouldn't hurt anything for you to throw out the hook.

Before you get mad, remember you asked for help. Lesson One: don't <u>ask</u> when you can <u>tell</u>. Asking is an underdog strategy. TELLING bluffs the opponent who then uses his own set of facts to decide what you know. He almost always overestimates your hand.

Sterling

❏

June 22, 1972

Dear Mom and Dad Fortner,

Thanks for your calls and your prayers. I hope you understand that Dagmar and I didn't want you to come because we thought it would be too upsetting to you, and Lou wasn't conscious anyway. He is awake more and more now. His sleepiness was not necessarily from the injuries but from being put under general anesthesia a couple of times to set bones and remove teeth. At first, the oral surgeon thought he could save and restore the two upper front teeth but, after four days, it was evident they were dead.

Still no idea who did this, but it seems obvious that it was a result of the housing report. An anonymous person phoned Lou's office and said so, giving unpublished details of the attack. Lou said it was dark in the restaurant parking lot—the car was toward the back of the building. He heard and saw nothing. The doctor said it is not unusual for a beating victim not to remember. His wallet was missing so we had assumed robbery was the motive. His keys were under the car.

He should be out of the hospital in a week and will be at home a while. That might be a good time to come if you still want to.

Love,
Quinn

❑

Friday, June 23

Dear Quinn,

We are sick about what happened to Lou. Quinn, we truly love him as a brother and feel outraged by the evil people who set upon him. It's incredible that people could feel such hatred. Our only consolation is that he is on the mend. Knowing Lou, his spirit will be undaunted. That's one of his most beautiful attributes. We have sent him notes, to the hospital, but wanted to express ourselves to you. Mindy, Lance and Sovereign colored a roll of shelf paper in happy pictures as a mural for his wall. Hope it's arrived by now.

Love and Kisses
Sterling

❑

June 25, 1972

Dear Roz—

No one has been more attentive than you have to both Lou and me. His hospital room and our house are full of roses and luscious fruit. We appreciate you.

This incident has given me new gratitude for family. I want to ask you again to reconsider your relationship with Sterling. Her tactics border on the outrageous sometimes but she is driven by a quest for justice. She's a good person.

Quinn

❑

July 2, 1972

Dear Mother and Dad,

No parents could be more thoughtful than you two are. We were delighted to find out you had paid the television charges for Lou's hospital room. Then, when we got home and saw the little TV set you had sent for the bedroom, we were doubly delighted. It has kept him company hours on end.

Lou's parents have arrived and are dynamically entertaining. I see him perking up.

Z. is rather theatrical herself. She goes in and out of his room wearing various items on her head and he loves it.

Now that I have time to think, I feel weak-kneed with anger and guilt. I shouldn't have pushed the housing problem so hard and made Lou a target. I should have known what was possible. I've seen racial violence over and over. It is hard to look at Lou's face and keep from crying. Only the understanding support from family has made this bearable.

XX
Quinn

❑

July 10, 1972

Dear Quinn,

I'm still waiting for that letter from you. Well, I know you are busy so I guess I'll have to get details on your life from Sterling when she finally has time.

We are totally wound up that they are going to move here! She called me on the fly last week. They were in town, house-hunting, and had a dilemma. The one they liked best was in the city. She said they never should have looked at it in the first place. Her kids would be bussed all over creation and the schools are mainly black. She said the reason they didn't go back to Charlotte was that busing was county-wide and they would have had to put their kids in private schools ($) to avoid it. Here at least you can escape. The city of Richmond is all by itself—not part of a county. The busing order only affects the city, not the surrounding counties. So they settled for a house out in Chesterfield. Less for the price, but what are you going to do?

See you when you come to visit.

Friends,
Joanne S.

❑

Aug. 24

Sterling,

I want you to hear this from me before you see it on the air. My documentary on abortion is about the physical aspects of it, specifically for the unborn child. I began researching in a balanced way, but after spending a week posing as a scrub nurse in a clinic, I had changed my mind. Don't ask me where or how I gained access; it is confidential and will not be named in the show. There are doctors doing this procedure who consider it an abomination, as I do now. Have you seen it for yourself? If you have, I am incredulous that you can condone it. I watched babies (not zygotes, as it says in your book) be sucked out—ripped—into a glass jar or brought out in raggedly-cut pieces and thrown away. (First trimester) I watched intentionally-crushed heads and decapitated bodies be drawn out. And whole babies with saline-solution burns be born dead. I watched induced live births in which the baby was not old enough to survive. (Second trimester) I watched gasping children, born by hysterotomy (C-section), placed aside to die. (Third trimester) This is murder.

Q

❑

Dear Quinn,

There was a tone of hysteria in your letter. The documentary sounds weighted and sensationalistic. Perhaps you should put it aside for a while to regain perspective.

Sterling

❑

S,

The story does not deserve "perspective." I have developed a real distaste for perspective. A real distaste for balance, which is so goddamned sacred in America—particularly to the media. Some issues are not worthy of balance. This is one of them.

Q

❑

To: Quinn Fortner, Los Angeles Bureau
From: Mary Barrington, Programming, New York
Date: October 2, 1972

The scheduling of A TIME TO DIE has been postponed due to court injunction by feminist interests who cite it as inflammatory, ill-balanced and possibly inaccurate. Review process in cases of this sort can be lengthy. Nevertheless, network officials stand behind your report and will air it as soon as feasible.

❑

Dear Rozzy—

Chomp, chomp. The sound you hear is that of words being eaten. I think you're right about Sterling.

Q

❑

October 23, 1972

Dearest Daughters,

It is our sincere wish that you remain close friends throughout your lifetime. It causes us deep sorrow to see, year by year, your gradual parting. For, whatever comes in this life, there should be one haven after the love of God, and that is the love of family.

Christmas is the time worldly concerns should be set aside for a sacred gathering of our spirits. But again this Christmas, you do not wish to worship together and we sense in you an even wider division. What family members individually endeavor, what we own, what we seek, what we hope and what we champion are merely trappings of an age.

Family love is ageless and an heirloom to be carefully passed along. What are we teaching the grandchildren?

Please join us this Christmas. Please join hearts.

Forever,
Mother and Dad

❑

Nov. 1

Dear Mother and Dad,

What we endeavor, own, seek, hope and champion is what we ARE. You are looking at this in a temporal sense and it is not temporal. The divisions in this family regard the most fundamental questions that can ever be raised.

Maturing means letting go, of situations and of people antithetic to our most basic beliefs. An even higher maturity demands that we oppose, with all our strength, those situations and those people. For such issues do not drift on air, they are in us to resolve.

Our philosophies are not hung upon us like tags, they are our bone and breath.

Quinn

❑

November 20, 1972

Dear Ros,

Dad Fortner's funeral was yesterday. I am writing this on the plane, with Lou and Zandria asleep in the seat beside me. We'll be home in an hour. The heart attack and subsequent events came at us so fast, they were almost like blows. I fear for Lou, who is broken.

Dad's funeral was almost that of a pauper. We held back on financial assistance, knowing how independent Mom and Dad Fortner have always been, how proud. But both of us were struck by the utter simplicity of the coffin and burial. Dad was a great man, in character and in talent, but he could barely stay even in life. This was because of his color.

I witness white men with less skill reach "the top" early on and use their achievements to glorify their own egos and to purchase gross material excesses. I hear Lou breathing loudly beside me through a nose so shattered by a beating that reconstruction could not fully remove splinters and spurs, and I feel determined to lift him up. He can't do it himself. He couldn't live long enough to surmount centuries of racial hatred and build a free life. I won't see him buried like his father. And I promise that the child I am carrying inside me will not be buried like his grandfather. Buried with his dreams.

We may not approve of Sterling's methods, but she has taught me that the only way to move ahead is to wrest power from those who own it. Since I am of the "accepted" race, I must do this for Lou, and hand it to him.

Q.

❏

PERSONAL

To: Winston Taylor, Corporate Offices, New York
From: Quinn Fortner, Los Angeles Bureau
Date: December 3, 1972

As you are aware, my task in the last eleven months has been primarily investigative. It has become apparent to me that this is where my main interests and talents lie. However, Los Angeles is not the ideal setting for a major investigative headquarters, New York is; and my title and my number of staff associates are not adequate to my vision.

In preparing hours of investigations and resultant programming, it has oc- curred to me that most people have situations in their backgrounds that they would not wish to be revealed. Even a person as esteemed as yourself might hesitate at the prospect of intense scrutiny and full disclosure. I'm sure you understand this basic concept and will give careful consideration to the following proposal.

1. That a New York investigative office be established for the purpose of bringing justice through media exploration of American issues.
2. That a new weekly prime-time program be established to bring such investigations before the public.
3. That the network grant this new endeavor an adequate and competent staff; and, further, that the staff be headed by an aggressive journalist who will be cultivated as a recognizable and respected television personality.

I look forward to your reply.

❏

1 9 7 3

Rosalind

9th Jan 73

Rozzy—

Guess where I am—New York City! In December, I tried to put a stran-
glehold on a VP in charge of network news. He flew me here to see what kind of
creature had such audacity. Laughed as he read the offending memo aloud to
me. But he's a sport. Gave me a desk for two weeks and some faint rumors on a
Wall Street fraud-in-progress. If I can sniff it out, he'll consider moving me up.
I'm staying in the company apartment. Want to come down and play?

QUINN

❑

1/18/73

Oh, Roz, I loved seeing you. You are beautiful, inside and out. Thanks for
taking me to A Little Night Music (how did you ever get those tickets at the last
minute?) and for the gorgeous black doll for Zandria. I've been keeping my
eyes open since, in the stores, but I haven't seen another. Where did you find
it? I want to get a couple for Lou's cousin's kids.

I'm winding up my two weeks and Taylor is jumping out of his skin. Thinks
we can scoop the Wall St. Journal. This stuff's tricky, tho. You don't want
to butt heads with the SEC which is obviously doing its own covert investigation. We're checking that out so we don't tip too soon and wreck them.
The name: Equity Funding. If you own any of their stock, get out. KEEP
CONFIDENTIAL.

Love ya,
Quinn

❑

January 22

Rosalind,

I was as uneasy as you were. I'm sorry you felt you had to leave early. I would
have been the one to do it, given two or three more minutes. I knew you were as
stricken as I was.

Somehow we have expanded our circles of friends enough that there is an
overlap. Next time, I would like the opportunity to say a few words to you
privately.

Paul

❑

January 27, 1973
Dear Annie,

Paul Cordner was at a large private party I attended this week. I thought I could small-talk with him, but I had to run away. He has enormous power over me. Still.

I could tell he had similar feelings. He wrote me a note which I didn't answer.

He's a special advisor to the governor of Connecticut. And he's married to Elizabeth. No children. That's all I know of his present, but the past is very much with me.

Talk me out of seeing him again.

Roz

❑

You remain the song of my heart and the Heart of my creations. To be with you is like no other experience. Join me at the Plaza for the Spring Preview, November 5, 6 and 7. I cannot show the line without you at my side.

Arch

❑

2-2-73

Rosalind:

Have inquiry on your NJ Turnpike real estate. Major developer considering for shopping center. Call me.

V. Doud

❑

February 7, 1973

Rozzy—

Taylor bought in. He's moving us to NY! I'll shuttle between there and DC (at least for now, because of Watergate).

I didn't get what I'd hoped for: a separate operation, but he's adding me into news and giving me a staff of two. Thinks my strong point is sniffing out plots. I think he's right.

Lou? Good natured and proud. Boning up for the NY bar exam. He can transfer to another office of the same firm. The only sad note in this is that Dagmar doesn't go for New York and won't be with us. She saw it once, on a school trip. A man fell out the rear doors of a bus at a stop. The other riders simply stepped over and past him. She said she can't live in a place where people are so jaded. She's going back to Detroit, to work for Celeste Dodson again (bodyguard). Celeste has called her weekly all this time. They are really pals.

New address on envelope. We'll be close!

X   Quinn

❏

February 13, 1973

Dear Roz,

Mom told me you and Quinn had a fabulous night on the town in New York. Great that she's moving East. Maybe we could all start getting together. We won't be far apart.

With the Supreme Court's pro-choice decision this month, the abortion issue should be behind us.

Richmond is to our liking. It's steeped in history. You can't escape the aura. At first, I was put off by these southern women asking, "And who was your grandmama?" Family is everything. You are measured by your people and your birthplace. They recoil slightly when they realize I'm a Yankee, but they have the grace to smile.

Traveling north from Charlotte to Richmond, you're actually going south. It's much more southern here because it's the Confederate capital and an older settlement. The power of the FFV is not a myth.

The women are known by three names: first, maiden and married. It's important to establish your ancestry right away. In self defense, I am research-ing the Hamilton genealogy, including climbing through graveyards and visiting ancient courthouses.

Love,
Sterling

❏

3/6/73

Dear Annie,

I'm pleased to be asked to be your maid of honor! I'm looking forward to meeting Steve. He must be ultra-special. You sure took your time locating Mr. Right. I am thrilled for you both.

You mentioned my years-ago lament about losing touch with my sisters after their marriages because we no longer had any privacy . . . It was sensitive of you to remember that and to say you'll make efforts to maintain our friendship on its former basis as well as its new one.

Quinn and Lou invited me to NY last weekend to help them set up their apartment. Annie, it was magical. Quinn and I sat up talking into the night. Lou was snoring in his bed. I'm going to be cautious that I don't come between them (Lou's a generous soul anyway, and dear to me) but I want to cultivate this relationship with my sister. It is so comfortable. And I'm getting a huge charge out of my niece. I need a child to cuddle.

I'm relieved you chose not to go through the routine of bridesmaids' dresses, etc. But do tell me what color you'd like me to wear.

Love,
Ros

❏

March 28, 1973

Dearest Rosalind,

Dad and I are elated that you and Quinn are having such a grand time together. We laughed at Quinn's description of you girls going to Macy's to have a complete make-over. The snapshot was amazing. We hardly recognized you two.

We've just returned from a long weekend with Sterling and Randy. His camping shop is doing a brisk business. He picked a good spot, across the street from a mall.

Sterling is heavily into researching family history. We haven't seen her so domestic in a while. I think she feels her main job in the women's movement is over since they were successful in their efforts to legalize abortion. She said, and I agreed, that she wished this would be the end of your differences.

Rosalind, please give it some thought. You and Quinn are enjoying one another and I believe Sterling sees herself as somewhat left out. Perhaps you could write or call her a bit more often.

The children are darling. Mindy is almost nine! Time goes by quickly. Important to remember. Cherish each minute and don't let small concerns stand in the way of happiness.

All my love,
Mother

P.S. I want to plant the
bug now: how about a big family Christmas here?

❏

March 29, 1973
Dear Rosalind,

I'm sorry you couldn't accept our invitation to the Los Angeles premiere of A MIXED BAG last winter. I hope you will consider coming for the next Brawley-Maeder film, CASSADAGA. Roz, this is a winner, guaranteed. I am having a script sent to you. Please treat with utmost secrecy.

The first paragraph of this letter is nice, eh? That's because I'm getting ready to hit you up. MIXED BAG did make a profit (in spite of the critics) and I want you to reinvest. I can pay you your capital + earnings now (don't make me do that) or I can put them into CASSADAGA. I wouldn't be recommending the latter if I didn't believe you would benefit greatly.

MIXED BAG had the misfortune to be launched alongside THE GOD-FATHER. And I was mistaken to cast Kensey opposite M. For CASSADAGA I got Simone Sharpe. No one can argue with her credentials.

Won't beg this time,
Thom

❏

Dear Ms. Morrow:

A friend of mine, Richard Beddow, recommended you as someone I should get to know. You may remember him from a fitness tour he was doing last fall. I will be in Boston May 10–12 on business and have no friends there. I would appreciate having a knowledgeable companion show me the city.

Will you please inform me as soon as possible concerning your availability.

Cordially,
Michael Naiman
3 April 1973

❏

Dear, dear, Ros,
Thank you!

Thom

❏

Rosalind,

I have something to tell you. It's important. Please meet me at the Cafe Dubonnet on Tuesday at two.

Paul C.

❏

4/20/73

Rosalind:

I wouldn't be too hasty in getting out of the market. Reconsider. Since the beginning of the year, you have sold all of your stock in the following companies: Avon Products, Black & Decker, Burroughs, Eastman Kodak, Emery Air Freight, Ingersoll-Rand, Phelps Dodge and Sears Roebuck. I know you know this, but I wanted you to see the tally in a sentence.

Watergate is only one factor in the economy. I am still bullish and feel you may regret you jumped out too soon.

Grab your calendar and make a date with me. I am doing heavy homework for you and will have a list of opportunities to consider.

Ruth

❏

April 28, 1973

Dear Annie,

Tremendous. A glorious wedding. I like Steve immensely. You can tell him I said so. Many thanks to you both and to both sets of parents for treating me like royalty. May your marriage be filled with joy.

Annie, when I got back, there was a card here from Paul. I met him for lunch, at his request. He said he had something important to tell me. He did: he knows exactly who I am.

He admits I was right to let him go. My career would have killed his.

The fact that we're still in love astounded us both. I have made the decision to accept him under these circumstances. We have an arrangement which should never interfere with our public lives. We will not meet often enough to arouse suspicion.

I know my future, Annie. I will always live alone. Call it destiny. In accepting him, I am accepting myself at last, the way I am, the way things are.

Ros

❏

My dear Ros,

A surgeon should be unsurprised, even nonchalant in regard to physique. After all, the human body is familiar terrain to him. He makes his livelihood managing it with confidence and authority.

Another theory shot to hell.

HMM

❏

May 18, 1973

Dear Ros,

There is nothing more rewarding than finding one's ancestors! The more I study and research, the more fascinated I become. I am almost back to the Civil War on the Hamilton family tree. There is evidence that they are related to Stonewall Jackson. Also, I have hints that if I go back far enough, I will discover Alexander Hamilton!

Will you do two things for me?

1. Keep a daily log of your life. While you may not think it interesting at all, it will be fascinating to your descendants.

2. Consider beginning research on the Morrow side. I haven't time to approach that project, and it would be wonderful to have some help.

I am sending you two books to get you started: a text on genealogy and an accompanying workbook. We owe it to those who come after us to have done some legwork on this important mission.

Love,
Sterling

❏

June 11th, 1973

Dear Rozzy,

When are you coming back? We have a favorite restaurant for you to try. Margaret (Zan's hired nanny) put us onto it. You'll like Margaret. We had to go through a lot of duds to find her but it was worth it. And she's willing to take on two when the baby's born.

Here's something you can only tell your sister: I am having a lot of fun kicking ass on this job. (Was I angry as a child? Refresh my memory.) Seriously, I've always had a sense of outrage at unjust, dishonest, hypocritical or sneaky acts. One of my earliest recollections is that of beating up Jimmy Blocker because he stole my trike. I didn't stop to think how much fatter he was than me. My fury did him in.

I have relished exposing Nixon's '73 inaugural as the most expensive in history ($4 mil), digging in the dung of Watergate and coming up with Segretti, and—my favorite—monitoring federal fund cut-offs to school districts and state college systems that have not complied with desegregation requirements. Basically, holding feet to the fire.

People are becoming afraid of me and I like it.

What day can we expect you?

XX   QUINN

❏

July 7

Dear Roz,

Thank you for taking such good care of my girls—and my boy. I'm a lucky man, having a sister like you.

I felt totally helpless, getting that call in Indianapolis, knowing the baby was coming early and I'd be too late to do one damned thing about it.

Quinn said you were there by the time she got into hard labor, and that you sat with her all the way through. Zan told me you celebrated with her at a "cook-on-da-tadle" place. Japanese?

I was one crazy ACP at that NAACP convention, loping around passing out ceegars, grinning and drooling. A son!

We've decided on a name: Dalin (because we like it) George (after my father).

LOU

❏

Ros,

If you can, meet me at the Inn the last weekend in August. Make two room res. I'll call Inn to check the week before.

Missing you.

Paul

❏

Aug 16th 1973

Dear Ros,

I am disturbed with Mother. She saw me on the John Mitchell interview and wrote to say she thought I should be careful—that I was dangerously arrogant with him. She doesn't realize what it takes to get a candid reaction from a subject. You can't be too nice.

She's always had the conviction that you get what you dish out. She thinks people will hurt me or that I'll sabotage my career. I can't make her see that investigative is different. If these characters are engaged in wrongdoing, they deserve to be exposed. You have to be a tiger.

Luckily, my assistants (Jean McCully and Don Griggs) are of the same persuasion: fierce. I'm giving them more and more responsibility because they've earned it. I can leave the office for days, on assignment, and find they've fired some accurate torpedoes while I've been gone.

I like the fact that you and I tell each other everything. It lifts the monkey off my back. Thanks for your ear.

Hugs,
Quinn

❏

Roz
I love you I love you I love you I love you

Paul

❏

Sept 14th 1973

Dear Roz,

Did you see my bit on Agnew? The end is near! No kidding. They've got this one red-handed. Only a matter of weeks til his demise.

Now, if we cd just stop Kissinger from becoming Secy of State. I feel sure he's the one who put the wiretaps on Kalb et al. I often wonder if I'm being tapped. This admin hates news folk.

I'm gathering quite a following, if poison pen letters are any indication. That's all I get except for a few ridiculous "tips." A note that arrived after UN Secy Gen Waldheim's address on human rights insisted he was a Nazi bigwig. I send straight replies to all this junk. Ack.

Come stay with us. Zan is asking for you.

Still kicking ass,
Quinn

❑

October 16, 1973

An Anniversary. Eight years since we started. May it never end. Ros, you are the best.

Chase

❑

October 25, 1973

Ros:

This is personal. Please listen and then bury it. I want you to stop research on the Morrow family tree. If you haven't started, all the better.

I've been making a big deal of this and Mindy has been so intrigued, as have Randy's parents. But many facts I have uncovered are shocking and embarrassing. No one would wish to claim relation to some of these people.

You may find that amusing, but in the South ancestry is a point of honor. One of Randy's maternal great-great grandmother's cousins was Mary Surratt, who was hanged with three men for plotting the Lincoln assassination. I found a photograph of the execution. She has a white bag over her head and her long skirt bound by a rope around her knees. For modesty, I suppose. But what stopped me cold was my investigation of the Keseberg branch. They helped open the West. Lewis Keseberg was trapped with the Donner party (1846) and later charged with six counts of murder for cannibalism. And there's more.

It's hard to explain to Mindy why I quit. I told her I got tired of it. Randy knows the truth and encouraged me to abandon the project.

Just toss the books away.

Love,
Sterling

❑

Ros,

I can't concentrate on my work. I am forever fantasizing about our meetings. Thank God the fantasies come true—but not often enough.

Being with you has changed my world. I have a million questions and no answers. I feel intense guilt regarding Eliz and intense jealousy regarding your companions. I want to quit being me and be with you. If I did, would you have me?

Paul

❑

R.—

Since you won't have me as your husband, I'll take anything I can get. Yes, Friday's good. See you at home.

P.

❑

Dec 2

Dear Rozzy,

I had to write to you. I've never seen you cry like that. Holidays are a blue, bleak stretch. I'm grateful you wanted to come here and stay a night over Thanksgiving.

I didn't think about it before you said it. I guess I saw you as content. It seemed as though you were choosing the life you desired.

But to hear you whisper, with such grief, that all you ever really wanted was to be a wife and mother, destroyed me. Totally. When I remember the men who let you down, I could kill them.

You were the one who asked Sterling and me to play house and "babies" over and over—long after we were bored with it and wanted to switch to hide-and-seek or circus. You were the one who was always dragging your chair to the counter to climb up and cook with Mother.

I should have seen it. I understand you better now and maybe I can be a better friend.

Your

Quinn

❑

12.11

Dear Rosalind,

I wanted to tell you this in person, but the whole thing came about so quickly that there isn't time. Don't worry when you read it in the newspaper. I haven't changed my mind about us.

I am being considered for a post (minor advisory) with Gerald Ford. It seems like a poor moment to be entering the White House, but I believe it's an advantageous one. Nixon will be removed—as Agnew has been. VP Ford will become president. He is an honest and well-known figure. He will be elected in '76. His future is unlimited.

It's what I've worked and waited for, Ros. Please go easy on me. If this comes through, it will necessitate a move to DC.

Somehow we will stay together. I will see you every time I come home. We will work out other ways. I remain devoted to you.

Paul

❑

I hoped you would say that. My heart was fearful when I wrote to you about the possible DC move. So sure I'd lose you. But now I understand that we are Forever. Merry Christmas, my Sweet. You'll be on my mind each minute.

P.

❑

12/31/73

Dear Annie,

I'm glad your Christmas as newlyweds was euphoric. I appreciated your calling me at Mother and Dad's Christmas Day. You asked how our family reunion was going. Forgive me for telling you the truth now that I can.

It was the worst Christmas I could imagine: 13 of us cooped up in the house because of the weather. The first full gathering since 1964. As you have known our family for a decade and have seen the clouds gathering, I need to describe the storm to you.

For the two days before Christmas, we were courteous and wary. On Christmas, hostilities began to surface. It felt as though Quinn and I were on one side of the fence and Sterling on the other, with parents and husbands hopelessly looking on.

By the day after Christmas, the three of us were at the boiling point. We put on coats, hats and boots and walked far away from the house into the woods where we argued until we shouted.

Sterling said Quinn and I had deliberately closed her out. She accused me of favoring Zandria and Dalin over her children. She thinks I have become a recluse with odd ideas. She feels I flaunt my money. She believes I only supported the pro-life forces to spite her. She resented my interest in Randy while they were divorced. Etc!

Quinn called Sterling a hypocrite on the race issue and brought out of her pocket a letter from a mutual friend describing Sterling's search for an all-white Richmond neighborhood to live in. She accused Sterling of meddling in her career, specifically of halting an abortion documentary she had put weeks into. She accused her of constantly upstaging the two of us for Mother and Dad's attention, of incessant drama and fickleness. Sterling countered that when it comes to drama, no one beats Quinn, parading self-righteously across the TV screen.

I, who am usually fairly placid, was drawn into the emotion and told Sterling that, indeed, she changes her mind too often. She goes "whole hog" for a cause then abruptly abandons it. She expects the rest of us to "forget," too.

Sterling said that we are grudge-holders. That we can't just let go of issues and move on. That we are rigid and unforgiving. That we never endorse the good things she does. A lot of times we never even see them, she said. She told Quinn she was instrumental in getting her the position as network correspondent.

Quinn laughed, and then turned livid, believing her. I noticed that the snow was literally melting where we were standing, we were generating so much heat. Half an hour later, Quinn had packed and was gone, family in tow.

I thought Sterling would leave, too. The roof was coming off the house. But then I remembered. She'd stay and lick her wounds in front of M & D. She's always needed their support more than we have. So I went. There was nothing else to do. This was not a tiff but an expression of years of division.

Quinn and I are not at all like Sterling and it would be a relief to stop the charade. I spoke to Quinn by phone when I got home and she said she wants to separate from Sterling. Permanently. She doesn't want to let herself in for any more "nonsense."

I was undecided until I received a package from Sterling, Federal Express, two days later. In it was $2500 with no note. The repayment of an old loan and, I presume, her last word.

ROS

❑

1 9 7 4

Quinn

January 7, 1974

Dearest Quinn,

I'm glad you were at home when I called. It's rare to catch you sitting down!

I could tell you were bothered by my asking again about Sterling. You feel you simply have opposite personalities and that it is the calmer choice to leave her alone. But I tell you: we never really know what's in another's heart. We can't look into their eyes and see what they've seen. We have to be merciful.

There's no mathematical formula for assessing people and for predicting the future. What I'm telling you isn't theory. It's based on events I've lived through.

We're here to do good works, to be accepting and—at the least—not harm one another. Please reconsider. I'm asking Rosalind to do the same.

Deepest Love
Mother

❑

Jan. 8

Quinn—

Idea. Agnew's secret service protection is unwarranted at this point. He's no longer vice president and he resigned as a result of illegal acts. Why should taxpayers foot the bill? I think this would make a nice package. Am already researching precedent and law. Can I go with it?

—Jean

GO!
QMF

❑

1/10

Jean

Saw in the Times that Paul Cordner of Connecticut is being considered for a post w/ Ford. Get what you can. Word is he's a schmuck.

Q.

❑

1—15—74

Quinn:

Congrats on the enclosed TV Guide article. You haven't changed a bit from college daze. Atta girl!!!

It's a wonder we haven't bumped into each other the past year. I'm prowling Washington, too. Was with the Baltimore Sun but started my own company. We provide news film for stations across the country. Right now, it's heavily Watergate-related. I married Judy Swain in 1970 and we have twin boys. She sends her best to you.

I hear Jean McCully is on your staff. We were co-workers at the Sun. Watch out for her. She's passive-aggressive and will step on your head if she gets the chance. The fact that this comment is out of character should underline its importance.

Lunch in DC sometime?

Bob Sherman

❏

Beauty and the Beast

by Aaron Foss

IT'S AN EXCELLENT camouflage, the profusion of frosted blond hair framing placid pale green eyes, the slow smile revealing pleasantly uneven teeth, the petite but busty build. Her face is round as a baby's, the tilt of her head a bit self-effacing. If you saw her walking in your direction and didn't know who she was, you'd think you were in for a sales pitch from a Jehovah's Witness. Or perhaps five minutes from your daughter's gym teacher, come to tell you how little Kimberly mastered the somersault.

Quinn Fortner, GBC's answer to today's political mayhem, sits quietly in her office at 6 a.m. perusing her staff's notes for an imminent live interview. She sucks V-8 through a straw from a 64-ounce can and blinks at the printed page. One has difficulty believing this is the woman Spiro Agnew called "a blunt object." Fortner, 28, has built a reputation for ambushing comfortably-seated guests on GBC's two-hour morning show, SunUp. Swift and sure, she disarms them only to follow with a gutpunch.

Last year, her first delivering a daily 15-minute segment on SunUp, she sympathetically interviewed a grieving Lady Bird Johnson then inquired about her newly-deceased husband's alleged womanizing, dismantled H. R. Haldeman then asked the name of his barber, called tennis star Bobby Riggs an amateur opportunist, and smacked three oil company presidents with the term "theater of the absurd" regarding the gasoline shortage. In her evening television commentaries, she has taken on everyone from suspended Atlanta NAACP officials ("traitors") to Robert Bork who finally stepped up to fire Archibald Cox in Nixon's infamous Saturday Night Massacre ("a pathetic drone").

She is always on the prowl for what she labels "the beast," that foul-smelling, nebulous, floating evil that settles "wherever there's money, politics or prejudice." To her detractors, she's The Knife, abrasive and undignified at best, vengeful and rude at worst. But her champions are an ever-increasing number. Her viewer mail, by latest count a hundred pieces a week, is running two-to-one in her favor. She says she appeals to middle Americans who are, plainly, "fed up" with the condition of our national life. Her boss and close friend Winston Taylor, vice president of news, applauds her "moral sensibilities" and her "courageous hammering" at untruth and injustice.

Fortner comes to network news from a four-year apprenticeship with stations WMTN-TV Memphis and KLAC-TV Los Angeles. She served as western regional correspondent for GBC two years before being promoted to director of investigative news in their New York headquarters. She lives in an Upper East Side condominium with her husband Lou Fortner, an attorney, and their children Zandria, 3, and Dalin, 6 months. It is a biracial marriage. She and Lou met during the Chicago race riots of 1965 when he was a student law clerk and civil rights activist, she a student reporter for WCHI-TV.

A check of her file at Merrill reveals a controversial personality who tackled the administration on such issues as the falsifying of a professor's credentials and the practice of automatically granting passing grades to athletes. In a tragic mistake, her live-television updates during a campus shoot-out disclosed the position of a police SWAT team member who was killed by the gunman as a result.

Taylor calls Fortner "an eyewitness to history" and says she has "the experience, right and obligation" to project her opinions. Indeed, she's survived fire and earthquake, stood over a dying Martin Luther King Jr., interviewed Sirhan Sirhan and Charles Manson, welcomed the Pueblo, posed as a scrub nurse in an abortion clinic, and witnessed devastation from nuclear blasts and plane crashes. "She can say anything she likes," Taylor grins, "within FCC guidelines." The network's news ratings have risen steadily over a 12-month period. That, along with a record four bomb threats to GBC's New York offices in 1973 clearly indicate that something noteworthy is happening within.

Fortner who, through it all, has kept herself aloof from alliances with powerful people is unmoved by the hub-bub. "I just tell it like it is," she shrugs, tossing the V-8 can into the waste basket. Seizing a hand mirror from the chaos of her desk, she freshens her pastey-pink lipstick, lifts her hair with her fingers until it resembles a puff of cotton candy, and strides toward the SunUp set.

One hopes whoever's waiting has been forewarned.

January 18th '74

Dear Sherm,

Fabulous to get your letter. And, yes, lunch is in order. I'll call when I'm down your way—which is frequently.

About Jean: I don't see her stepping on my head. We get along perfectly. And I think I know her pretty well. Maybe you two had a personality clash.

Ask Judy to lunch with us. We always hit it off. Is she still a comic?

Best,

QUINN

❑

1/20

Dear Quinn,

I have to ask you a favor. Paul Cordner came to see me regarding your investigation of his private life. Please, could you stop?

I have the feeling you are doing this to him on my behalf but I have no desire to hurt him. I forgave him long ago for whatever unhappiness may have been between us—and he forgave me.

Please let it rest.

Love,

Ros

❑

January 24, 1974

Dear Roz,

I understand your point of view but I feel this way: if he has something to hide, let him beware. If not, he shouldn't be afraid.

The public has a right to know the type of man their vice president is choosing.

It's my guess you still have a twinge for him and he's using that to get to me. Why else would he have the audacity to contact you after four years?

Rozzy, don't let people ride over you this way. You are a gem but you have a flaw. You are too kind, too gentle—especially with the opposite sex. They take advantage of you. I resent it and think you should, too.

QUINN

❑

Cordner no longer in the picture. Passed over. No news value. Sorry.

Jean

Feb 4

❏

2/13

Jean:

It delights me to report that the bill restoring the death penalty—with any kind of luck—will pass the Senate shortly. Get a jump on this. Review death row inmates and find a group for our story. Pref. you select ones most deserving of the ax. No milk toast. I've waited a long time for this. Take Don for film.

QUINN

❏

Quinn Suzanne,

You been winding up yourself too tight. It's all, run here, run there. And Lou's chin in his shoes.

I don't say my thoughts for a long time but. You been running on top of yourself and Lou, too. He has his own pace.

That Jean who ate with us thinks he's slow. I caught the look. Made my eyebrows fall out. Don't let her in between.

I'm sending this to work, PERSONAL. Hope it's OK. You = still my favorite chum and I liked visiting. Give my Dalin and Zan some aunty kisses.   Dagmar

❏

I know it, Dag, but I'm impatient. Lou's too meek. He's got to push like hell for redistricting in Brooklyn and Manhattan or it'll never happen. Two Congressional dists and several state legislative are drawn along discriminatory lines. This has to be fixed before elections.

Jean McCully means well. Her trouble is she's exactly like me. Ambitious. No one could stand two of us. I'm not surprised you felt like you had a dose.

Lou's aware of her attitude toward him but tolerates her, for my sake. She dances to the same music I hear in my head.

No one's going to come in between.

Love you,

Quinn

❏

2/27
Don
    Your film in death row story: exquisite. U. R. a arteest.

                    Q

                  ❑

2/28
Jean:
    Kissinger's intended, Nancy Maginnes—who is? I mean REALLY. Wedding scheduled for Mar. 30. Priority.

                Quinn

                  ❑

                Mar. 8
Quinn
    Previewed your Death Row series this a.m. I was on the floor by the end of it. God, you're great. God, you're good. And I thank you.

              Winston

                  ❑

Oof. Oof! Your friend Jean didn't like me a bit. She made it clear, don't you think? But I couldn't figure out what put her off. Anyway, thanks for a glorious weekend. You and Lou are absolutely the best friends I could wish for. I adored going to see Raisin with you and, of course, rocking and playing with the children. They are precious people.

                  Love,
                  Rozzy

Maybe I offended her? Do
I owe her an apology?

                ❑

3/26/74

Dear Roz,

This is the second time this year I've had to explain Jean to people. She's different, that's all. Her emotions are close to the surface. I don't know what she thought—she was guarded in her comments. I couldn't figure it out, but I noticed her pique. Sorry! I won't subject you to her again. Believe me, she's great at the office. And even in private moments outside. But when others are with us . . . ? If you are thinking she has a sexual thing for me, you're dead wrong. Dead. Wrong.

Lou and I loved having you here with us. Zee you zoon.

XXX   QUINN

❏

4/6

Winston:

I'm not interested in

a. Patty Hearst kidnapping

b. The Xenia tornado

c. S. F. Zebra killer

You have News for that. Use them.

And, while I'm complaining: I NEED MORE AIR TIME. How bout dumping junk. Start with Danny Culpepper's inane commentary. He's aged out. All he does is whine long lists of vaguely related items. Come on now.

QUINN

❏

April 13, 1974

Dearest Quinn,

Oh, I was thrilled with the flowers you and Lou sent for my birthday! A spring bouquet, tulips and daffodils. Marvelous!

Rosalind called and we talked for an hour. She told us again how many adventures she has with you and Lou and that she treasures those times. Honey, it would be the greatest gift I could receive to see you share your life with Sterling, also. She is in a state of transition (as we all are), maturing and learning. Please grant her grace.

Since the oil crunch and downturn in the economy, Randy isn't doing as well with the store. They are on lean times and they have four mouths to feed. Try to relate to her where she is, we beg you. You girls were always so close. Sterling will be a fast friend for you, forever, if you let her.

Are there still long lines at the gas stations in the city? We wait 30 minutes and more and pay atrocious prices. And the new 55 MPH speed limit seemed incredibly slow when we drove to Richmond last week. You are fortunate not to own a car at this time and to have easy access to public transportation. We gave up our plans for an auto trip this summer and, instead, are going to Europe for an early 35th Anniversary fling! Autumn.

We send our dearest love to you, Zandria, Dalin and your wonderful LOU.

Mother

❏

5—1—74

Quinn,

Thanx for lunch. It seems appropriate that we were streaked in DC's best restaurant. Class somehow eludes us. God, wasn't he the fattest, fastest nude you could imagine? Judy and I whoop, remembering.

I was musing on the tidbits about Jean McCully. It fits. I didn't see it before. She picks an idol, like you, and then wants to chase everyone else away. Blow them up, even. To have the person to herself. If it doesn't work, she feels rejected and tries to blow up the idol. Don't say I didn't warn you.

Stay as sweet (smile) as you are. And—next time—we want you to come to the house for dinner. Make sure.

Sherm

❏

5/14

Jean:

Don't use that slant on Assoc. Milk Producers. Yes, we're in first and in deep but everybody's going to have this story eventually. Question isn't what but who. So Nixon traded higher federal support price on milk for big campaign contributions. Yawn! Bring me the who.

Quinn

❏

J—

Now you're thinking like me. Shovel out every last living fact on Connally and his connection w/the milk bribes. We'll stick it to him.

QUINN

❏

June 5

Dear Quinn,

Los Angeles! Thom met me at the airport with his current flame, Trecia Gamble. Trecia is a new breed of actress—less beautiful, more intellectual. I thought her a good match for him.

I stayed at the Beverly Hills Hotel. The premiere of CASSADAGA was that eve. Thom had an escort for me, Kevin Price, an actor. (No romance.)

CD is a brilliant piece. Don't miss it. CD's a small town in Florida which abounds with psychics. Jett plays a drifter who spends three of his last bucks to have Lily Grace, a medium, contact his dead brother. The effect is spellbinding, the story sensual and poignant. Can't tell you more or I'll spoil it.

Jett was humorously obnoxious at the midnight dinner. He vaguely remembered me, he said. That's silly. I hadn't seen him before, except on the screen. Mostly, he was busy being The Center, dipping asparagus in his coffee, kissing countless cheeks (men's, too), dancing barefoot in his tux.

We ended up at his house—castle?—about a dozen of us. It's a monument to Ego, but he treated us well.

Thom took me to the plane—sans Trecia—and seized the opportunity to wring a few more dollars out of me for THORNY, the next Maeder spectacle. Thom's worried CHINATOWN might beat CD for the Oscar. Also, GOD-FATHER II is a threat.

Grisly details in person.

Rozzy

❏

6/16/74

Dear Rozzy—

Your LA letter was fascinating. I saw CD the first night. Agreed—it's a piece of work.

But, I question your generosity to Thom. He's not been supportive to you since you lived together—except when he wants money. Can't you see it?

OK—I'm meddling. But you're too accommodating. The recipients of your beneficence should earn that privilege.

I leave this afternoon to cover the Kalmbach sentencing tomorrow. Nixon's days are numbered. GBC's helping turn the screws. I'll be in the thick awhile and probably won't have time to write.

Take care.

X   QUINN

❏

7/25

Rozzy—

Get out of the stock market. Nixon is closer to resigning than anyone thinks.

Q.

❏

To: Quinn
From: Jean
Date: August 15, 1974

Ford will be retaining most, if not all, cabinet members he inherited from Nixon. They are clean, I guess. Already scrutinized by media. More fertile ground wd be this list of prospects for cabinet and other vacancies surrounding the President.

Benevento, Marcus R., Florida
Coleman, William T. Jr., Pennsylvania
Cordner, Paul W., Connecticut
Dunlop, John T., Massachusetts
Hathaway, Stanley K., Wyoming
Hills, Carla A., California
Iorio, James H., Arizona
Kleppe, Thomas S., North Dakota
Knebel, John A., Oklahoma

Levi, Edward H., Illinois
Mathews, Forrest David, Alabama
Morton, Rogers C. B., Maryland
Richardson, Elliot L., Massachusetts
Rook, Arthur M., Washington
Rumsfeld, Donald H., Illinois
Tryon, Jonathan F., Ohio
Usery, Willie J. Jr., Georgia

❑

Jean:
   Paul Cordner. Exhaustive search, please.

                                    QUINN

❑

Dag, Roz is very sick in the hospital with pneumonia. Not getting any better,
she says. Wants us to come lean on the doctor for her. She called me here in DC
and I didn't recognize her voice. I've been trying to get you. I hope to goodness
you're not away. I am stuck here with this Watergate mess and Mother and Dad
are in Europe. Lou's with the kids. Roz would die before she'd ask Sterling.
Sending this Overnight Mail and please respond as soon as you get. Can you go
there? Call me, day or night. I'll stick a card in here with numbers on it. If you
can't go, I will.
Quinn
Aug 21

❑

Quinn Sue—
   Rozzy is poorly. Like a corpse dug up. I been holding her, petting her head.
I bring her my oxtail soup, but she won't eat. Cough with a sound like her ribs
breaking in her mouth.
   Roz an angel for sure but too nice. This man doctor able to bully her with
voice only. She'll be OK, he says. Takes time. I am thinking: Smart Ass. When
I question, he looks at me like my color made me stupid. Getting nowhere.
Maybe you better come.

Dagmar

❑

9/4/74

Dear Mother and Dad,

No need to cut your trip short. Ros is going to be okay. I just got back to DC from Boston. Dagmar is staying with her. My time was limited because we're in the aftermath of Nixon's resignation but I had it out with the doctor and got another one. The new dr. said she had been on the wrong antibiotic for her type of pneumonia and no wonder she wasn't well. She turned around in 24 hours and they let her go home. She'll make progress now.

Please have a dream vacation.

QUINN

❑

September 17, 1974

Dear Dagmar,

A million thanks for staying all that time with Rosalind. You took perfect care of her and none of us will ever be able to pay you back the way you should be paid. But please know how grateful we are.

When I think of that doctor getting the best of her, I could pull hair (his). These men deserve comeuppance. If only she could give it to them! She is an angel, as you said in your letter, and that seems to invite people to mistreat her.

Speaking of mistreatment, I finally wised up to the fact that Jean was mistreating Lou with her attitude. By not saying anything, I was condoning it, so I approached her about it. She was cool, but I could tell I was having an impact. We're on strictly business terms now.

You were right, Girl.

Guess who else she didn't like: Rozzy. She alluded a couple of times to Roz's sophisticated appearance and quiet manner as a facade. Burned the hell out of me.

Dear, dear. And this started out to be a thank you note! Well, you know Quinn Sue.

QS

❑

9-19

Quinn, off the record—How low do you want to go? Cordner's been waiting in the wings nearly a year. Passed over for Ford vice presidential advisor (remember?). Relisted for possible presidential advisor. He's intellectual, aristocratic, pristine. Except! He has a mistress. And she's a Lady of the Evening.

Too smutty for us?

Jean McC

❑

9/23/74

Jean:

"Lady" EXCELLENT. Cordner moving up fast on the list of hopefuls. I'm in a position to know: in the middle of the White House press room. I'll never get back in time to do the research and pull the trigger on this one. You do it. Don't miss. Use whatever ammunition you can find.

QMF

❑

HONEY, THIS LETTER FROM DAGMAR ARRIVED YESTERDAY AND I THOUGHT I SHOULD GO AHEAD AND FORWARD IT SINCE YOU NEED TO BE IN WASHINGTON 10 DAYS OR SO. I COULDN'T DECIPHER IT. WILL YOU ANSWER HER? I AM RUSHED OFF MY FEET. MISS YOU. LOVE EVER, LOU

❑

Quinn and Louis G.

I got a pure feeling about Rosalind from being at her house. Her closets & drawers spangles, fur and perfume. The phone rings too much.

You two know what is the truth and I want to know it, too. Who is Rosalind? With who?

I can take it. Tell me: She not going to be any different in my mind.

Dagmar

❑

10/9

Jean—

I know you've been out digging on this Cordner thing, but I hope you got my message to hold up. Don't go any farther until I talk with you. Urgent. I need to check something. We could make a dangerous mistake.

QUINN

❏

November 7, 1974

Dearest Quinn,

We have made the decision to close up Rosalind's house and go back to Pittsburgh. Dad can't stay away from his practice anymore.

It amazes me that she hasn't called us. Surely she must know how desperately worried we are. Dad says Rosalind probably believes we are ashamed of her.

Since you were here last week, nothing's changed except the continual falling of the leaves in high wind until the trees are almost bare. Her scent lingers. Her mail is overflowing the cardboard box inside the front door. The phone has stopped ringing. It's eerie that she left a whole house full of belongings. One has to believe she will come back. Meanwhile, we pay her bills.

The police make us angry. They are half-hearted in their attempts to locate her. They say it is absolutely typical for a person surrounded by negative publicity to disappear and, since Paul disappeared at the same time, it seems obvious they are together. But Dad and I feel alarmed that she severed her ties so sharply and we want the chance to tell her how much she means to us.

It is hard to watch your grieving, which is like an illness in which you are making no progress. I realize what is bothering you the most but Rosalind couldn't possibly believe you would hurt her on purpose. If only you had had the chance to speak with her. Jean knew how to fatally wound both of you at once. I'm relieved she is no longer in your office.

You have tried every avenue to find Rosalind but there must be other ways. Let us think on it.

My hope is that Rosalind will come home Christmas Eve. I'll open the door and she'll be there in the twilight, in the snow, and I'll wake up with her under our roof. That would be the greatest gift.

Much love,
Mother

❏

1 9 7 5

Sterling

January 2, 1975

Dearest Sterling,

I am aware of your upset at not being with us this Christmas. I would have
been grateful to have you and Randy and the children here, or to visit with you
in Richmond, but Dad is absolutely beside himself about Rosalind. With each
day, he becomes more angry and fearful—angry that she hasn't contacted us,
and fearful about her well being. Don't say I told you this because he likes to
appear the strong one. I am trying to help him through.

I've been over the events of the past few months—and years—a thousand
times in my mind. I can't believe I didn't really know Rosalind, missed all the
clues. Maybe I saw it and denied it, but I don't think so. It is a strange feeling.
Each of you, growing up, was totally readable to me. I perceived your thoughts
through your facial expressions, through your posture, through a slight change
in voice quality. I never wanted to "catch" you, only to help you. I couldn't
stand to think there was unhappiness lurking anywhere in your hearts or
minds. I thought I could control present and future events, and emotions. And
I did, for a long time. I thought I was still doing it.

Another fact I've found it hard to accept is that families don't live close
together now. I can't expect that of you. But look how many of your Dad's and
my brothers and sisters are in and around Pittsburgh. It's where they were
raised; I don't think it occurred to them to leave their parents and friends. I'm
not trying to hand you guilt. But if something's amiss among us, we know it
almost as it's taking place. Can occasionally be maddening. When I was a
young working nurse, I had lunch one day with a cousin's husband who arrived
unannounced on a business trip from Erie. Your Dad heard about it within the
hour and showed up in his greens to have dessert at our table. Wanted to see
who "the man" in the rumors would turn out to be!

I guess at this point I need to thank you for your honesty. You have always
exposed your inner self to us, particularly to me. I'm sure your sisters would
agree we have an unusual relationship. You have wanted to share more of your
thoughts, year after year. And, although we haven't been together geograph-
ically, we have mingled our experiences so thoroughly that I feel I know you
very well.

I love you.
Mother

❏

Jan. 3

Sterling—

I could hear stress in your voice when you called at Christmas. Believe me, I wanted to be with all of you for the holidays, but your mother was suffering greatly. She just didn't feel up to it. To tell you the truth, I'm more than worried about her. She is still losing weight, over 10 lbs. now. Usual for depression— can't eat, can't sleep. I'm in there fighting but you can give her a lift, too. A couple of suggestions. I've never deceived Diana, however I must ask: if you can't patch your differences with Quinn, could you give the appearance of having done so? Mother needs the security. I'm asking Quinn the same thing. Also, I realize you and Randy are in a temporary financial bind and it is of deep concern to me, but please—whatever may be going on—try to reflect satisfaction to Mother. She can't take any more bad news.

The last request is: if you can imagine a way to locate Rosalind, do it. We can't continue with the private investigator we hired. It's draining our resources.

Thanks, Honey. I miss you & your gang.

Best love,
Dad

❏

Jeff—

It is time for you to pay back the money you owe me. $2500 plus 5 percent annual interest for 7 years. Total $3517.75. Send within 15 days c/o P.O. Box 563, Richmond, Virginia 23235.

Sterling Hamilton

❏

1/22/75

Sterling and Randy.

I went up to see Paul. Had to look in his eyes. My opinion, he's telling the truth. Doesn't know where she is. Did not "go away" with her. Etc. Anyway, his wife has taken him back but things are so tense I had to talk to him on his front porch in sleet. God, I felt sorry for the man. Sorrier for Roz, who counted on him.

Quinn's out of her slump and gone the other direction, galloping around trying to get someone to kill her. Three days ago, the police were dismantling a bomb planted at Rockefeller Center. She used her credentials to get close, then slipped through NYPD lines and walked directly up to bomb squad at work. Winston—perverse creature—loves it. Makes for great stories and—he hopes—high ratings. Even higher if she martyrs herself.

I'm waist-deep in education problems. System's integrated, it says here. Fact: within individual schools certain classrooms have minorities only. In typical government fashion, HEW is "studying" the mess. Meanwhile, the city of New York teeters on the edge of bankruptcy.

Brighter side: Zandria's chewing them up in nursery. Favorite activity is painting. They do tempera, at an easel, wearing smocks. We've got a wall of her masterpieces. Abstract. Luckily, the teacher writes the title across the bottom of each one. "Eggs on a stick." "A Mexican skyscraper." "Infinity-decker hat." (Our favorite.)

Dalin's my babe. Smiling Buddha. Both kids ask for Rozzy constantly. Quinn and I have leaned on everyone we know to find her. Amazing that we can't do it.

Am enclosing original art by Lady Z.

Peace,

Lou

❏

Dear Fan:

I want to sincerely thank you for your kind expression of friendship. Letters like yours provide tremendous encouragement for me. I will strive to continue to be worthy of your attention and please know that I am always grateful to hear from you. The large numbers of letters I receive make it impossible for me to answer each one personally, but I am enclosing a hand-autographed photo as a token of my appreciation.

Jett Maeder

❏

FOR GOD'S SAKE, READ THIS. IT'S NOT A FAN LETTER!

Jeff—You owe me money and you know it. Send it NOW. $2500 plus 5% interest for 7 years = $3517.75. Send to: Sterling Hamilton, P.O. Box 563, Richmond, Virginia, 23235.

❏

January 27, 1975

Dear Mother and Dad,

Thought you would enjoy having this darling picture by Zandria. Isn't it colorful and cute? I got a kick out of the title, "Good Shoes and a Purse." We enjoy hearing all about her activities and Baby Dalin. Just got a letter this week. Did you notice Quinn's taking a new, "up front" approach to her stories? Gets us close to the action. Did you hear about HEW's study of NY schools? I admire the work Lou's doing with equal opportunity. Be sure to ask him about it.

Randy has decided to expand his line at the store to include sports uniforms for schools. He feels this will help us over the rough spots and he's very excited about new opportunities. Bobby Hughes lent the money to get him started. We should be able to earn it back in a short time.

The children send love.

Sterling

❑

February 4, 1975

Dear Sterling:

Great running into you at the Bd. of Ed. Bldg. Sorry I was on my way to a meeting. Tried to call you a couple of times after. Let's get together. Tea and crumpets?

Want you to know an insider's view. You may have a long wait due to the teacher glut (nationwide). In Chesterfield, we have dozens of applicants for a single position. Many have masters degrees and are taken first. Guess everyone our age was told in college to major in ed because of the teacher shortage! I'm sorry. If I could pull strings for you, I would. Same game in the other counties.

Thought you'd want to know the truth about what's going on so you could get into another field for now, since your situation's urgent.

In friendship,
Joanne

❑

February 9, 1975

Dearest Sterling,

Just a quick note to tell you how pleased I am that you and Quinn are communicating again. You are doing the right thing in forgiving her. All will be well.

Congratulations to Randy on his new venture. Sounds promising. Glad Bobby is such a good friend and that you're on the road to financial recovery.

Love,
Mother

❑

Dear Randy and Sterling,

I have given it a lot of thought and don't see how I can lend more. As it is, I'll probably have to close one of my stores. What I sent was all I can do, I'm tapped out. I hate like the devil to tell you no, you with family involved. There's only me here and I am peddling fast. You tried the banks, how about another friend or relative? Keep in touch. I'm with you.

Bobby

2—18

❑

Dear Fan:

I want to sincerely thank you for your kind expression of friendship. Letters like yours provide tremendous encouragement for me. I will strive to continue to be worthy of your attention and please know that I am always grateful to hear from you. The large numbers of letters I receive make it impossible for me to answer each one personally, but I am enclosing a review of my new book, along with information on my appearances in your area. I hope you will come out and give me a chance to get to know you.

Jett Maeder

❑

Maeder's Poems Simple, Compelling

By Sibyl Downey
Los Angeles Times

NOT SINCE ROD MCKUEN burst upon the national consciousness with verses directly from and to the heart, has a lone poet captured popular America's fancy like Jett Maeder. One may speculate that the instant success of Maeder's first volume, "Prisoner of Your Smile" (Belkirk, $6.95), is due to his recognizability from the silver screen. Yet acclaim for "Prisoner" has reached beyond the wave of movie-goers into an untold sea of buyers.

It has not, however, reached into the community of literary critics who brand the effort "soda pop," "graffiti" and "sky writing." Translated, these swipes refer to the utter accessibility of Maeder's poems, precisely the trait that is causing the crush at book counters. A poll conducted by the publisher reveals an interesting perspective: most copies of "Prisoner" are being purchased as gifts. This, then, is a love offering, a piece of the collective soul.

"Prisoner" contains some 90 poems which span 1960–67, the years Maeder was incarcerated at the North Carolina Reformatory at Statesville on a manslaughter conviction he says was circumstantial. His live-in companion Jocelyn Yates, who was under psychiatric treatment, plunged to her death from their apartment balcony in 1959. Maeder—whose real name is Jeff Mather—testified that Yates intended to frame him and that he physically tried to restrain her from jumping. The jury focused instead on the testimony of an elderly male passerby, nine floors below and across a congested street, who insisted she struggled desperately with a second party before she fell. The jury was further swayed by the accounts of neighbors who heard her scream for help seconds before she died.

Throughout "Prisoner," Maeder's belief in his own innocence is as penetrating as winter mist. It gets in the eyes and down the throat, lingers heavily in the lungs. We are breathing a man's presence, his thoughts at times indistinguishable from our own. We relate to his imprisonment even, and especially, of the ordinary sort: of affection and affectation, of temperament and unreason and flesh. What moves us most about the book is not the vision of confinement but the winging of release across the bulk of pages, a buoyancy not gratuitous but native.

The title smile belongs to an unnamed woman who visited and wrote to Maeder regularly during an unspecified number of months while he served his sentence and the sharpest emotions are evoked in the poems about her.

"Prisoner," it must be said, has occasional lapses into the kind of pictureless, general statements which constitute weak writing ("See me/ seeing you,/ seeing through/ your eyes,/ your pretty, pretty eyes") and into overdrama bordering on melodrama ("I have not seen a flower/ since 1962/ but there is a picture/ of one/ in the infirmary./ I have been there twice"). Nevertheless, one comes away with a portfolio of solid images and a lasting impact from witnessing the starker side of life quietly and poignantly contained.

❏

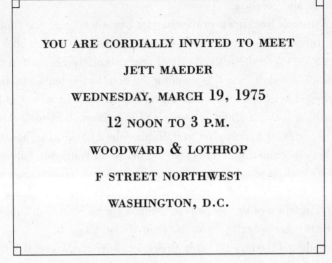

YOU ARE CORDIALLY INVITED TO MEET

JETT MAEDER

WEDNESDAY, MARCH 19, 1975

12 NOON TO 3 P.M.

WOODWARD & LOTHROP

F STREET NORTHWEST

WASHINGTON, D.C.

❏

S. —Here's your $. I couldn't believe it when I looked up from autographing and there you were. I swear I never got your letters. Wonder what people thought, both of us starting to cry like that. What a shit I am. As I said, I thought constantly about paying you back but I didn't want to plunk the money down into your life and cause you more embarrassment. I treated you badly and I apologize again. I was an envious, desperate person. I thought the best thing I could do for you after that was leave you alone.

It haunts me about Roz. But I wouldn't hire a PI if I were you. That route's been exhausted by your dad, right? How about Lily Grace? The psychic. The real one, I mean. She was a consultant to us the whole time we filmed in Cassadaga and she's uncanny. Don't dump this idea until you think it over. I'm enclosing her address and phone #. I'd offer again to pay for any investigation you want but you made it clear how you feel about that.

Deja vu, this PO box of yours. I've opened one of my own, not accessible to my staff. Write me there. I won't be a jerk this time.

J.

❏

4/11/75

Dear Randy and Sterling,

Even Winston's freaking over the chances Quinn's taking. She's out there in disguise, buying drugs from street people. In the past month she's slogged through a toxic waste site without proper gear and offered herself in trade at a bank/hostage standoff. She was opening the door to the bank building when police dragged her back. She's conducting her own investigations of killings, some of which may be Mafia-related. NYPD is down Winston's throat. He, meanwhile, is trying to decoy her w/ fluff. She lobs it back in his face. Can't say I blame her on some of this. He's coaxing her to do Watergate follow-up—all those jokers getting off after having served only 3 or 4 months. Strictly in the Who Cares category. And carcinogen stories. Like recalls of TV sets for radiation, depletion of the ozone layer by hair sprays; estrogen supplements, DES in cattle and polyvinyl wrap on fruit. Good God.

I am reading Pilgrim at Tinker Creek (exquisite). Maybe if I read long enough, when I glance up again she'll have worn herself out. It's painful to watch.

The kids are fine.

LOU

❑

April 17th

Dear Mother and Dad,

Am hunting for a job while helping Randy at the shop. The uniform business is promising. But, of course, we are in competition with other suppliers who have been around longer. It's kind of fun being there with Randy. He's easy. Thinks everything I do is marvelous! Ha! A superb employer. Gives me short hours so I can be home when the kids come in from school

I almost hope I don't find other work. After being totally available to the kids for a couple of years now, I would miss it terribly.

We're here together most evenings. Money being tight has cemented us. We play board games, hide and go seek, make cookies and bread. Pinching pennies has made us creative. We don't toss out a box or spool or jar without imagining further uses for it. The other night we did a family collage from junk we found in desk and dresser drawers: tickets, photos, news clips, letters, announcements, ribbon. Turned out swell. Big. $2' \times 4'$.

Have you seen the interesting stories Quinn is doing? She's amazing. Did Lou tell you he's reading Pilgrim at Tinker Creek and finding it delightful?

Hugs and kisses,
Sterling

❏

Mindy Hamilton
Grade 5

For Mother HAPPY MOTHERS DAY

My mother is pretty and smells like coffee. She says Who wants to dance with me? My little sisters like that. She dances with both at one time. I play a record. My brother thinks its goofey but he laughs. Her dance makes us happy. She gave us each a wish. Mine was a trip to Nabisco factory. We went. She takes my picture every day. I didn't like it but now I see how I grew.

❏

Jeff—

Are you sure about Lily Grace? I paid her plane fare to Richmond & met her for breakfast at her hotel. She wanted a bag full of items Roz had used. I got them through Lou, who has a key to the house.

She showed up at the dining room in an old robe and fuzzy slippers like it was the most natural thing in the world and didn't comment on it. Her hair was a high, rusty-red nest. No make up. She drank orange juice & ate grapefruit. Three of them. That was her total consumption over an hour. The bag went under the table and she didn't refer to it again, although she did take it with her. Wouldn't accept a down payment. Seemed insulted by it. Said, "Everyone is psychic. You could find Roz yourself." Not sure what that means or how much money she'll want if she's successful. Reassure me.

I told her to write c/o PO box. Randy would have a fit about this. He doesn't believe in anything—except God—that he can't see, hear or touch. He lumps ESP with flying saucers and the Loch Ness monster.

S.

❏

May 21, 1975
Dear Sterling and Randy,

This is a critical time for us with retirement coming. We could lend you some, but not all. Randy, would you consider rejoining me in practice? When I retire, I'd leave you my equipment, 100%. Patient load assured.

I respect your wishes and right to pursue another career choice but you are a fine dentist and I would welcome you back.

Your Dad

❏

Jeff—How long do you think I should wait to hear from Lily Grace before I call her? It's been weeks. The farther I get away from meeting her, the more I think I've been taken for a ride. Maybe she just wanted a trip to Richmond. Uh.

Sterling

❏

Jul 12

Sterling

No one hurries Lily Grace. She's totally disassociated herself from the clock. Will not go back and look at anyplace she's lived or worked before. Won't even look at photos. Never visits graves. Won't go to weddings or funerals—nothing that marks time. She believes it detrimental to her powers.

Wait. And don't get on the wrong side of her.

Brawley thinks the world should "leave Roz the f- - - alone!" Says she's immensely resourceful and capable, doesn't need meddling and will come back when she wants to. (We were discussing her one day—I didn't tell him you and I were in touch.) He's in an off-hand, magnanimous mood about Roz because he doesn't need her money, if I may be so frank. CASSADAGA was a gold mine.

We're ready to release THORNY, which I'm skittish about. The dude's an alcoholic salvage diver. Script isn't balanced and Thorny's not truly likable although I played the hell out of the role—if I do say so myself. And I can't stand not to be likable, even in a film.

I'll shut up now. I could always talk to you better than anybody.

Jeff

❏

8th Aug.

Jeff—

I haven't heard a word from Lily Grace. Is this a joke? Her phone's been disconnected.

Bad mood today. Can't find a single job in this backward school system and been applying to day care centers. Ahgh! Poor little people. This is warehousing. In the one today, the kids lined up single-file for lunch and passed a warm washcloth down the line, wiping their hands and faces. I was standing with the kid at the end of the line and almost puked. Such nonchalance! One caretaker will tend a whole room full of children. Kids sleep with no one watching them. They are dejected sacks, lying heaped on mats. The pay is minimum wage. No wonder they get who they get—no education and don't give a rip. I saw teachers (?) conversing on the playground while kids fell off swings and whacked at each other. Odor in those places is another thing. I clung to my kids when they got home from school. They clung back. You should know my kids, they're great people. I don't think I can work at day care. I was offered jobs. My main instinct is to get legal recourse on these centers and shut them down or clean them up. I can't ever be a follower. I have to soapbox.

Blab! Bent your ear, didn't I? Can talk to you better than anybody, too, but don't get ideas.   S.

❏

Dear Sterling:

I'm sure you noted that the National Academy of Sciences released a report in May that demonstrated a significant decline in maternal deaths and injuries related to abortion since abortion laws were liberalized. There was also no corresponding increase in mental health problems among women who underwent abortions.

We at Nova believe that your book THE LOGIC OF ABORTION was a milestone in the journey to this enlightened state. Accordingly, we feel the time is right to update your work with supporting statistics and reissue it at the earliest opportunity. Would you be willing to undertake this immediately?

Give me a call and we'll talk.

Best regards,
Rachel Gooding
Senior Editor
Nova Publishers
August 13, 1975

❑

September 9, 1975

Dearest Sterling,

Our visit with you did us much good. When I visualize your beautiful family, it relaxes me and restores my optimism.

I see growth in your relationship with Randy. You are considerate of each other in a very mature way. Your high regard for one another shines through. What a generous and thoughtful wife and mother you are. We especially relished the humor you and Randy have cultivated. Many laughs. The children are benefiting from it, that's evident.

I enjoyed curling Mindy's hair and talking music with Lance. We are still chuckling about why he chose the cello as his instrument: you don't have to work hard . . . you get to sit down and you don't have to hold your arms up!

We marvel that Sovereign and Laine are so similar facially—almost like twins—and yet have such diverse builds and personalities, Sovereign sturdy and acrobatic, hurling herself from activity to activity, Laine quiet and delicate. Serious. Amazing intellect, and that's not just a grandmother's pride speaking.

Oh, we loved being there. God bless you.

Mother

❑

September 9, 1975

Dear Mother and Dad,

Just a note to thank you for your visit and for all you did for us while you were here. You organize and energize us!

Sovereign wrote the enclosed poem for you. Don't fall off your chairs.

Love,

Sterling

❑

Treasures

Treasures, Treasures,
Are always pleasures,
The milk from udder,
Can help you make butter,
The cattle eat grass,
Because of the milk they pass,
Between the Chicken's legs,
Out comes the eggs.
Treasures, Treasures,
Here are the pleasures.

❑

9/11

Jeff,

My parents were here and my mother looks scary. Her clothes hang. I have GOT to find Rosalind. Let's face it, Lily Grace dropped the ball.

On top of being unstrung by Mother, Laine broke two fingers yesterday! And it was her birthday, too! She was in a neighbor's yard. A playmate ran over and told me. When I found her, she was lying on the ground, doubled up and silent. My heart left my chest. I picked her up. She was so little against me. I hurt clear through. All of my children are precious to me, but Laine is special. Gorgeous and sweet but never very strong or well. What happened was that a boy had hit her across the knuckles with a stick! I wanted to choke him! I thought as people got older they got braver. I'm not. I'm going the other way. Life is incredibly fragile. Seems harder and harder to hold the pieces together.

I need to share like this with you. Don't have any friend but you. Lots of relatives, no friends. I'm not trying to drum up pity, merely stating fact.

Sterling

❏

September 13, 1975

Dear Rachel,

I appreciate your letter and the chance to update THE LOGIC OF ABOR-TION, but I wish to decline. I would like the book to remain out of print, for personal reasons.

With every good wish,
Sterling Hamilton

❏

Dear Mrs. Hamilton,

Your sister is in a large city, possibly in the Northeastern United States. Her essence comes through to me as extremely vital, however currently possessed by profound sorrow bordering on despondency. As many people do in such a situation, she has relaxed her natural caution and is placing herself in various degrees of danger. I see much of this as deliberate. For balance, there is in her sphere a compassionate person with an essence equal to hers. It is most certainly a male, of large physical stature who works with or around the scales of justice. My strongest visual perception of him is that he is black skinned. These two people have children in their keeping, one of each sex. Very small children. I will tell you more as I am able to discern it.

Lily Grace

❏

Lily Grace:

That's my OTHER sister, Quinn—the person you described. She's on national television. Quinn Fortner. She's married to that man and those are their children.

What about Rosalind?

Sterling Hamilton

❏

Well, I'm trying to drum up pity. Did you see THORNY? It stinks. You're in a damned vacuum when you're doing a film. Scenes shot out of order. Script changing daily. And when you think it's in the can, an editor gets hold of it and your best work ends up on the floor. Then the viewing and premiere. People licking your hands. You're hot. This is your zenith. The reviews come out and say what you thought all along: Deadly. Trite. Mistake. It starts when you pick a project: tough to know what's good. You read a script and think you can pull it off. Or think Pacino will snap it up if you don't. (He's probably already turned it down.) Or you listen to your agent, the producer or another actor who bought into the package. It's weird that I can't tell whether a script is slop or Oscar material. Biggest film this year is about a shark chomping tourists. Figure that out.

I don't have a friend either. Except you. They've all got hidden agendas. Even Thom. I'm sorry about your baby Laine. I'm putting a silver dollar in here for her. Tell her it's from Santa Claus.

J.

❑

Dear Mrs. Hamilton,

Sometimes my gift does not work exactly as I wish, but it always works. This sister whom I am perceiving takes precedence at this time because she continues to place herself at the edge. Her spirit is closely aligned with Rosalind's. If I am to locate Rosalind, your sister Quinn must still her own soul. Faith is a circle.

You are searching for a piece of jewelry you mislaid. It seems to me to be a promise ring. You took it off for a water activity. Washing dishes? It is up high. In a container. A vase?

Lily Grace

❑

11/4/75

Dear Quinn,

I know you want to find Rozzy as much as I do and I feel I am close to a breakthrough. I have hired a psychic with a reliable track record but she tells me she cannot concentrate on Roz while you are putting yourself in all kinds of jeopardy. Could you please let your insides get very peaceful so the psychic can work? I will let you know as soon as she comes up with a lead.

This probably seems strange to you, but she found a ring for me so do it, OK? And don't tell anybody because Randy doesn't know about her.

Sterling

❑

Sterling,
You've always been in La-La Land, but this takes the prize.

QUINN

❑

November 15, 1975

Dearest Sterling,
Thank you for the invitation to spend Christmas in Richmond with you. We would love that but feel it best to stay at home in case Rosalind chooses Christmas to return to us. Will you come here? I am asking Quinn & Lou, also. We haven't seen them since they had the brief visit here last summer. She has been stand-offish, but we understand what is causing it.

We have been blessed with the reconciliation between you and Quinn this year and we believe that this could be a memorable and meaningful Christmas for each of us if we are together.

My love,
Mother

❑

Dear Mrs. Hamilton,
You must tell your sister Quinn that she will be in great peril, not of her making, directly following Christmas. The danger passes by the end of the year. She is not to go out during that time. The vision I have is of explosive device or fire in a public location.

Lily Grace

❑

November 30, 1975

Dear Lily Grace,

Thank you for the warning. I want to reassure you that the incident you are describing happened at Rockefeller Center earlier this year. Quinn was unhurt.

I appreciate your concern for Quinn but I want to respectfully ask you if you would please focus on Ros.

By the way, you were right about the ring.

Sincerely
Sterling Hamilton

❏

Dear Mrs. Hamilton,

Your sister Quinn must not go out between December 26 and 31. You must tell her.

Lily Grace

❏

12/10

Quinn,

You'll think this is because I don't want you at Mother and Dad's for Christmas but if you do come, you'll be in danger. The psychic says you may be in proximity of a fire or explosion in a public place between Dec. 26 & 31. You are not supposed to go out.

I'm aware you've been pretending to Mother—as I have—that we got straightened around this year. Please tell her you have to work and then stay home. It's plain you're trying to do yourself in, but I don't want to be responsible.

Sterling

❏

December 16, 1975

Dearest Sterling;

We are elated that both you and Quinn have agreed to come here for

Christmas. She called last night. They'll arrive the 24th and stay til New Year's Eve.

I believe with my whole heart that Roz will be home, too.

I've been working on the children's wish lists and I am excited!

Love,
Mother

❏

I hated calling Mother's but I knew you would see it on the news.

I did that to "show" you, leaving Pittsburgh early, saying I had to work. I'm thankful Lou and the kids were still there with you.

Had got my luggage in the claim area at LaGuardia and walked into the parking lot—a hellish rumble and flash stopped me. I turned toward the building as huge windows lining the front blew out, instantly slicing people to death along the busy roadway. I went partially deaf. The bomb in the locker was equal to 15 sticks of dynamite. The fire burned for an hour. You know this.

What you don't know is that I could not react, could not do a story on it, could not be interviewed for one. Bodies and parts of bodies lay mingled with glass in puddles of blood for two hundred yards. A head. A leg. A foot.

My hearing didn't come back for five minutes. When it did, I heard only the rushing of water into the street. People didn't speak. Children sat, stunned, against suitcases on the grass. Emergency vehicles had not yet arrived and, in the cold dark, survivors slowly lined up to use the outdoor phones.

When I took off my coat that night, it glistened with splinters. So did my hair.

You have my attention.

❏

1 9 7 6

Rosalind

1–22

Dear Roz,

Quinn's asked me again if I know where you are. I have to keep sidestepping her with non-answers like, "Don't you think I'd tell you if I knew?" Not sure why she keeps coming back to me. Maybe she smells a rat.

Anyway, I'm not trying to be judgmental but you really need to take some action. Your house is still sitting there & your folks are running in circles.

I've got first-class guilt about this since I'm supporting you. Aiding and abetting. Harboring.

Hey—I do it cheerfully. You deserve homage for investing in me when I was a grunt.

I may be a grunt again shortly. THORNY's fallen on its technicolor face and the well is dry. No idea worth touching has come across my desk lately. What I should do is create my own (as I did with CASSADAGA) and commission a writer. Jeff swears he won't leave me but will wait it out.

Stay warm in cold country.

Thom

❑

January 26, 1976

Dear Mrs. Robinson:

This letter will signify our acceptance of your packet of hand-colored pictures by the children of Toksook Bay. We found them to be beautiful in their simplicity and touching in their depiction of Alaskan life.

Our check for $500, made out to the Toksook Bay Elementary School, will follow shortly. Please tell the children that the pictures will be reproduced on first-quality, textured-weave note cards and sold in our shop. Each child whose artwork was selected will receive three packs of the note cards as a gift.

Many thanks,
Rosalind Lowry for
Maylene Brinker, Owner
Native Alaskan Art

❑

February 3

Thom,

I have first-class guilt, too, but I need more time. Being basically alone is a tremendous relief. I was so weary of other people's expectations and my own. I don't expect anything now but tranquility. The vast wilderness of this state and the nearly round-the-clock darkness match my mood. I am in Anchorage as little as possible. I prefer the out country.

For the moment, I am trapped in the city by weather. The bush pilots won't fly. I meet my broken dreams here. Panhandlers fill the sidewalks with odors. They accost me verbally and would touch me if I let them, in their determination to have a few cents from me. I rebuke them with wordless walking, charging past, my hands in my pockets, my shoulders knocking theirs. So far, I have won.

Don't push.

Roz

❏

2/9/76

Rosalind-

Remember me? I flew you to McGrath last Sept. You asked me to tell you about crafts I encounter.

I've been along the pipeline a lot and met one Matthew Patrick, born in Barrow. A photographer of wolves. His stuff is worth a look. I gave him your card. He has no permanent address.

Jonas Krull

❏

2–18

Rozzy

Quinn and Sterling have hired a psychic to find you. Wah! It's someone I know—Lily Grace, our consult from CASSADAGA. I wouldn't turn gray over this. Her magic's a little shopworn. So's she.

Your arrangement with Maylene to merely keep a tally of your earnings instead of paying you should prevent Quinn from tracking you through your

Soc. Sec. # and hitting you before you're ready. Don't know how else she could do it.

Sleep tight.
Thom

❏

3/5/76

T.— A man who looked like a panhandler opened the shop door yesterday. I gave him a scowl. He went away and returned a few minutes later with an armload of magnificent 8 × 10s. Turns out, he's the one who tracks the wolves. I have heard of him from several sources. He has little formal education but has studied the wolves for six years, lying in trees and ditches, migrating with them. He's accidentally met packs and individuals head-on many times. They either regarded him with curiosity and then sprinted away, or ignored him.

His face has the wise, wary expression of a wolf. He seldom speaks. His name is Matthew Patrick.

I bought "The Snow Trek," the shot of nine wolves traveling single-file across a white field. The one with his tail held high is the pack leader. I'll mat and frame in 16 × 20. Already have a buyer for it.

Check out these photos. AND SEND THEM BACK.

Roz

❏

Roz!

The idea of Matthew blows my mind. Here's this guy, by himself, communing with wolves. Can you put me in touch? Lie. Tell him I'm respectable. If I can use you as a character reference, I'll be in your debt again.

Thom

❏

March 15, 1976

Dear Mr. Flagg:

In answer to your inquiry, we are always in the market for furs and pelts. We have our own workroom. Our coats are handmade of native Alaskan product only and each is an exclusive design.

When you are in Anchorage, please stop to visit us.

Very sincerely yours,
Rosalind Lowry for
Maylene Brinker, Owner
Native Alaskan Art

❑

Thom,

Don't do this, about Matthew. He's not story material, he's real. I won't ask him. Why are people and events only grist for your mill? Next you'll want <u>my</u> life story. Have a heart.

Roz

❑

I'll take it! Your life story. How much? I'm not kidding. Your biography would put me on Oscar turf. You understand I would do it with reverence. It would be art, a poignant comment on our times. I'd start with Glenn. Believe me, I'd treat this gently. I do have a heart. But I view life through a camera. I see irony.

Matthew's safe. If you don't want me to use him, I'll drop it.

God's honest truth: I'm not so bad. Am I?

THOM

❑

April 3

Thom, DON'T TELL QUINN

Sterling is <u>here</u>. She was staring through the shop window at me. Her face seemed so young surrounded by the furry hood of a parka—she looked twelve years old. That's what got me. I felt ten years old gazing at her.

I went outside. Neither of us said anything, she just followed me in. I knew she would find me before Quinn did. I knew it. She said the psychic sent her. She had described to Sterling the sign on our store.

Maylene fussed over her and gave her a jade worry stone. The heat and brightness around us, the jumble of objects, seemed to glaze Sterling's eyes. She was very quiet. After a while, I took her the few blocks to my apartment. That's when she became upset. She wouldn't sit down. Insisted that I come home with her. She grabbed my shoulders and shook me. Surprised, I stepped off balance. She thought I was shoving her. We waltzed around the room that way, bumping into furniture, muttering, cursing, muttering, finally laughing.

She slept with me last night. I have only one double bed. She smelled like the sister of my childhood. Her hair has a heavy fragrance, of clean springtime earth yielding a few chilled roses.

I felt comforted.

R

❑

April 9

T.

This will be a fight. Sterling believes that, because we were born to the same parents, we own each other. She's possessive of me and my space, is clashing with Matthew. He's a symbol of the forces that are holding me in the evil void, away from my family. She doesn't see this as my choice. She acts as though I'm a mental patient, too big to carry.

Matthew hangs around me when he's in Anchorage. Right now, he's here a lot. He's not especially verbal, and he lives in his car. Two strikes. In decent weather, he tents all over creation. I told her, but a tent doesn't count as a home. To her, he's a bum.

He uses my shower. Not much to ask. But the first time she encountered him, she slammed the door on her way out. Didn't come back for two hours. The second time, she booked a hotel room for him, paid, and brought him the key. He wouldn't go. Got his dander up. They don't pass closely in a room now. They circle each other.

I showed her the wolf photos. She wasn't impressed.

She packs my clothes while I'm at work. I unpack them evenings when I get home. I wonder how long she will stay.

Rozzy

❑

April 14

T.

Matthew left but Sterling's here. Can't imagine how she got the money for this, but it moves me that she did it. She said Randy is helping her and that she swore him to secrecy.

She burned herself out quickly, is no longer at me with advice and instructions. Instead, she watches and listens, weeps because she says I haven't been loved enough, hides trinkets for me under my pillow.

We are alone for hours at a stretch. Mostly, we don't talk. During a break in the storms, I had a friend fly us to Homer, the end of the world. It's a crooked spit of land jutting into Kachemak Bay. Across the water, the mountains loom as large as you can imagine. It's eerie, even desolate there in winter without the plentiful fireweed blooming along the roads, without the crush of fishermen. But exquisite: gray and white, black.

Sterling's patience and hope are large between us. She's waiting for me to go home with her but I can't.

Ros

❑

April 18

T.

S. is going, day after tomorrow. Too soon. We are barely beginning to recapture what we had lost.

Childhood is a journey into privacy and time. Playmates wind through an entire summer of adventure by themselves. There is opportunity to know deeply: an arbor, a book, a person. This is what we had.

Adulthood is crowded, hurried, filled with responsibility. Even those who leisurely shared earlier seasons with us flatten to the eye, become landscape. Uninterrupted hours are shared only by lovers. Friends, sisters, stand in line indefinitely.

R.

❑

April 22, 1976

Rozzy,

I thought of nothing but you all the way back. Oh, it's so far! Mile upon mile of glaciers. Hour after hour of fields and cities and rivers. I feel as though you are on the moon and I am staring up at you, lonely.

That last night, when you told me about the baby, I stood inside your soul. I was you, making the decision, regretting it, changed unalterably in a few heartsick minutes. I will never be the same, hearing this from you.

Much of what I pursued and fought for seems foolish and wrong now. I was coming to it on my own, but you brought it into focus. Forgive me.

I will honor your wish for a few more months of rest. I won't tell Mother or Dad or Quinn where you are and I won't write to you until the new year.

Be kind to yourself.

Love,
Sterling

❏

5/12/76

Dear Matthew,

I hope this letter catches up with you. When Maylene pointed out the pup you had left as a present for me, I was overwhelmed. I know how you feel about taking them out of the wild. I can't properly care for him, I'm sure. Can you return him to his den?

I thought it was a dog; he was curled in the box, gnawing on the braid-rug lining. I picked him up and he licked my cheeks. When Maylene commented that wolves make better pets than dogs, I almost dropped him!

Everyone who visits the shop babies him but I refuse to name him because I don't want to get attached. I think he should go back. Will you come get him?

Rosalind

❏

June 8

Thom,

Matthew gave me a wolf pup. It is growing fast. Blue eyes, thick coat, a regal animal—very devoted. Its family was shot for the hell of it by some unknown person.

Matthew is an enigma. Solid and silent. I decided to go with him on a one-week journey, tracking, to try to see through his eyes, to understand the photos he brings me. It is spring here, water pouring off the glaciers. I saw the soil in flower. He treated me as a guide would treat his charge. Squarely. Personal service impersonally rendered. Maylene kept the pup while I was gone.

The wolves are, if not friendly, tolerant of humans. We searched for them on foot and tented near a den. Wolves are not man-eaters. They hunt mice, rabbits, deer, caribou, mainly at night. They are loyally familial — mate for life and closely guard their pups. We were able to observe them first-hand. I felt safe the whole time.

I have named the wolf pup Luke.

Rozzy

❏

June 10, 1976

Rozzy —

We agreed not to correspond but I have to share something with you. When I got home, Laine was sick again. She's still not completely well. She's had a weak body from birth — is small for her age and doesn't grow at the normal rate. We've had test after test but no one can tell us what's wrong.

Only you would understand this: it's my fault. I didn't want her. When I was pregnant and couldn't get a legal abortion, I prayed for her to die. It affected her development.

Now that I know her, I would die for her. She is special.

I don't expect you to answer. In fact, it's best not to, because of Randy. But it helps to tell you.

Love,
Sterling

❏

Thom

You promised me Matthew was off-limits. How did you contact him directly? You stink, you know that.

He isn't cut out for your commercialism, you'll ruin him, his spirit. He doesn't belong to anyone, and shouldn't. Especially you. Stay out of here.

Roz

❏

Now, wait a minute. He's not an idiot who can't fend for himself. He's perfectly lucid and not in your keeping. I simply asked him if he would camp with me and show me the wolves. Stop jumping around. I'm paying him well.

Are you too bent out of shape about this to meet me at the airport? Am enclosing a copy of my ticket. Be a love.

Thom

❏

July 7, 1976

Rozzy,

I'm not supposed to be writing to you, but Matthew's behind my mirror, staring at me. I shouldn't have left you. He has the bearing of a predator. I worry about it a lot.

You are very vulnerable right now. I don't think you know how vulnerable. When I get out the snapshots I took in Alaska, I see you more clearly than I did when I was there. The resigned curve of your back, the half smile.

I don't have a photo of Matthew but that red unkempt beard under those cool brown eyes sears my memory. The idea that you might be involved with him bothers me. He would not be a logical choice under any conditions— especially not these.

I love you.
Sterling

❏

July 14, 1976

Dear Mr. Maupin:

Today we sold your block print, "Moose Swimming," and will be forwarding a check to you the last day of the month. The print went to a private collector in Seattle who owns six of your originals. She was delighted.

Have you more offerings? We are down to one, "Sleeping Lady." Your work draws additional admirers daily.

I will be in your area soon and would like to meet with you again.

Every good wish,
Rosalind Lowry
Representative
Native Alaskan Art

❑

You look like death warmed over, girl. I had no idea you were so bad off. You belong in a hospital. No wonder Sterling stayed two weeks. I told you and I'm telling you, you'd better move down here with me or go home. If you want a plane ticket, it's yours.

We're doing the wolf story for sure. I have a writer. That Matthew's one weird dude. You're not sleeping with him I trust.

Smooch.   Thom

❑

Announcing
the birth of
Sierra Rosalind Fortner
8 lbs. 13 oz.
July 20, 1976
New York City

Parents
Lou and Quinn

Rozzy—
I thought you'd
like to know this.
Sterling

Sterling

Please don't send me anything else. I want to vegetate. I thought we had an understanding.

Forget Matthew. I'm not involved with him.

People constantly invade my life without my consent. Thom's been here scouting Matthew for a movie. Jesus.

Give me a chance.

Ros

But I have to explain why I sent the birth announcement. I was hoping you'd respond to Quinn. She isn't good. The network is sort of tolerating her. She was wired—in a scattered way—for a while after you left and then she crashed. I've watched her on SunUp. Her delivery is uncertain, like she can't remember the facts or like they don't make sense to her. Interviews nosedive. She used to be irreverent and abrasive. She's neither. She's being trampled with glee by her former victims. It's embarrassing. GBC doesn't have a cubbyhole for her and may put her out. The baby seems to be an offering to you.

I'm choking on my word but I'll keep it.

Love,
Sterling

P.S. You're not with
Thom again, are you? He's
not worthy.

❑

Sterling—Stop! I promise you I won't take up with anyone. You promise me you'll leave me alone and guard my location. Deal? Rozzy

❑

Deal. Heaven help us.
Sterling

❑

11—10

Roz—

Script is half finished. A jewel. Am bringing Jeff to meet Matthew and study him for characterization. Will be there next week. Stand up for me or stand back.

THOM

❑

12-1

Roz,

Nice visit. You were more than civil and I thank you.

Far be it from me to meddle, but the man is wrong for you. You're hooked, no doubt. That was fast. I have imagination—my specialty. I can imagine this duo five years down the road. Total disaster. Listen to me.

Thom

❑

December 7, 1976

Dearest Rosalind,

Sterling asked us not to write to you, but after careful thought we've decided that we must. Seeing our continued sorrow led her to break her silence. Please try to understand the divided loyalties she suffered this year.

We accept you under any circumstance. Whatever you choose to do, you do with our blessing. We have no wish to surround you except with caring.

There is a new serenity in Sterling regarding her relationship with you. We hope it will continue. Whatever was said during the time you were together has had a healing effect on her. We only want to ask you please not to forget Quinn, who knows none of this. We leave it to you to contact her. May it be soon.

Treat yourself well. You're our darling.

With Great Love,
Mother and Dad

❑

Rosalind

In continual free fall
from first memory, I,
ears and mouth stopped
with plugs of wind,
lungs stopped, heart stopped

as earth angles closer,
long to fly. Pieces of sky
snag my suit, my best tie,
the grin I strive to maintain.
If there was a plane
from which I leaped, confident, new,
it is gone now into the blue
widening space of God's yawn.
What seemed true has turned a few
degrees, a curious view. And
what seemed breeze in the canting doorway
slices through bone. Mute, alone,
I seek you,
the invisible cord that hides
in the nightmare of my waking,
the string
to shield me from the taking,
bringing the stone-sudden snap of silk
billowing overhead. A thread.

Jeff

❑

1 9 7 7

Rosalind

Thom—Unable to reach you by phone. Married Dec. 28
in Pgh. Honeymooning in Bermuda. Sorry you had
to get our news on a post card! Home to LA on 10th.
Roz & Jeff   1/3/77

❑

Welcome home. Champagne in fridge.
Thom

❑

January 12, 1977
Dearest Rosalind,

What a beautiful Christmas. To answer the doorbell and find you standing
on the porch was a vision from a dream. Of course, I recognized Jeff at once—
but could not figure out why he was with you!

Thank you for being kind to Quinn. The way you ran to her and hugged her
thrilled Dad and me. To think that our family is together again fulfills our
deepest longings.

Love makes everything right, doesn't it? Jeff's love seems to have trans-
formed you. There is such peace in your countenance.

Thank you, too, for your gentleness to Sterling. She was so afraid you would
be angry because she had told us where you were. I still feel a little concern
about her. Did you notice that she seemed to be more shocked by Jeff's

presence than the rest of us? She was pale during your wedding and left our house very quietly shortly after you did on the 28th. I think events moved too swiftly for her. She likes to be in control of what is happening—a trait which endears her to us but causes her anguish sometimes.

Wishing you and Jeff many blessings,

Mother

❑

January 14, 1977

Dear Annie,

The Oriental rug you and Steve sent is marvelous—a splendid blend of colors: those seacoast greens and blues crossed by royal red. It's too nice to walk on. We have hung it on the wall of our foyer to admire.

Wish you could have been with us for the wedding, but we understood why you couldn't just drop everything! My parents reacted to Jeff with surprise but open acceptance. My sisters were typically off center, although they attempted to give support.

Quinn is overweight and morose. The network took away her investigative staff and tossed her into news proper, a demotion. I feel responsible, in part, for her condition. Guilt perches on my shoulder. To make sure it stays there, she is distant with me.

My relationship with Sterling is in better shape. I think!

Thanks for being my friend in all circumstances. Your loyalty never wavers and the thought of you has sustained me in both low and high moments.

God bless,

Ros

❑

Dear Rosalind,

Best wishes. I saw it in the paper.

Chase Holling

❑

Dear Rozzy,

I've just witnessed the grossest, most shameful event. Gary Gilmore, tied into an old office chair (!) and shot to death. Did you see my story?

For ten years, I've been championing capital punishment and boasting that if there were ever another execution, I'd attend with bells on. Last week, Winston slapped a plane ticket onto my desk and winked at me. I couldn't refuse to go.

I had pictured a scene with romantic mystery to it: a cold morning's walk to a stone wall outdoors, the condemned man staring down his executioners, making them nervous.

But it was held inside a defunct cannery on the prison grounds. Outside: a media circus. Inside: a bunch of witnesses mundanely stuffing cotton in their ears. I was one of them.

Gary came in and was loosely tied into a wooden chair in front of a dilapidated mattress and sandbags. The weapons pointed at his chest poked through slits in sailcloth which concealed the executioners. A bag was placed over his head.

The horrendous loudness of the shots stopped my heart. I had to double over to start it again.

Although blood flowed copiously from Gary, he didn't die immediately. We watched his death throes.

Now, I wonder what we are that we can be so easily disposed of. We are told in church of our miraculous spirits and minds, of an essence worth nurturing and saving. It disappears in a split second—the unique composition, the specialness which will never be seen again. I knew this once but had forgotten it over years of following death around as reporters do. I think of it when I look at my children, their radiance.

For the first time, death frightens me because I have realized it will come to people I love. Rozzy, please, could we get together?

Quinn

❑

2/5/77

Dear Rosalind,

Your call to Quinn elated her. Asking her to help you clean out your Boston house was a good thought. She needs that island of time with you.

Our marriage has been taking some lumps—not your fault. I've pressed hard for three years on this investigation of NYC schools and when HEW charged the system with discrimination in January, I saw my reward. But Federal money for education will be withheld from NYC—as a penalty—and that, too, has its downside for minorities and handicapped.

I've been obsessed. Am still obsessed. Quinn spends most week nights alone with the children. I've been so busy defending my race, I missed all eight episodes of <u>Roots</u>. (Humor.)

I'm not asking you to smooth our road, just to endorse Quinn. She's a fine person who didn't know what she was getting into when she married   LOU.

❑

February 11, 1977

Dear Mother and Dad,

Jeff is all I had hoped for. Wise, funny, protective. It is strange to be plunked smack into the center of his life, which is in motion in a hundred directions. I'm learning everything at once: names and faces, habits, schedules, geography, finances. He is totally opening his affairs to me, adding me to house, car and bank papers. I know now how it feels to have what you have: complete devotion. Thanks for embracing him as a son.

Your loving
Rosalind

❑

February 19, 1977

Dear Sterling,

Your silence is deafening. It was obvious how you felt at the wedding. I am asking you to please work with me on keeping the closeness we regained in Alaska.

You first knew Jeff as a convict. I understand that. But he is not the man he was years ago. He has changed, as we all have. We've got to let go of the past.

I'm asking you to believe in Jeff as I do and to grant us your support.

All my love,
Rosalind

❑

Feb. 22

Rozzy—

I'm set. Lou will tend the home fires.

I've been ruminating on your question as to whether I've outgrown my occupation. I think it's a matter of being misplaced in time. Vietnam and Watergate are over. Carter is shaping a lackluster White House. I need another cause. I doubt I could be the bitch I was, though, and that's what it takes.

I envy Lou, whose zeal never flags. In addition to education issues, he's been pursuing real estate. With the city near bankruptcy and individuals affected accordingly, the man who couldn't buy the home he wanted in LA now owns a couple of buildings in Manhattan. Through it all, he's the same sweet guy, but distracted—and famous. Infamous? When I think of my resolve to win power and "hand it to him" I have to laugh.

Quinn

❏

Rozzy—
    With you always.
    Sterling

❏

March 6, 1977

Dear Annie,

Just got back from Boston. Quinn helped me sell off my furniture and pack. Relics of another era.

When we first unlocked the door and stepped inside, it came to me that I had made a mistake in asking Quinn there, that we would not be able to find our footing in that place. We were saddened immediately—strolled once through the house, then closed it and went to lunch. Each of us had a salad and four glasses of wine. Sat in the booth til three o'clock when they threw us out.

We stayed at the house. Couldn't sleep. Didn't try. Worked all night, dismantling the pieces of our unhappiness, putting them in boxes, to be shipped or sold. By dawn, the walls and tables were bare. That satisfied us, the way it is satisfying to discuss a nightmare, reducing it to parts and laying each part aside as unrealistic, finished.

I decided to keep nothing. We phoned a service that buys contents of estates. They came within a day and gave me a check for the whole thing. On the way to the airport, I mailed the key to the realtor.

Quinn waited with me for the plane. Suddenly, she cried and said there was something else, and that she wanted to be rid of it. When she and Lou were married in Los Angeles, he was 1-A for the draft. She had a friend on the draft board and he engineered it so that Lou's file disappeared. Lou does not know this. He believes that, for some lucky reason, he simply was not called.

She could hardly speak for weeping. It amazed me that the memory had such power over her, nine years later. But she said she was ashamed of her cowardice. After all, I had lost Glenn.

To me, my situation and hers were not connected. I did not feel she had injured me by this, but it was evident she needed my pardon.

Why should she cheat to keep Lou, she said, was he more precious? Her self-hatred made me cry. I said nothing, merely held her hand. By the time I left, there was a lot of healing between us.

Rozzy

❑

Roz!

Good morning! I worship you! Will call you mid-day!

What a party you thought up! This town hasn't seen class like that since the 40s! That's what Thom said! He was ecstatic! We hit Marion Tingley's column this AM! Society page, not entertainment!

Jeff!

❑

Roses are red.
Violets are blue.
I take it all back.
He's perfect for you.

Thom

❑

Dear Thom,

Thanking you in person didn't seem like enough, hence this note. The Thunderbird is elegant and the verse that came with it sufficient apology. Our friendship has undergone many changes but remains strong. I value it, and you, more than I can express.

Rosalind

❑

April 8, 1977

Dear Annie,

I am happy, clear through my soul. Jeff and I are more than infatuated newlyweds. We are possessed by the concept of eternal love. I had intended to give him a lot of space, but discovered—to my pleasure—that his idea of marriage is nearly constant togetherness. This may seem sappy to some, but suits us perfectly.

We spend hours sunning and talking in seclusion, preparing and consuming ceremonial suppers alone. I accompany him everywhere. It is met with mixed reaction, especially at business lunches and meetings where I am frequently treated like a child he is babysitting. I simply smile at it, and am learning much.

You're right. Marriage is way ahead of whatever's in second place!

Love,
Rozzy

❑

Dear Rosalind:

May I appeal to you again to regroup these funds? Shifting this much of your assets into motion picture stocks is tremendously risky.

Nevertheless, I am enclosing packages on MGM, Columbia and 20th Century Fox. Don't know why you need the info. You're convinced this will fly and you're seldom wrong.

Cheers,
Ruth
4/13/77

❑

April 24, 1977

Dearest Mother and Dad,

The sale of my home in Boston is complete and I am enclosing a lump sum to cover the outlay you had while I was gone.

Repaying you cannot compensate for the terrible uncertainty you felt while I was out of touch and for the inconvenience I caused you, but you have made it clear that you accept my apology and accept me. You are an inspiration, models of how to live.

Best love,
Rosalind

❑

Rosalind and Jeff, I made you one quilted pillow for an empty spot. Coming in mail. May your marriage bring the dance of the spirit. I am a guard for the Moulton sons, 3 & 6. He is a judge in Det. Willie Dodson doesn't box now and he left Celeste. I see her sometimes.

Dagmar

❑

Roz

I appreciate your agreeing to read these books and scripts. They pile up fast. I'm getting antsy about having a project to launch when we get back from Alaska. Glad you've decided to go north with us.
Thom

❑

May 13, 1977

Dear Aunt Rosalind,

I like the music box you sent for my birthday. "Feelings" is my favorite song. You are my pal.

I am trying to earn money for Camp Blue Jay this summer. Could you please ask Uncle Jeff to sign these pieces of paper? I can sell his autograph. I hope he won't mind.

You are in some magazines. You look fancy and kind but I don't like how they call you Queen of Hearts.

Love,
Mindy

❑

Thom—My comments on the stuff you sent over:

Til Then
Whiny romance, built around late-bloomer female lead. Pass.

Lip Reader
Murder mystery, deaf male lead. Interesting premise but not complex enough in second half. Pass.

Shirtsleeves
Saga. Too many characters. Not enough of a showcase for Jeff. Pass.

Red Arrow
Soviet, Japanese and American spies in Asia. Bondesque, but you need a scorecard. Pass.

Walking against the Wind
The old "priest in slum" theme. Priest? Jeff? Pass.

Matrix
Semi-clever. Crack inventor of eavesdropping devices steps unknowingly into mortal danger. Talky. Pass.

My Camel's Thirsty
Comedy set in Middle East. PASS!

American Joy Ride
Folk-hero appeal. Southern California setting. Mixture doesn't work. Pass.

❑

May 23, 1977

Dear Mindy,

Here are the autographs. Uncle Jeff sends his love with them and I do, too. Your Mom told me wonderful things about you when she called last week. She said you are a model for Miller & Rhoads department store and are going to be in their ads. Congratulations on your success. I think you are a simply grand young lady.

Hugs,
Aunt Ros

❑

Roz—

This is THE ONE! It knocked me right on my can. Read it quick and comment. You could do the legwork on putting a package together while Jeff and I are in AK.

Thanks, partner!

Thom

❏

Thom,

I read this and am against it. The plot has enormous holes in logic which will make the lead appear unintelligent. Sorry.

Roz

❏

June 27, 1977

Rosalind:

I've been watching your Twentieth Century Fox stock double in the past four weeks as a result of Star Wars.

You drive.

Ruth

❏

6/26/77

Dear Rozzy,

Winston's fixed it in his head that if he sends me to enough murders I'll regain my aggressiveness. It's having the opposite effect. I'm locked into this Son of Sam case and keep being called out of bed to the scene of a shooting. I dread hearing the phone ring. I'm considering resigning, but don't know where I'd go or what I'd do.

You see it on the news, I'm sure. It's nothing like being there. Sometimes the victims are still on the street. Most of the time, I end up at a hospital, intruding on a very desperate, very private moment. Since I saw you in March, I've covered three deaths by the same gun: a 20-year-old woman shot in the face as she walked along a sidewalk, and a young couple who were parked.

Last night, I was called to Queens. GBC immediately sent a van around to pick me up, so I got there quickly. Another couple had been fired upon while sitting in a car. The 17-year-old woman had staggered out and was lying at an intersection, conscious although she had been wounded in the head, neck and shoulder. I almost broke down, seeing how young she was.

I'm not cut out for this anymore. Why am I doing it? Why don't I stop?

Q

❑

7 July

Dear Benj —

As you know, Jett and Thom are on location but I have taken the liberty of reading the scripts you sent over and am returning them herewith.

Rosalind Maeder

❑

Thomas

Not one in the second batch worth considering either. Why are we connected to Benjamin Sillers? He doesn't know a good story when he sees it or he's deliberately feeding us trash.

Roz

❑

7—21—77

Dear Heart

Miss you. Good we're shooting this thing in halves and you've promised to be with me for the winter scenes.

No one's cherished me the way you have. No one. Only you and I understand why you're sitting in LA reading instead of sitting in Alaska with me. I trust your instincts and love your wanting to find "the break-out role" for me. You will.

Thom and I finished our copies of the book you sent up. I felt a kinship with the character and thought there were several incisive scenes, but Thom nixed it.

Matthew asked to be remembered to you. He's got Luke with him. I took a photo so you can see your pup full grown.

Husband!
Jeff

❑

7/26

Dear Roz—

Sillers is on my neck about us turning down so many offerings. Maybe you'd better leave the search until I get back. Benj can be a peddler of inferior material but, unfortunately, he's the senior agent on the golden list. We can't just zing scripts back to him.

Your husband needs you here. This is a long, complicated shoot. The wolves have no stage presence or sense of timing. We're tired of playing cards and would welcome your pulchritude. Come on up.

Thom

❑

August 1, 1977
Dear Rozzy,

I haven't slept in two days. Another shooting. Another leap out of my bed in the middle of the night. They're just kids. You saw it, no doubt. The whole country is watching this. I don't think the woman is going to make it and the man's lost his eye.

I've spent this afternoon with a NYC detective who has worked on the Son of Sam case from the start (July '76). His name is Tony Malerbo.

In the beginning, of course, no one knew there would be a series of killings. But Tony investigated that first murder with the thought that there might be more. He is a remarkable person. In a few hours, he's given me perspective on why I should stay in the middle of this.

His job is to study the lives of the victims so closely that he feels he thoroughly understands them. He showed me photos, letters, pieces of their lives. I think of them differently now, not simply as victims but as people whose spirits remain with us. They want us to find their killers. We must.

There's a seed sprouting in my brain tonight that is suspiciously like my old rage and it feels right.

Q

❏

Aug. 12, 1977

Hi, Rozzy!
Lou said you called with praise for my Son of Sam story. Thanks! No other network was there when they grabbed him. Tony put me on the inside of that one. The photographer and I rode in his car and sat with him during the stakeout. Did you see Berkowitz smile? Oh, my God.

QUINN

❏

August 25, 1977

Dearest Rosalind,
I've been looking at my calendar and see that Jeff gets home a week from today. I know you're anxious for that! Did you find a part for him yet? Maybe you could consider something off-beat. Who would imagine Mary Tyler Moore giving up her show this year and doing a serious role? When I heard that Elvis had died, I thought perhaps his story would be a possibility. Dad and I have been to a lot of movies this summer. It's more fun now that you're involved with them. We saw *Close Encounters*, *The Deep* and *Saturday Night Fever*. I believe it when you tell me this is the most financially successful summer for the film industry in a long time.

I regret Dad and I haven't been able to fly out and stay with you yet. I'm after Dad to slow down. His practice is extremely busy. Dr. Bryant did come on board as a partner, so that should help. Anyway, we wondered if you and Jeff could be here for Christmas. Sterling said yes. Since Randy and Bobby merged and began to publish the mail-order catalog, Sterling's calmed down. Fewer money worries. Quinn said she'll try. Have you seen how she's dropped most of that extra weight and let her hair go natural? Quite nice.

Love always,
Mother

❏

Dear Roz,

I'm so mad I could <u>spit</u>. Nova reissued my book without my consent. I didn't even know it until a friend sent me a review which called it "The Bible" of the movement and praised the new version as "meticulously updated." They had asked me to modernize it. I refused.

Went back to my contract and, sure enough, they have the right to do this!

A reporter from the Richmond paper phoned to ask for an interview. That's the last thing I need. Will this shadow me my whole life?

Sterling

❏

Roz

Herewith, A MASTER TRAP. Breathtaking concept. Anxious for you to read. Visualize the setting! If you're as enthused as I am, we'll make a move for it.

Thom

❏

9/28/77

Rozzy—

Oh, geesh. Tony called me at the office today. I went down to the diamond district with him. In a 15th-floor workroom, the body of a missing diamond broker was found stuffed into plastic garbage bags and a wooden crate. I was there when they opened it.

One more scoop for GBC, a possible raise for me. What a vulture I am, feeding on these events. I have to believe and keep reminding myself that I'm more than a reporter. I'm an instrument by which justice might be accomplished. If I care enough, if I dig enough, what I discover and what I say on television may bring an answer. A clue. An arrest.

QUINN

❏

Rozzy—

Look at this article. The reporter dug around until he came up with ancient pictures and quotes. Some kid in Laine's class brought the clipping to her. She was devastated. I had to tell her the whole story from my point of view and reassure her over and over that I wouldn't trade her for a billion trillion dollars. Lance and Sovereign demanded to know if they were planned! Mindy's heard the infertility tales so many times she's secure. It's been hell around here.

S.

❏

Oct. 27, 1977

Dear Annie,

I appreciated your call. It's lonely without Jeff, but the weather's cooperating and they're zipping along on the snow scenes. I hope I can have a project lined up for him when he gets back. I'm going through a lot of bottles of Visine, reading, reading, reading.

Since we talked, Thom's returned THE RAIN SHIP to me. Can't understand it. This is an unforgettable book and would be a classic on film. It's a mistake to let it go.

Remember I told you about DESERT HUNTER, which Thom despised and I loved? Harrison Ford snapped it up. Ooooo.

Rozzy

❏

11/8

Roz—

We're in the bush, away from the phones but mail goes in and out by float plane. You can write c/o camp.

Benj sent me CARMEN MIDNIGHT and I flipped for it. He said you turned it down. Am taking an option on it. It's ideal—you'll see. Wanted to tell you before Benj did.

Thom

❏

Thom,

CARMEN MIDNIGHT would be professional suicide for Jeff and for you, too. I called Sillers and stalled him off until we talk.

I respect your talent but you have a tin eye for scripts. So does Jeff. He admits it, you don't. Only CASSADAGA was alive.

Why can't you let me help you?

Rozzy

❏

Nov. 30, 1977

Quinn—

Answering service gave me your message. Yes. Stay with me. Jeff's still in Alaska. You and I can have a special visit together.

How far you've come this year—from nearly quitting to being sent here to cover Hillside Strangler.

I saw your feature on "motives." It was brilliant and lingers in my mind.

I'll meet you at the airport. Send me your info.

Love,
Rozzy

❏

December 1
Thom,

Woke up in the night thinking this: Why would a person with your brains, education and ability have turned down four great scripts since June? The answer isn't simply that he has no perception. That's too easy. The answer is: because I found them and pushed for them. Isn't it? Our struggle hasn't been about literary or cinematic taste, has it? It's been about control.

Today, I cancelled your deal with Benj on CARMEN MIDNIGHT.

Roz.

❏

12/9/77

Dear Rozzy,

Sorry I missed Jeff, but his decision to sight-see on his own a few extra days after filming ended gave us a much-needed spot of privacy.

Rozzy, you guessed right about Tony. I lied to you when I said there was nothing going on. But then, you know that. You have a sixth sense. I haven't slept with him and won't. You caused me to really think about this. Forget it, okay? Please?

It was a good visit with you—all that quiet time together. You're the best.

I hope you got straightened out with Thom. My cab was just pulling out when he ran up the driveway toward you. I hadn't seen him coming! I made the driver stop, and I stared through the rear window a minute or two. Thom sure was mad—but so were you—both waving your arms around. It seemed like an even match to me, so I stayed out of it. As soon as I could tell you had the upper hand, I felt safe driving away.

KISSES
QUINN

❑

1 9 7 8

Quinn

Fri. 6th Jan.

Rozzy,

Oh, how we missed you and Jeff at Christmas! But you did the prudent thing by staying home. The first couple of months are critical. It's a good idea not to travel. Have you thought up any names yet?

We had a terrific week at Mother and Dad's but it wasn't the same without you. I had to talk to Sterling. Couldn't avoid it! Just kidding. We got along pretty well considering there's a generation gap between us. She's changed a lot—mellowed, you might say. For the first time, I see her acting like a parent toward M & D. She watches over everyone. The children—hers AND mine—adore her. Gosh, she reminds me of Mother!

One day, Sterling and I went out for groceries and we drove by the Belleville Avenue house. It was strange to park across the street, staring as members of another family came and went from it. Sterling said she slept under my crib the night I was brought home as a newborn because she felt so protective. Viewing myself through her eyes gave me some perspective on her.

Thanks again for the children's marvelous gifts. You always know what they like.

Love,
Quinn

❑

January 11, 1978

Dear Quinn,

I feel closer to you after our time together. Memories of the Belleville Avenue house keep popping up now, even when I'm not thinking about it. I spent kindergarten through twelfth grade there. It has my whole childhood in it. Since you were between eighth and ninth when we moved away, it's no wonder you didn't experience the same nostalgia. But you were patient listening to my reminiscences!

I got Mama's Bank Account from the library yesterday and am reading it to Sovereign and Laine. I had forgotten until you reminded me that it was a favorite when we were growing up.

One more story I thought of about Belleville Ave. Remember when Molly Bailey's prom date came to our house by mistake because he'd never taken her out before? He was so nervous, rushing into the room, shaking hands with everyone, sweating, practically unable to speak. M & D didn't have the heart to tell him she lived next door! Wasn't it clever of Dad to go out the back and get her and bring her in through the kitchen? He even slipped her a key so she could be brought "home" to our house after the dance. Don't you giggle when you think about it?

Love,
Sterling

❑

January 30, 1978

Dearest Quinn,

We are sorry you and Lou are having problems. We hope that you can work things out. I appreciate how lonely you must be without him at home even though you have Zandria, Dalin and Sierra to keep you company. We have written to Lou expressing our support and concern.

I respect your decision not to let your co-workers and friends know about the separation. It may be brief and this would save a lot of explaining. I especially concur with your choosing not to tell Roz just now because of her condition.

Call us if you need anything. We adore you.

Mother

❑

Quinn

Because I have been through a separation, I understand your turmoil. May it be resolved soon. Please write to me and tell me how you are doing. It is good you have your nanny Margaret to help you with the children. Take care.   XXX

Sterling

❑

2/4/78

Dear Quinn,

Family has been on my mind. I have done a lot of reflecting on how close we all are and what a blessing that is. Since I became pregnant, I've been thinking about Jeff's folks. I've never met them and Jeff isn't in touch with them. Both parents and a brother live in Texas. He says he drifted away from them when he was in prison. I can't picture people letting go of a son for any reason. He says it wasn't like that. They didn't let go of him, he let go of them.

Anyway, I want this baby to have all its grandparents as much as I want it to have all its fingers and toes. I'm working on Jeff, but he's silent about it, distant—which isn't like him.

Thom backed down and let me pick a script: WINGS ON THE MOON, an original screenplay about a college professor visiting a Navajo reservation one unforgettable summer. Filming starts in New Mexico in May.

Love to you and Lou and the wee ones.

Rozzy

❑

Feb. 15, 1978

Dear Sterling,

You invited me to share and I have to—I really have to. Lou comes and goes, to see the children, to get his belongings. He only took a suitcase full of his clothes and papers at first but, little by little, he is emptying our home of his presence. Today, he removed some certificates and photos from the wall. The blank white spaces shocked me.

He is preoccupied, as usual—wrapped up in the fight over Queens District 26. The school staff is more than 90% white and the school board president, Caulfield, hell-bent to keep it that way. C's filed suit against the city. Lou says we'll talk after this "big one" is settled (perhaps in March), but he goes from project to project with his head down. During the few moments that he does focus on me, I see caring in his eyes and he says there's no one else—which I believe. There's no one else for me, either.

I am not blameless. As he gradually disappeared into his work, I became resentful and found other interests. When he said that maybe he should move out, it didn't seem that it would make much difference. I thought I wanted freedom from him. I don't.

It helps to write to you.

Quinn

❑

Dear Quinn,

Your letter was heart-wrenching but please continue to share with me. I wish

I could say or do something that would renew your marriage but I believe that will come in the long run. Maybe this is a natural, albeit torturous, working out of your long-term relationship.

Love,
Sterling

❏

March 1

Dear Quinn,

I didn't want to talk about it when you called, but now I do. The doctor termed it a "miscarriage," but that's not descriptive enough. It's too euphemistic, too sterile for the death of a child. People discount my grief because they—and I—never saw my baby.

In the bank, walking down a long flight of stairs, I saw the blood before I felt the pain. It was on my shoes, it was on the carpet. I couldn't climb up or down the steps—I was afraid I would faint and fall the rest of the way. People ran to me, held me by my arms, shouting for help. Don't tell Mom and Dad how bad it was. I gave them only the briefest details.

We're buying a gravestone for our daughter and putting her name on it. Caroline. The doctor finds this bizarre but Jeff wants it, too.

Ros

❏

Dear Quinn,

You are the best sister a person could have. Your call was very special to me. It must have seemed odd that what I wanted to hear most from you was simply the everyday vignettes of your life. It was soothing and comforting to me when you described walking in Central Park with Lou and the little ones on a Sunday morning, the children's fascination with the boat pond, you and Lou dancing to the music of the disheveled and elderly violinist holding forth near a park bench, the frigid air on your faces, the surprisingly warm sun on your backs. Your satisfaction brings peacefulness to my soul.

Rozzy

❏

3-11-78

Sterling—

Met Lou last night for dinner. He was elated because the city suspended the entire school board of District 26 for insubordination. He smells a kill. I suddenly realized that he was exactly like this when I married him. It's the characteristic that attracted me: the dogged pursuit of right. He mirrored me then. He's a dear person but he's never going to lose his political zeal.

We started growing apart when I changed, lost my thirst for the kill. It takes a lot of idealism and egoism to maintain the prosecutor's pose. Winston wisely sidetracked me into straight news. Still, no matter how good I get at covering homicide—and I do have a sixth sense for it—this isn't my turf. In the final analysis, I'm a political creature like Lou, but without the bite. I wish I had it back. I feel boxed and restless.

Quinn

❏

Dear Quinn,

Of course you're a "political creature." Always were. And you have a penetrating intelligence and depth of emotion that are vital to this country. If only you could feel comfortable with yourself again.

Admiring you.
Sterling

❏

March 29, 1978

Dearest Quinn,

Dad and I were both alarmed at your frame of mind when we visited you last week. It was upsetting to us to see you losing ground. I must be frank with you. Take care of yourself! All the progress you made last year in your health and ambition seems to have disappeared. We wish we could have had a chance to talk with Lou.

Sweetheart, it is difficult for Dad and me to realize that we cannot solve this for you. We can only give you support. Please, count on us for whatever you need.

With great devotion,
Mother

❏

April 2, 1978

Dear Quinn,

I'm glad I called you and could cheer you up. You sounded so down when I first heard your voice. Don't ever hesitate to pour it all out. I'm a willing listener. I hope the rough spots at work will smooth out. You can't help but have carry-over from your personal situation. I understand.

Guess who's coming to New York. Me! Randy, Bobby and I decided to publish a color catalog. I'll be selecting merchandise. Mail orders are the bulk of our business now. With the rise in women's employment, couples don't have time to go out and browse.

We're changing the Camp Shop name to simply CAMP because our expanded catalog will feature clothing, bedding and luggage as well as trail supplies. We're getting into making our own stuff, too. The first item is a goose-down vest. The idea is to control quality and guarantee it. If all goes well, we'll close the store and do business solely by mail. It is exciting. I am working almost full-time for Randy, buying goods. We shut down the sports uniforms division.

Will call you with dates shortly. Am enclosing an envelope of orange Pop Rocks for the kids. Have you seen them in NY? It's candy. You put the pebbles on your tongue & they sizzle & snap. A weird sensation.

X
Sterling

❑

4-19-78
Dear Sterling,

Your visit couldn't have been more perfectly timed. I was so depressed I was eating my shoes. What a lift you gave me and the kids! You were unfailingly jolly with them, even when I knew you must have been exhausted.

And dragging me to Bloomingdales for make-overs was a stroke. I look ten years younger. So do you!

Thanks.
QUINN

❑

Quinn

Read your 10th anniv piece on ML King Jr in TV Guide and wept. You're one hell of a journalist. Still.

Was I weeping for myself? My kids don't remember King—or RFK. Or Vietnam. I'm a relic at 35. They say your memory is the first to go but I doubt it. It's the insidious waning of enthusiasm that gets you.

Judy left me for a tag-team wrestler, which renders my existence somewhat of a joke. She has the kids but I have a 22-yr-old live-in. A nearly equal exchange.

Hello to Lou

Sherm

❑

Quinn—

Take that new job! You need a change. You say you aren't up to it, but attitude follows action.

Go for it.
Sterling

❑

Dear Quinn:

Received a call from Winston re. raiding his network to stock our own. If it's getting too hot over there, come on board sooner than July 5.

I'm pleased that we could talk you into leaving GBC for greener pastures—or browner, as the case may be. Our first order of business will be to send you to Love Canal. As you are aware, this situation is urgent.

Enclosed are contracts for you to examine and sign.

Congratulations,
HAP
Howard K. Melton
Vice President for News   May 18, 1978

❑

Tony, you almost took my ear off. What ever happened to positive reinforce-
ment and words like "Congratulations"? I'll still help you solve your puzzles.
But I don't want to live inside them anymore.

You taught me more about murder in a year than I could have learned from
others in a lifetime. We're comrades indefinitely, have no fear.

Send me something nice like a flower.

QUINN

❏

May 22, 1978

Dear Hap,

Signed contracts enclosed. Am looking forward. Let's aim for July 1st as
Berkowitz trial will most likely end in June. I like to leave things tidy.

Winston's sorry for himself, glad for me. No problem.

QUINN

❏

May 27, 1978

Dear Quinn,

The anniversary card you sent us was as special as you are. I can't believe
I've been married 15 years! I want you to be happy, too. Let me give you some
of my happiness. Take it, and feel better. Life is amazingly splendid.

Think about Mindy going to her first dance last Saturday . . . her blond
shiny hair drawn back from her elegant face . . . the silver-white flashing of
braces as she grins . . . the serenity of her bright blue eyes. Her dress is
medium-pink satin with puffy, ruffled sleeves and slight V-neck, long fitted
waist, waltz-length gathered skirt. She wears pink satin shoes and white
rosebud wrist corsage. She is not even a tiny bit nervous. I am. I take her
picture a dozen times, until she — and Randy — protest. "But," I say to Randy
after she goes down the walk with her date, "she will never be more radiant!"
He laughs. "Yes, she will," he says. I can't imagine.

Sterling

❏

Sterling,

Your enthusiasm and contentment feed me. I get energy just from holding the pages of your letters in my hands.

Quinn

❏

June 6, 1978

Dear Quinn and Lou,

We're two and a half weeks into filming near Ship Rock. I'm enclosing pictures for you. The colors are much more vivid than this. Wish you were here. Sunrise and sunset are awesome artistic events. Light spills like molten gold in the morning and creates pockets of greenish purple in the evening. The night sky is crammed with diamond stars, as though a veil has been peeled back and we can view the heavens clearly. We sleep well.

The magic of the story has gripped the actors. At the end of a scene, they don't want to speak but sit alone. We all feel it. Thom put his hands on my shoulders yesterday while watching them work: his way of saying he is pleased. The script is powerful, the setting supernatural. We are gathered in purposeful unity out here.

Being on location has been good for me. I don't think about the baby as often and, when I do, I am calm.

Love,
Ros

❏

7/5/78

Sterling,

I opened the door to my new office and there was the gorgeous Ficus tree from you! It is full and healthy, as though someone had polished every leaf. And it's six feet tall. Luckily, I have a nice BIG office. The tree is the ideal touch.

Love ya!
Quinn

❏

Dear Mother,

I thought it over, as you asked, but I don't want to tell Rozzy. I wouldn't add to her sadness for anything. And she's trying to get pregnant again. She doesn't need to know.

Love from Quinn

❏

July 20

Lou and Quinn—

The 40th birthday is rough but you got me through it in style. Such sensitive gifts. Ex-Lax. Dentu-Creme. Rubber underpants. You two had at least as much fun wrapping this stuff as I did opening it.

Sorry you and the Hamiltons couldn't be here. Quinn, your mom and dad made sure the champagne allotments for you guys didn't go to waste. We gave them a hand.

Roz got me a camera that records on videotape cassette. I can take the tape out right after I shoot and stick it in the VCR and play it back. Hi-tech, huh?

We miss you and the critters. Specially you, Lou. You're never there when we call. Dial us up sometime.

JEFF

❏

Quinn!

I saw you with President Carter in NYC. I took a picture of the television set when you were on. Hope it comes out. I'll send you one. Way to go.

Sterling

❏

8/14/78

Dear Sterling,

Talking to you is a balm. I feel that I'm collecting those normal, warm, funny pieces of your life as you speak and putting them in a bag to look at later, as many times as I want. I wonder if my life will ever be whole cloth again.

I'm worried about Lou. He's progressively haggard and lean. With no family to interrupt him, he's working around the clock. His eyes are glassy red, his emotions muted.

I'm definitely in my niche on this new job. But with the newspaper strike— all three papers, I'm doing overtime. Don't want to. Am trying to keep my schedule in balance. The longer Lou's out of the house, the more attention the children need from me. I am relying heavily on Margaret. She stays with us now.

Tomorrow, I leave for Florida on assignment. Haitian boat people are coming ashore at an alarming rate. Sunbathers watch, amazed, as old boats roll in with the tide. Their occupants pull the vessels up on the beach and scatter to the streets. We'll probe lax patrolling on the part of Immigration.

Love to all,
Quinn

Quinn and Lou

Ten years ago,
you
built roof, walls and floor,
windows, door
against the snow,
the winds of time,
the slow climb
of frost,
that nothing should be lost
but taken in and fed.
You wed,
and in that marriage grew
gift after gift,
not just for two,
but for the stranger and the friend
you welcomed to your feast.
Mine is a future you helped mend.
I am the stranger you released
from yesterday

and called a friend.
To the grace of your house
and the joy of your home,
may there be no end.

HAPPY ANNIVERSARY

Jeff

❑

Quinn—

It's presumptuous of me to send an anniversary gift but I just know that Lou will come back soon because you want it so much. I am thinking of you with love.

Sterling

❑

August 25, 1978

Dear Quinn,

I'm sorry the anniversary was a disappointment. It takes time to resolve problems.

Caught your report on the Haitians. It was vintage Quinn. I'm proud of you. Mother called me right away.

Asian boat people are being helped by the churches here in Richmond. Randy and I hired a Vietnamese man who told of hardship he suffered while escaping. His extended family was with him. Only he and a cousin survived.

We took him to lunch at a cafeteria shortly after he arrived. He put nothing on his tray. Said he didn't see anything he recognized! Also, he had a humorous line about cooking. He wants to learn to make American meals. We suggested starting with hamburger. He said he couldn't make burgers because he doesn't own a charcoal grill.

LOVE!
Sterling

❑

September 20, 1978

Dear Quinn,

You've been doing so well. I see you on TV. Your confidence is showing, whether you realize it or not. You even managed to make the report on airline deregulation compelling.

On a bad day, think about Sovereign and Laine's delicious anticipation of Halloween. At 9 and 10, they're still enchanted with costumes and spend hours dreaming them up for me to sew, drawing them on paper, coloring them. This year, Sovereign wants to be a flapper and Laine a fairy princess. I'm buying satin, tulle and sequins.

Think about Lance having to shave his face now. My little boy!

These are the glorious, the ice cream days with the children. Don't you agree?

Has your crew seen the new shows, TAXI and MORK & MINDY? Guess who's glued to that one!

Love,
Sterling

❏

October 3, 1978

Dear Quinn,

We went to see Jeff's family. After the baby died, I wanted this more than ever.

We decided not to write or call, but to simply go—in case we changed our minds at the last minute. Jeff did it for me. He was sick with apprehension.

The Mathers live in a log house on forty wooded acres. The driveway travels at a right angle, up to it. By the time we made the turn, three dogs were running alongside the car, barking.

Jeff's father came out on the porch as we pulled up. When he recognized Jeff, he grinned and ran to meet us, tugging his son from the car and embracing him. Jeff's mother and brother came out then, too. The brother moved slowly. I could tell at once that he was mentally handicapped. Jeff's mother left the porch and threw herself happily at both of us. The brother, David, let himself down the stairs as quickly as he could by hanging onto the railing and stood smiling. I didn't know how to approach him, what he would be comfortable with. But he began clapping with glee and I clapped, too!

No one asked any questions. We blended into their home as though Jeff had only been gone a few weeks. We ate by the fire and told story after story, the way people do at any kind of reunion. There was no mention of Jeff's prison days. Jeff and I slept in the guest room and woke to bird song, dappled sunlight and the smell of bacon cooking. It was incredibly easy.

His father's an insurance salesman, his mother a librarian. David, at 42, is a landscape assistant. They are beautifully ordinary, this family. Their house is Early American antiques and china cupboards, polished wood and buckets of flowers. Quilts. Books. I can't understand what Jeff was running from by shutting them out. Perhaps he felt he had embarrassed them beyond limits when he went to jail, although he was innocent. I'd like to understand more of what happened but I don't want to push Jeff and it doesn't really matter.

Best love,
Rozzy

❏

You knocked me off my chair with that piece on Paisley, the CIA employee who committed "suicide."

Sterling

❏

October 17

Quinn:

You're not the reporter I thought you were. You're twice the reporter I thought you were. Leaping on the Paisley suicide was masterful. The average person might have suspected foul play but only you would suspect the body might not be his.

My compliments.
HAP

❏

11-4-78

Dear Sterling,

This is a thank you note. You have encouraged me so thoroughly. I've been thinking back on the visits, the calls, the advice, the gifts and the praise you've given me. It has made a difference. I am stronger because of your caring.

It is gratifying to me to see your life also green, flourishing. Most of all, I know you so well—something I could not say before.

QUINN

❏

Nov. 10

Sterling

Last night, I was grieving for Lou so deeply that it was unbearable. I got out of bed and got dressed. I knew where to find him: at the office. The guard, who recognized me, let me into the building.

Lou was sitting by himself, working. He saw my reflection in the plate glass window over his desk as I walked up behind him. He took off his glasses and laid them on a stack of papers, turned off the reading lamp and stood up wearily. I helped him into his overcoat and we went home. It was that simple.

Suddenly, mysteriously, this siege by outside forces is over. It is as though all I needed was the courage to claim my husband and my career.

QUINN

❏

November 18th

Sterling:

I'm writing this in the airport. Am leaving for Jonestown. Tried to get out of it but it's the story of the year and the southern correspondent asked for backup.

I am remiss in not calling you. Haven't had a letter from you in a couple of weeks. Your schedule's hectic, I'm sure.

Will be in touch when I get home,

Love,
Quinn

❏

11/27/78

Dear Quinn,

Forgive me for not telling this when you called. Sterling didn't want me to. Our Laine is in the hospital at UVA—the 4th time this year. Tests do not reveal what is wrong with her. It was Sterling's desire that you be spared knowing our difficulties.

Sterling has hardly gone out of the house the past months because Laine is sick all the time. Laine goes back to school and, a day or two later, she's in bed again. She is progressively weak and thin, as though life is draining from her. We have had her to a lot of doctors and have been told her illness is probably not of physical origin. I can't understand this and don't believe it.

Your mom is with Sterling and Laine. Rosalind also offered to come, so there is nothing for you to do right now but pray if you will.

I'm remaining in Richmond with the other children to try to give them a sense of normalcy and to keep them in school. Will stay in touch.

Randy

P.S. Your dad and his colleagues also looked at Laine this year and were stumped. We are sorrowing.

❏

December 5, 1978

Dearest Quinn,

Your anger is shaking this family to its roots. Sweetheart, no one ever meant to slight you and this is surely the wrong time to take the matter up with Sterling. She has been through enough this year. I'm asking you to take the role of peacemaker. Sometimes we have to do that even when it isn't our turn.

You had been upset and faltering for so long that we all felt you didn't necessarily need to know about Laine. It wasn't a secret, but there was no need to bring it into your life when you had your own troubles to contend with.

I hope you can believe that we had your best interests at heart.

I love you.
Mother

❏

Sterling—

Why can't you understand? I feel betrayed. You lied to me! Mother says this is the wrong time to bring it up but I am sick and tired of this family because no one tells the truth. Our whole way of communicating is to sidestep, omit, alter or gloss over facts. It's never the right time to reveal who we are. Someone might be frightened. Someone might be offended. Someone might interfere. Strangers know more about us than we know about each other.

Perhaps it is none of our business what our relatives do. Then, why dress our relationship in the guise of honesty? It is a hurtful charade.

On the phone you kept using the term "white lies." White lies are lies.

QUINN

❏

Quinn,

I won't argue with you. It's true, we do that, we lie. To protect each other? To protect ourselves? It's not from spite, I'm sure. The opposite. It's misguided kindness.

So, I'll be honest. I believe Laine is dying, being pulled away from me by some force of justice that has found me guilty. She and I have been in this hospital, this pediatric unit, forever—a limbo where the corridors are filled with dark unanswerable questions.

Life breaks you. That's the truth.

Sterling

❏

Quinn

I still see you coming down the hospital hallway, catching sight of me, holding out your arms for me.

I will always see it.

S.

❏

1 9 7 9

Quinn

Jan. 3

Dear Rozzy,

When Lou and I and the children arrived at the hospital Christmas Eve, we had no idea that Mother and Dad and all the Hamiltons—in-laws included— would be there. Most of them were in the lobby because they could only get four visitor passes at a time. Someone called Laine's room and Randy came down and gave me his pass.

Randy's parents & Sterling were with Laine. She was apathetic, almost unresponsive as she lay in bed. She didn't care about her presents. Sterling opened them and held them up for her to see. Laine barely smiled. I didn't describe Laine's state to you on the phone because Sterling was with me and I was trying to be chipper.

Sterling stayed with Laine each night. Only one parent can sleep in the room with the child—the other has to leave because the hospital doesn't want hanky-panky going on. Can you picture that? Anyway, the rest of us took over an old hotel nearby. We were almost the only guests. In spite of the situation— or maybe because of it—Christmas was especially memorable. There was a lot of tenderness.

When everyone else went home on the 26th, I stayed a couple of extra nights—one of them with Laine while Sterling took my hotel room. S. was bone tired. I didn't dare sleep. I watched Laine til morning. She seldom talks, as though she's saving her strength. She wanted me to hold her hand most of the night. I kept trying to transfer some of my health to her with my touch.

Sterling said that, when they were first there, she closed her door and hid with Laine. The atmosphere of illness on the pediatric floor terrified her. She didn't want to meet the other parents and patients. But, gradually, she blended into their circle.

Time is suspended within those walls—each day the same as the one before. So many of the children have life-threatening conditions that the outside world seems far away. There's no talk among the mothers about fashions or new cars or recipes. Those things are distant, from another life. They talk about their situations, live moment to moment, do one another's hair as therapy.

The children are sweet—too sick to be rambunctious or belligerent. They have heart problems, kidney disease, cancer, cystic fibrosis, nothing con- tagious. At bedtime, the sound of the nurse's hands beating gently on the CF child's back echoes through the hallways.

The kids, if they can, play like any others. There's an activity room but it's only open during the day. In the evening, the corridors come alive with kids riding trikes and chasing toys. The nurses are good-natured about it, even motherly. Some long-term-care patients spend many nights without a parent. The financial burden keeps the parents home, working, or the parents have other children to tend.

The whole experience was devastating. I am both glad and sorry you weren't with us.

Love,
Quinn

❑

To: Quinn Fortner
From: Howard Melton
Date: January 11, 1979

This memo will confirm the details of our meeting yesterday.

1. You agree to produce a quarterly investigative report for television on an aspect of American life. Length: one hour.
2. This report will be in addition to your regular duties.
3. You will be provided with support staff from News to assist you on each report.
4. You will furnish, in writing, a description of each proposed report and submit it to me nine months prior to its scheduled air date.
5. The first in the series will be aired in December 1979.

❑

January 20, 1979

Dear Quinn,

Your letter about Laine made me so sad. Imagine having all that trouble and being only nine years old. I'm sorry you were upset at not being told of Laine's illness during its many stages. I wasn't told either until December. I think Sterling didn't want to alarm us. I see your point that this has gone too far. We need to stop being so protective of one another.

We missed you at Christmas but this was a golden occasion for us. Jeff's parents and brother had not spent the holidays with him in twenty years. They were grand house guests, lots of fun—and every one a chef. Too many cooks definitely do not spoil the broth. We ate like kings.

Jeff and David are extremely fond of each other and seem relieved to be together again. They went fishing one day while I walked the beach with Paul and Lillian. David is a dear, dear soul. I give P & L a lot of credit. They obviously have been faithful and loving to him. He passes that affection on to others.

The editing of WINGS ON THE MOON is complete. We had a private screening over the holidays. Quinn, it's the best ever. Took the top of my head off. It's scheduled for release in early summer.

Thom has stepped back into the director's role and let me manage Jeff's career. Negotiations for the next package are underway. Script is an original screenplay titled A RECIPROCAL AGREEMENT. What happens when a man makes a deathbed confession to his wife and then doesn't die? I was a little afraid of this story. It has wry humor to it and Jeff's style is more suited to serious material. But it's engrossingly clever. I think it'll go.

After AGREEMENT, I'll choose a topical subject. Trend is for films to make a social statement. The Vietnam movies—DEER HUNTER, COMING HOME—are front runners for Oscars this season. And there's one due out in March called THE CHINA SYNDROME, about the danger of nuclear power plants.

Perhaps we should do one on the problem of infertility. I have been trying for months to get pregnant. Haven't lost hope yet, though.

X X
Rozzy

❏

Dear Aunt Quinn and Uncle Lou,
    I like being home. Thank you for reading to me. You are nice.

Laine

❏

Dear Quinn,

I am desperately in need of an oasis where you and Rosalind and I can be completely alone for a while. I am exhausted from Laine's constant weakness and discouraged that no cause can be found. I long for my sisters. Randy has suggested that I take a week or two at Easter as recuperative "leave." He will keep the kids. I mentioned this to Rozzy and she thinks she can borrow or rent a place in Florida. Will you come?

Sterling

❑

February 8, 1979

Dear Quinn,

I've talked with Sterling, as you have. It's set. We'll "hole up" somewhere, just the three of us, for a number of days. We haven't had an opportunity like this since we became adults. I'm sure that's part of what's been wrong. We need to get back in touch. Years, miles and events have come between us. I want it to be a time of renewal, both of our relationships and of our individual selves. I want for each of us to come away from the visit with strength and happiness we haven't felt for a long time—perhaps ever.

I am working on renting a house in Florida, at Palm Beach, for the two weeks surrounding Easter. Also, Jeff asks that he be allowed to give us the gift of having every meal out, if we wish, so that we don't have to shop and cook.

The Academy Awards are April 9, but I can meet you on the 10th. Easter is the 15th. Please let me know as soon as possible whether this will suit your schedule.

Lots of Love,
Roz

❑

Tony—

Take a look at this tape—it's footage from a fire at a warehouse in SoHo. There's a man standing to the right of a fat lady in a yellow coat. He's partially bald and has a cigarette hanging out of his mouth. They are onlookers, at the fringe of the crowd. Isn't that Pete Babb, the guy you're hunting in connection with the Gilfoyle murders? If so, I've already checked him out for you. (Don't worry, he didn't get wind of it—I did it personally.) Turns out he was only in town for one day and News caught him in living color. If you bring me a whole strawberry cheesecake from Poli's, I'll give you his address & alias.

Quinn

❑

The cheesecake was delicious.

QUINN

❑

3/9/79

Hap,

I'm not big on formal memos, so here's the subj. for Dec. invest. report: Agent Orange. As you know, class action law suit was filed Feb. 1st in Fed. dist. court (NY) on behalf of 4.2 million Amer vets who served in Vietnam. This will not be old news by Dec. This is only the beginning! I want to talk to some of these men and—more important—find out if & how this stuff was tested, etc. Sounds like typical govt. shoulder shrugging slid it through and now they're trying to deny responsibility for resultant cancers.

Quinn

❑

March 30, 1979

Dearest Quinn,

I am elated that you and Sterling and Rosalind will be together for Easter. It is the answer to my prayers that you three are developing a supportive friendship.

God bless you in this endeavor.

Love,
Mother

❑

Wednesday

Dear Lou,

The atmosphere here is charged with promise and tension, hope and regret.

The house itself is glorious, right on the beach — close enough to the surf for the gentle, steady sound of the waves to pulse through the screens. There is plenty of room inside, which is good. We will need space for being separate after times of intense sharing.

At the last minute, Sterling brought Laine with her. A surprise. Roz and I were taken aback by it, but Laine is a walking shadow. Quiet. Frail. I think Sterling was afraid that if she left Laine, she might not see her again. Having her among us may interfere with our communication, but I don't think so. She is willingly self-sufficient, has brought books and likes to be alone in the shade of the palms, on a lounge chair. We would entertain her more but she can't stand much activity. We played cards with her last night and she liked that. Sterling seems relieved that we have not made an issue of Laine's presence, or even mentioned it.

I miss you and wonder what these weeks will bring. It is strange to be with my sisters again in isolation. I don't know what to expect.

Love always,
Quinn

❏

Thursday

Dear Lou,

After a period of polite chit-chat, we are becoming more open. I am amazed that there is no anger, none of the volatility that marred earlier meetings. Perhaps we have matured. We are poised in readiness but no one has ventured into deep topics. We do, however, admit we have essentially been lying to each other for a long time. We are formulating reasons why we have this behavior but so far have not hit on one we all believe.

We are making new ground rules, the first of which is that we will be completely candid in the future.

Love forever,
Quinn

❏

Friday

Lou,

Laine is an exquisite human being.

You have seen her physical beauty—the bluish tint of her pale skin, the graceful limbs and floating gait, the attentive tilt of her chin. You have heard her speech, which is at once wise and childlike. But, in spending hours with her, I have moved into the realm of her personhood.

Her thoughts are occupied with seashell patterns and hibiscus petals, the pelicans who herd fish by skimming the ocean, the rhythm of the tide. Whatever is lovely captures her notice.

She listens for my thoughts and carries me pieces of my dreams: water-worn stones, smooth against the hand, sea grapes plucked from a round-leaf tree.

She runs her fingers along my cheeks as if memorizing them. Her words are shaped with kindness. She likes many friends at school and writes them all letters, tucking sand into the folds of the paper.

She is enchanting.

Q

❏

Oh, this hurts, Lou. It's shock after shock. It can't be a good idea to unearth all this stuff, can it? We are not attacking each other, just sharing secrets and sorrows. What is being told now will never be told again. It's too painful. I think we all have the same instinct—to stop baring our souls. But we have missed so much of one another's lives that we need to bring out these experiences. Starting fresh can't work if we don't say what shaped us.

Q

❏

Sunday

Lou,

We have spent a whole day not talking, except to Laine. No one is upset, we just need time to absorb all that's been said and to decompress emotionally. We've been sunning, sleeping, baking cookies. It's very comfortable.

Give my angels hugs from their mama. I adore them and you.

Quinn

❏

4—17—79

Darling,

Your letters fill in the gaps. I can't get from your phone calls what's really going on. I guess that's natural. Keep writing.

This is an interesting time for me, too. Much as my mom loves you, I think she's relishing having her baby boy and the grandkids all to herself, under her roof. Well, almost to herself. Dagmar drops in and chases the kids around. They shriek with excitement. Well, the little ones do. Zan has suddenly turned demure. Dag, recognizing the signs of ladyhood, has taken to painting Zan with make-up, in front of a big mirror. Lots of rouge, lipstick, bangle-dangle bracelets and blond wigs. Pierced her ears with safety pins, too. Sorry. I was consulted after the fact.

Dag's ready to move on from guarding Judge Moulton's sons. They view her as a babysitter and they're too old for that. To run her off, they play tricks — hide from her and take elaborate risks in front of her.

Your kids send you sloppy wet kisses. Me 2.

Louis

❑

Wednesday

Dear Lou,

It has been raining for two days, which has sent us into a pensive mood. We haven't been able to rest well. Last night, we ended up in the living room at 3 a.m. for cheese and crackers and wine. Laine was sleeping.

Sterling began to cry about Laine's health and we cried with her. Sterling believes she injured Laine in the womb by not wanting her. Further, she believes they are part of an equation, a balancing of nature. Sterling championed abortion: her child will die.

Rozzy and I protested, held her, tried to talk reason into her but, in the end, were affected by her philosophy. It is this: As children we were wanted and nurtured, catered to, humored, treasured, adored. As adults, we have been entrusted with cherishing the next wave of children and we have failed. Ours is the first generation that has fought for and won the right to terminate the life of any child. A fetus most certainly is a child, complex and sacred. A gift.

Sterling's anguish taps our own guilt and grief. In the end, we answer with our conscience. We are filled with emptiness.

Quinn

❑

Thursday

Lou,

Being responsible for Laine frightens me, as it does Sterling. Laine has weak spells. Even sitting down sometimes, she feels she cannot get up without help. I am ready to take her anywhere, to the best clinics, but Sterling says they have done this.

We have fallen into a collective suffering, as though we are connected spiritually the way a spring runs underground. But there is power to it. We concentrate so hard on Laine that we can hear one another thinking.

Rosalind and I now sense the inevitability Sterling has sensed, the folly of struggling.

Quinn

❑

Lou—

Something terrible happened. We had Laine with us in the surf. We were riding swells in shoulder-high water, laughing. Occasionally, one of us would get caught by a wave and go under, but it was exhilarating to be pushed and pulled by the warm water. It was a game. Laine can swim, still we kept her within arm's reach because she is so delicate. She had begged to go with us. We were careful.

Once, she turned her back against a large wave and smiled as it curled over her head. She held her arms forward as if she were going to dive toward shore. She didn't come up. We stood staring, disbelieving, waiting, looking in all directions. We couldn't run, couldn't swim, the undertow was suddenly so strong. We were in slow motion, screaming her name across roaring water.

We moved arduously away from the spot, searching. The current had a drag to the north. I drifted with it, treading water. Sterling was swimming now, far from shore. Roz was standing about 20 yards south of me, in water up to her chest. A gold sunburst floated between us. Roz and I realized at the same time that it was Laine's hair, fanning out from the back of her head. Roz, who had the advantage of the current, approached Laine. As she reached for her, Laine's face rolled upward. Roz said Laine's eyes were open, glazed, but all I could see was the glint of sun on skin as she was sucked to the bottom again.

The force of the water held me in place. I watched Roz be yanked under, as though by her feet. Laine's head appeared and shifted in the torrents. Roz surfaced near her. They slid rapidly along, parallel to the beach, Laine bobbing spine-up in the shallows, eluding Roz. That's when it occurred to me that we might lose both of them. Roz was sinking, crawling through the waves. I recognized her awkwardness as exhaustion. I looked for Sterling, who was crossing behind me, horror in her expression. Only Roz was close enough to Laine to catch her.

What I can only describe as an enormous energy passed among us, Sterling and Rosalind and me. And then, Roz grabbed Laine, drawing her up and out with such determination that Laine vomited water.

It is evening now, and we are unable to speak of it. We have called no one, although we had Laine treated at a hospital and brought her home. She seems to be all right.

Quinn

❑

April 25

Quinn—

It was hard to part with you and Sterling and Laine. I have never wept like that! I should have changed my ticket and stayed the extra day with the three of you.

Jeff met me at LAX and we flew on to Hawaii. Filming began immediately upon our arrival. The backdrop is lush: green velvet mountains and valleys, framed by shining sea. The island glitters with reflected light from the vast Pacific.

I think of you.

Roz

❑

Dear Quinn,

My heart literally feels strong in my chest, solid, like silver, because of you and Roz. May we always be this close.

Sterling

❑

Quinn—
Read the file on this one and spark me up, OK? The kid was only 12—
delivering papers before dawn. Jonathan Burris. Throat cut. No one saw
anything. We've interviewed customers, neighbors, acquaintances and relatives. Find the hole. Your intuition is better than a hundred man hours.

TONY

❑

May 18, 1979

Dear Aunt Quinn and Uncle Lou,
    Thank you for the check you sent for my 15th birthday. I am saving for a
Commodore computer.
    The newspaper wrote a story about the pictures of me. We have over 5000.
When my parents were away anytime they had someone take my picture every
day. Kids used to tease me but now they think it's awesome. A man from
Guiness Book called me up. I might get in.
    Laine has been going to school. My Mother said to tell you and Laine eats
really well. Mom is going to call you soon.

Love,
Mindy

❑

Tony,
    The second cheesecake was even better than the first. Send me the Burris
suspect's comments after arrest, list of evidence from his apartment, etc.
Don't quote me regulations. I want this scoop. I won't reveal the source.

QUINN

❑

    Quinn!
        I got pregnant in Hawaii!!!
    Rozzy

❑

6/26/79

Hap,

Appreciate your suggestion but everyone's doing nuclear power since accident at 3 Mile Island in March. It'll be passe by next March. I'm on the inside of some toxic waste stories that haven't broken yet. Let me do that.

Quinn

❑

July 10, 1979

Dear Quinn,

Our Pittsburgh trip provided a visual symphony. Mother & Dad took us on a river cruise the Fourth of July. It was a dinner dance and the kids were jumping to the music! At ten o'clock, the ship paused on the Ohio River and we could watch from on deck a spectacular fireworks display in the dark sky over the city. The running lights on hundreds of anchored small boats sparkled in the black water of the three rivers. It was a precious moment for me. Laine was standing on a bench so she could see. I had my arm around her. She was amazingly sturdy under my touch. Her health continues to improve. She is a paper doll come to life, slowly taking on color in her flesh and sheen in her hair, growing firm in the limbs, smiling more. It is mysterious.

Sterling

❑

My, my, Detective Malerbo. Aren't you getting adventuresome in your old age? I didn't believe what was coming over the phone at me. Couldn't comment on it at the time—my colleagues were within earshot. In regard to your proposal, network "regulations" prohibit me from lying to a subject in an interview. And waving a phony crime lab report under his nose to get his on-camera reaction compromises my ethics, not to mention yours, and which is not even to mention offending my finer sensibilities.

Mrs. Quinn Fortner

❑

Q.

Did I perceive a sporting tone? Davenford's guilty as hell and, legally, my hands are tied. I'm sick of giving these sleazeballs due process. He smothered his five-year-old niece while he was molesting her, for Christ sake. Listen, I'm ethical. If I weren't I'd have choked the SOB by now.

T.

❑

August 13, 1979

Dear Detective Malerbo,

Thank you for the strawberry cheesecake. It was very good and my family enjoyed it, too.

Come and see me again sometime.

Sincerely,
Quinn Fortner

❑

Quinn. There has always been an adversarial relationship between law enforcement and media. You're violating a sacred precept. We can't use this network's resources to help NYPD solve crimes. Don't do that again.

Hap

❑

Aug. 23, 1979

Dear Quinn,

This is a fantastic time for Randy, Bobby and me. We've finally closed all the stores and are strictly mail order now. Bobby is in the process of moving here as part of the consolidation. As we gear up for Christmas, we are already selling beyond our projected numbers for the entire year.

We are going to have a big 10th birthday bash for Laine on Sept. 8. Her newfound health is a miracle. Come for the weekend and bring your family, if you can. Mother and Dad will be staying with us. Roz refuses to travel and I think it's sensible. Her pregnancy has gone perfectly—I'm sure she tells you how thrilled they are.

The only thing Rozzy says disturbs her is that Jeff still has a manslaughter conviction. She doesn't want the baby to have to live with that. The woman jumped—she was a mental patient, after all. Knowing Jeff as we do, how could it have been otherwise? She says Jeff won't hear of reopening the case. He wants to enjoy his present life, not dredge up the sad times. But it continues to bother her.

Please don't tell her I told you about this. Yes, we promised to be honest, but we need to use discretion on some matters. Right?

Give the children hugs from me.

Sterling

❑

9/1/79

Hap,

My report for June '80 will be called "Reasonable Doubt." Focus will be on people unjustly accused and convicted of crimes. Purpose will be to spotlight gaps in law enforcement and the judicial system.

QF

❑

Quinn Sue,

Can anyone jump in anyone else's doodoo like you at top form? No way. I saw you giving it to Hooker Chem. on TV. You had them to the wall for that dumping against the law. I was bug eye at 28 Long Island drinking wells closed from their junk. You looked ready to chew that man's toopay off and spit it on his fancy suit. Girl you got your sass back proper.

Dagmar

❑

9/8/79

Dag—What a doll you are to write to me. You're right about my sass. I found it again & am using it liberally.

Lou's doing great. Sassy in his own right. I'm sure he's told you about the big fight he's in over IQ testing. It's discriminatory. Doesn't measure native intelligence, only measures certain skills—many cultural. But IQ is used to classify many black students as mentally retarded. It rags Lou to death. NYC's goal is to certify more & more kids as handicapped in some way so the school system can collect Fed. funds. There's a test case in front of Judge Peckham in California, so it's wait and see.

I'll call you in a week or so and we'll talk til midnight.

Love,
Quinn

❑

Quinn—

I've thought it over and your idea stinks. If your brother-in-law doesn't want anyone fooling around with his case, leave it closed. I'm sure he's a great guy and took a bum rap, but—hey—they're all innocent. You know what I mean? No offense intended, only caution. I owe you one but let's drop this. Give me another assignment.

Tony

❑

October 9, 1979

Dearest Quinn,

We saw you in the middle of that anti-nuclear protest in New York. It is incredible that 200,000 people turned out. Your interviews with Jane Fonda and Ralph Nader impressed us. You are more forceful than ever and we are proud of you.

Dad has tickets for one of the World Series games and we're excited about that. The Pirates should take the Orioles easily in 4 or 5. Pittsburgh needs something to perk it up. The economy is dropping rapidly. With interest rates up past 12 percent, nobody can afford anything. The steel mills are in danger of closing and, as you know, they are the heart of the city. We hope for the best.

Will you and Lou be available for Christmas this year? Rozzy wants us all to come there, even Mrs. Fortner and Dagmar. Wouldn't that be fun?

All my love,
Mother

❑

Quinn

The paperwork on Mather is endless: trial transcripts, etc. I need a longer period of time. Just doing homework will take a month.

Tony

❏

November 12, 1979

Dear Quinn,

David has been with us for a week. What a joy he is. At his request, we let him order plants for our rock garden and porch. He has worked at a leisurely pace all week, replacing basket and pots, setting in mums and marigolds, geraniums and angel-wing begonia, Swedish ivy. I had books and scripts to read for Jeff but laid them aside for the companionship of digging in the soil with David. He speaks slowly but has much of value to say. He has a precise memory for his delightful childhood adventures with Jeff. David is excited about becoming an uncle. We talked about it a lot.

I am radiantly well with this pregnancy and believe the baby is, too. The doctor suggested amniocentesis because I am 36, but I refused. If there is something wrong with the baby, I wouldn't abort it anyway, so what's the point? I am confident.

Love,

Rozzy

❏

Quinn

I've been trying to get hold of you. I had a colleague in NC check leads. The old man who watched the incident from the street died in 1973 but another eyewitness has turned up. This one's a woman who was a child at the time and playing on the balcony of an adjacent building. Her mother, now deceased, kept her from getting involved. My friend said she clammed up on him three minutes into the interview. Won't say anything else without an attorney present. Double jeopardy or no, I have a bad feeling about this.

Tony

❏

26 Nov.

Quinn:

Caught your report on the Tucson cover up. I should have listened when you told me your theory last spring. But who would believe a factory would be leaking radioactive tritium into the works of a kitchen serving all of Tucson's elementary schools?

People told me you were infallible, like the Pope. I'm almost convinced.

HAP

❏

Tony

You said yourself that my intuition is worth a hundred man hours. Jeff is not guilty. Prove it.

QUINN

❏

12/3/79
Hap,

Subject for next Sept. is "Backsliding into the 80s." Report concerns the fact that civil rights and women's rights are losing ground, beginning to revert to pre-70s conditions. There is plenty of evidence.

QUINN

❏

December 6, 1979
Dear Quinn,

We're glad everyone will be here for Christmas! This has been a marvelous year for our whole family. I am elated that the honesty we promised each other has been forthcoming. We are richly blessed.

Since WINGS ON THE MOON was released in June, it has been surrounded by tremendous hoopla. We believe this is the finest role Jeff has done. We are caught up in glory!

Strangely, I keep having the old dream in which I live my entire life in despair and loneliness because I have not met the right man. Then, I wake up beside my husband, with whom I am completely happy. He is kind and generous to me, always. Perhaps the loss of Glenn still affects me although I seldom dwell on him.

Thom and I will be giving a special Christmas gift this year. In April, a group of Vietnam veterans started a fund to build a memorial in Washington, D. C. The site will be chosen next summer. We can't imagine what design could possibly begin to represent the magnitude of tragedy and sacrifice in this war, but we are anxious to support the effort.

Best love,

Roz

❏

Quinn:
We need to quickly produce Xmas feature surrounding American hostages being held in Iran. Since initial shock of Nov. 4 embassy seizure has worn off, some family members have agreed to be interviewed. List of names & addresses in attached file. Zaremba was assigned to do this before his car accident. His plane tickets are enclosed. I regret the short notice.
Hap
Dec. 10

❏

Quinn, Where the hell are you? Call me right away. On gut, I flew to NC. Witness met with me privately. She became agitated recalling the incident. The woman, she said, was struggling with the man and shouting for help before she fell. Description witness gave matches Jeff's. I don't have a doubt. I stopped short of handing her a photo. BACK OUT OF THIS. NOW.

Tony

❏

Tony—
    Deep six that, for God's sake.
    Q

❏

1 9 8 0

Sterling

January 6, 1980

Dear Rozzy and Jeff,

Many thanks for hosting us at Christmas. It was perfect. I will always remember turning into your long driveway at night and riding through a dreamland of twinkling white lights, Santa on his sleigh, the Sugarplum Fairy, brightly wrapped presents hanging from branches, frosted topiaries laden with bows. Inside, a Christmas tree in every room, each with a different theme! You outdid yourselves.

In spite of California's splendor, I was content to come home to Richmond. I have grown to cherish the South as Randy does. The sights and the people are unique: the rose-like pink camellias blooming in winter, the waxy white magnolias magnificent in summer, green pepper jelly, red eye gravy, country ham, a tradition of gentleness and kind hospitality. I appreciate Randy's folks now that I understand them. And now when a Southerner tells me a space is "too small to cuss a cat in without getting fur in your mouth," I don't snicker, I smile.

Happy New Year.

Sterling

❏

January 6, 1980

Dear Mother and Dad,

Wasn't our week at Rozzy's fabulous? The children were ecstatic. And, oh, Roz is so casually glamorous — even her bathrobes silky and sweeping. Being Roz, she doesn't seem to know she looks special. She's as natural and generous as always.

Thank you for my scrapbook. You must have spent days sorting through baby photos and report cards and dance programs for the three of us. The kids are poring over my album, laughing at my dresses and boyfriends.

I am excited about the new year. I have a gut feeling it will be a significant one for me. I have energy to spare and am looking for ways to express myself. At 15, 14, 11 and 10, the children don't need me quite as much and the Camp catalog is prospering under Randy and Bobby. I can share my abundance with others.

Next year I hit the big 4-0. On the brink of adventure!

Love,
Sterling

❏

January 13, 1980

Dear Sterling and Randy,

Yes, it was the ideal Christmas. The thing I liked best about it was that it combined so many family members including Mrs. Fortner, Dagmar, Paul, Lillian and David. I wish your parents had been able to be here, too, Randy.

Sterling, David adored you. You really have a touch with people.

Did Dagmar tell you she has agreed to be bodyguard for our baby? She was looking for a job and we scooped her up. Since WINGS catapulted Jeff into a higher career level, we have had to tighten security — as you saw. This will put our minds at ease.

Our Hawaii movie, A RECIPROCAL AGREEMENT, is finally scheduled for release, at Easter. It's been ready but we've held it so Jeff would not compete with himself in '79. WINGS had a long run and we are hoping for Academy nominations. Release is April 1 and the awards April 14: they should dovetail nicely.

Thanks again for being here. What a good thought to tape a Susan B. Anthony dollar to each package as a keepsake from 1979.

Best love,
Roz

LAINE LOOKED TERRIFIC!

❏

Sterling

Good thing we never closed our P.O. boxes. Just when I think we should comes another occasion that warrants speaking to you privately. What is wrong with Quinn? She froze me out at Christmas. (Of course I asked her.) Roz didn't seem to notice. Did you?

Jeff

❏

January 29, 1980

Dear Quinn,

Excuse my sending this to your office, but you weren't quite yourself at Rozzy's and I am concerned. For one thing, you appeared to be avoiding Jeff. I

334

hope I am not overstepping my bounds to ask what the matter is. We promised to be frank with each other, including asking when we see rough edges. You can trust me. Write me at home. Randy and I don't open each other's mail.

Love,
Sterling

❏

February 3, 1980

Dearest Sterling,

Dad and I support you in your efforts to find an avocation. It has been our intent from the outset to finance any education our girls wish to receive. Therefore, if you would like to take a course or two, you can count on us for the tuition. We want to reiterate, however, our belief that "wife and mother" is a well-rounded identity in itself.

This will be a landmark year for us, also. Dad has decided to retire in August! You had spoken to us at Christmas about a 40th Anniversary party. Anytime after Labor Day would be fine and we can celebrate his "liberation" then, too.

Perhaps we should set a date shortly. Quinn's calendar is busier each year. She's been told that she will soon have her own weekly program. Did you watch her ABSCAM report? She's incomparable in her investigating and interviewing. I think I am seeing her in perspective: her name is as big as the stories she covers.

We miss you all and hope to be with you again before too long.

Love,
Mother

❏

Jett and Rosalind Maeder
announce with pleasure
the birth of their son
Adam David
February 8, 1980
at 9:45 a.m.
Weight 9 lbs. 1 oz.
Length 22"
Cedars-Sinai Medical Center
Los Angeles, California

❑

Sterling, You asked. Take this letter somewhere and read, then flush down the john. I have more than a hunch Jeff was responsible for the death that sent him to prison. I've been in torment for months. I am working on the documentary I told you about at Christmas — "Reasonable Doubt." Well, I shouldn't have but I started by investigating Jeff. I thought it would be a favor. I believed I could exonerate him. What I found was damning. Now I am torn between my apprehension for Roz and my remorse at setting it all in motion again. Ros always did pick the wrong man. Why should this be any different?

QUINN

❏

February 28, 1980
Dear Sterling and Randy,

Thank you for the marvelous baby quilt! You should see this little boy. He is an angel. He is constantly in our arms. If Jeff and I aren't cuddling him, Dagmar is. His hair is soft like milkweed. He has that distinctive "baby fragrance," of being brand new and lightly powdered. We are thrilled with him.

Steve and Annie will be here for the christening. They have consented to be godparents. M & D are not able to travel because Dad's practice is hectic.

Doorbell and phone are ringing and ringing. Adam's birth and Jeff's Best Actor nomination seem to have stirred the whole world into contacting us. It is overwhelming and humbling.

I am utterly content with my life, at last.

Much love,
Roz

❏

Quinn—I want you to totally erase that from your memory. You did not investigate Jeff. You did not find evidence of his guilt. You did not tell me. I did not write this letter back to you. We will NEVER speak of it again.

Sterling

❏

Jeff:
Congratulations, Dad!

Sorry it took me a while to answer. I asked Quinn in a discreet way why she seemed to be ignoring you at Christmas. Turns out she's been preoccupied, for personal reasons.

Don't give it another thought.

Sterling

❏

Dear Mrs. Hamilton:

I was pleased to meet you. I have reviewed your résumé and would like to invite you to a second interview, with some of my colleagues who have also read your application. Your background, particularly your volunteer experience with prison inmates, seems to make you an excellent candidate for volunteer participation in Lifeline Services. As you are aware, the people who call Lifeline are seeking immediate help in a crisis. It is our job to listen attentively, provide unjudgmental feedback and refer the caller to a professional counselor. In my opinion, you could do this very well.
I hope that you will contact my office to set up a conference.

Yours truly,
Scott F. Grogan
Director

March 15, 1980

❏

April 17, 1980
Dear Sterling,

Thanks for your consoling phone call. I'd be lying if I said we weren't disappointed that Jeff didn't win. But Dustin was certainly deserving. KRAMER VS KRAMER is powerful.

Just between us, sometimes I wonder if Jeff's criminal record is restraining the Academy's enthusiasm for his work. Letting it stand implies that he is guilty, which he certainly is not. I have begged him to put some money into reopening his case but he wants to leave past sorrows behind.

On the plus side, the release of AGREEMENT has been met with acclaim and Jeff's gone right into working on EASY MARK. Filming begins shortly. It's the story of a boy who grew up in the streets of LA because he was raised by a widowed, negligent mother. As an adult, he answers a newspaper ad placed by an elderly man who is trying to locate his son, long ago given up for adoption. The younger man pretends he is that child, for the purpose of inheriting money. What he does not foresee is that he will begin to develop an affection and respect for the old man. Looks like a winner.

Love,
Roz

❏

Sterling

Pardon use of PO box but I want to tell you alone—

I am the luckiest person alive. I have Rosalind, a healthy child and a rewarding career. None of this would be mine if it hadn't been for you. I thank you silently, profusely and often. Almost as often as I thank God. I think of you whenever I really look at all I have. Because you are One of a Kind, you brought out the worst and best in me. That's a compliment, and a tribute. You seem to be flying now, too. Only we can know how far we journeyed to this place.

Jeff

❑

4/30/80

Dear Quinn

How I missed you when I heard your voice! There was much celebrating at our house after you gave us the news that you got your own program! What a triumph and justified reward for your years of diligent, brilliant service.

Don't let anything mar this moment. Especially, don't fret about Jeff. I feel confident he is innocent. It will all "come out in the wash," as they say.

You have a tremendous instinct for plot but I have an equally strong instinct for people. It's been endorsed lately by volunteer work I am doing on a crisis hotline. I was born with this facility for instant comprehension of human behavior but I've only recently begun to recognize and use it.

You're the best.
Sterling

❑

Dear Sterling,

Since Adam arrived, I have been thinking more and more about Jeff's conviction. It is agonizing for him to look squarely at that period of his life, so I don't ask him to. But I would like to approach it on my own, secretly, through a detective. Surely I can clear Jeff's name. There must be someone who can support him by testifying that Jocelyn committed suicide. They lived in a heavily populated high-rise. There has to be more than one person who saw what happened.

I'll buzz you next week during the day and you can give me your opinion.

Roz

❑

Sterling,

I don't understand why you are upset. What harm would there be in trying? Either I'd come up with the facts I need to verify Jeff's innocence or I wouldn't. He's not guilty, certainly. You're not thinking anything like that, are you? You wouldn't have stuck by him if you had thought he was.

You've got me off center now. I'll mull it over.

Roz

❑

Sterling:

Was listening to tapes of your interactions with callers and I had to write you a compliment. You are remarkable. You have the ability to cut through the haze of what people say and look keenly at who they are. Specifically, I am intrigued by your ability to discern the "central issue" within a short length of time. I checked, and your referral followups are high. In other words, callers are acting on your suggestions that they contact the professional counselors on our list. This means that they perceive you as sympathetic and, further, that they trust you. This is difficult to achieve using only the telephone. We are handicapped by our medium.

Good work. And continued good luck. You have my sincere appreciation.

Scott

❑

May 21
Dear Sterling,

David is here. I am watching him out the kitchen window. How gingerly he tends the flowers, how reverently he turns the soil. It is an eerie day. His silhouette moves in the ash from Mt. St. Helens, a gray screen of particles combined with mist, much worse than our usual smog.

I am slowly determining to ask David about Jeff's prison years. I have tried it before. He became mute, tense; I changed the subject. But we are closer now.

Even Paul and Lillian do not speak of it. Their expressions harden with pain when I try. It must be like a death, this shutting away of one's child in the hostile climate of a jail. The mourning changes form eventually, but never ends.

This is the better way: to talk, to attempt to talk. I can't betray Jeff. You were right to stop me.

Rozzy

❑

5/26/80

Dear Sterling,

Thank you for the pendant watch. I like the scrolls of the gold case and the Roman numerals inside. It is classic and classy.

How fitting that you should give me this to mark the granting of my honorary Masters Degree at Merrill. When I stood up to give the commencement address, I could feel the watch against my breast bone, under my gown. The passing of time brings ironic twists.

I think the secret of the 60s was that a generation gap existed between siblings. The four years that separate us comprise an enormous span because the world changed cataclysmically. We were caught in it without understanding it. It separated us. I'm grateful we found each other again. I said to you once that you could have done anything I did, all you had to do was put one foot in front of the other. It wasn't true. The path was not open to you when you were ready. It was a different era.

Please know that having you there ahead of me enriched my life.

Quinn

❑

Sterling—I sincerely sympathize. Empathize. The whole staff is upset. We don't like to lose one. But Jordan Diehl was well known to us because he had tried to do away with himself before. He succeeded this time, that's all. It doesn't mean we did a poor job of reaching out. He simply couldn't respond.

You feel you misread him. I listened to the tape. He did sound calm. It would have been impossible for any of us to tell what horror was about to take place. Don't blame yourself. If you want to take a few weeks off to rest, I'll understand.

Scott

❑

Quinn,

I am a person with a fever. Obsessive thoughts run through my head, unbidden, even at night. Especially at night. I am not 100 percent sure of Jeff. I am not 100 percent sure of anything.

I want to hear about your investigation of him. Roz is the best of us. You and I agree on that. We can't ignore what Jeff might be.

Sterling

❑

6/28

Quinn—

I understand when you say you don't have a minute to deal with this right now because of your new show. Let me do it. I'll go see the woman if you get me the proper credentials. She's right here in my territory—Raleigh's two hours away.

Please. I have to learn directly from her who Jeff is. He's our invention, yours and mine. I brought him into our lives and you brought him into the limelight. We are morally responsible for what happens next.

S.

❑

July 1, 1980

Dear Mother and Dad,

I'm having fun planning parties! I've invited the entire free world to Randy's 40th on August 1 and half the free world to your 40th on October 11. Thanks for sending the list of names and addresses. I'm going to get the invitations out of here in early August to give out-of-towners plenty of time to get their plane tickets. Should be a terrific success.

Randy's gagging around like he's afraid of being 40 but he's actually supremely satisfied. CAMP is having its biggest year ever. Our line is the highest quality one can get by mail. He and Bobby are slightly self-congratulatory, but it's nice to see.

You know all that fooling around we've been doing with the Guinness Book? They finally took Mindy. They say. I hope it gets into print. It's a safe bet no one else has had her picture taken as many times as Amanda Melissa.

The kids are having a grand summer at the swim club. Laine's one of the best on her team. She's going to write you a letter about it.

Take care.

Love from
Sterling

❑

S-
Here's the stuff. Don't let me down. Act credible. She has to trust you. Tell her to call me if she has a question. Reiterate to her that
- he can't be tried again
- he has served his sentence
- her anonymity is assured
- she will not be called on to give a sworn statement nor placed in a public position
- she will not be named and will not be referred to by document or media
- we need her for verification purposes only.

Q.

❑

July 28

Dear Sterling,
Jeff's home with Adam and Dagmar and me. Filming on EASY MARK was halted by the SAG/AFTRA strike. It started July 21 and no one knows how long it will go on. Jeff was immersed in the part and is restless, itching to get going

again. But this strike is necessary. There are inadequate provisions for home video; the actors should rightfully get a percentage of their work in this burgeoning market.

It is strange to have stopped motion. Delightful, in a way. Thom is eating with us most nights. The evenings are filled with chatter and humor. Dagmar's antics continually stimulate us. Even the baby laughs.

I thought I was an "old" mother, having Adam in my late thirties, but it's in vogue. People magazine will take over the house next week for a feature on 40-ish first-time moms.

I paint pictures in my mind, capturing the color and joy of these minutes. I am concentrating on remembering the faces, the dough on the bread board, the moonrise.

Rozzy

❏

Quinn, call me from wherever you are. Took the photos of Jeff to the witness yesterday. She looked at his picture and grinned—thought I was putting her on because she recognized him from the movies. Even a 20-year-old shot of him got the same response. But when I flipped through the stack of pix there was one of Jeff, arm around David, snapped last Xmas. Her eyes widened. She frowned and put a finger on DAVID. It makes sense. They have similar build and coloring.

S.

❏

August 7, 1980

Rozzy and Jeff,

Your gift stole the show at Randy's 40th. The belly dancer was gorgeous, charming, talented—not the least bit lewd. No one had the slightest warning. She just came in prancing to music from her own boom box. You shouldn't have!

Prize for best gift goes to Bobby, however, who presented Randy with a buyout offer from Cargill & Hill. It suddenly struck me what a valuable enterprise CAMP is. We've decided to pass because we're intrigued by making the company flourish. We're not ready to let it out of our hands.

I mailed the invitations for Mom & Dad's dinner dance. I hope a lot of their friends will attend. Thanks for providing the florals. I'll give you a table count as soon as I know. Also, will need one for the cake table—and a corsage and boutonniere.

Love,
Sterling

❏

Sterling

Am in Fla with Cuban Freedom Flotilla. If you had called Lou he could have given you the number. Office not permitted to.

Your letter burned my hands. Jeff is, at least, fairly predictable. As gentle as David seems, we can't be sure. I worry about the safety of Adam and Roz. Dagmar's pretty able. Am checking David's background.

The other factor: Jeff, without a doubt, knows this. The incident happened at his place—he was arrested there. Did he take the rap for David? It's obvious Jeff's emotional about him, over protective.

A mess. A can of worms.

Q.

❏

Sterling:

One more plea to come back to Lifeline. Your self-flagellation is unwarranted. Your condition is the condition of being human. We can't know another's nature until he reveals it. But we keep trying. The alternative is isolation.

Scott

❏

S——I don't like your sudden announcement that you've thought of the "best" way to let Roz know about David. I'm in this, too. I have a right to hear what you intend. You caught me at the office, off guard. Your call left me sputtering. Look, it doesn't have to be solved by the anniversary. Why do you say that? For your own comfort? You're too impulsive. Call me back, damn it.   Q

❏

Jeff,

Only David was with Jocelyn when she died. Please don't deny this. I am disappointed that you haven't been straight with me.

You don't need to answer me, but Roz deserves to learn the truth from you.

STERLING

❑

September 12, 1980

Dearest Sterling,

In less than a month, our darling family will be together. We can hardly wait. Thank you for orchestrating this magnificent event. Dad and I are like newlyweds since his retirement—exploring the days together, eating lunch out. Our spirits are dampened a bit, though, by the state of the Pittsburgh economy. Church bells toll throughout the city at noon in commemoration of the steel mills that have closed and the workers who are jobless. Pittsburgh is significantly changed. The great black sheds of Jones & Laughlin along the Monongahela River are abandoned now. The flames that leaped from their smokestacks at night are gone. The men with metal lunchboxes and heavy boots no longer march to the mills over the high, fenced crosswalks that span the parkway. I hope Reagan is elected. With interest rates over 20 percent, Carter has no platform.

It's not like me to be blue but the sense of emptiness is pervasive. The thrill of seeing our loved ones will be double this time.

God bless you,
Mother

❑

Sterling

You did not run across this information by accident and I resent it. I am closing this post office box. Stay out of my personal life.

Jeff

❑

October 2, 1980

Dear Mother and Dad,

See you in just a few days! I'm enclosing your list with YES or NO written by each name. You'll see that most of the people we invited are coming! I'm also enclosing the menu we chose for the smorgasbord. Tempt your taste buds.

Schedules are perfect. Jeff's still on strike and Quinn is prying herself away from the Superfund fiasco. You'll see all our shining little faces.

Love, love!
Sterling

❑

Sterling—

Roz won't return my phone calls—Dagmar says she doesn't want to. How dare you tell Roz without consulting me first? And right before the anniversary dinner, too, in the parking lot! What were you thinking of?

Thank God it was dark and the kids had gone inside. What did you say to her? You two walked away as I was locking the car. She was so instantly furious, her voice changed altogether. It was a weapon! A deep growling scream.

Look, I had to grab her—maybe too hard but she was choking you wasn't she? Shaking you, shouting in that deranged way, "How do you know? How do you know?" Scared me shitless.

Why couldn't you calm her down? You had to go on and tell her what I did, for Christ's sake! And then she's on me, beating my back, knocking the breath out of me. She slammed me into the pavement like a man would, with that amount of force. I have shreds of stockings in my knee wounds. I still have stones in my hands.

You know what made me sickest? Us following her into the ladies' room, cleaning up in there, none of us speaking, we were so full of spite. It was a conspiracy to the end, even though we couldn't stand the sight of each other in the mirrors—even though we avoided each other's eyes. We were afraid Mother would come in, afraid she would find out. We were determined to sit at dinner composed so she wouldn't know! It was ridiculous, banging in and out of stalls, taking off torn panty hose and throwing them away, using wet paper towels to stop bleeding. All that damned witless washing, combing, smoothing.

Did you see Mother grimace when we told her I had tripped and fallen? She

believed it. She smiled blindly at us through the meal and the dance, she is so
determined not to see any rift between her children. I hate it. I hate you.

QUINN

❑

Quinn,

All I said to Roz was that she should check whether Jeff was a stand-in for
David, that I had received some clues about it. I thought she would just listen
and nod. We had discussed it by mail and on the phone several times. I thought
we were still in dialogue. It wasn't a matter of "picking" the parking lot for the
conversation. It was the only minute we had her to ourselves, without a parent
or husband or child to overhear us. Frustrating as hell. When we do get
together, there's almost no chance for a quiet word. I am sorry! I don't hate you.

Sterling

❑

October 21, 1980

Dearest Sterling and Randy,

No anniversary party could have been more meaningful than ours. Thank
you for your generosity in inviting our many friends and for being here with our
grandchildren. Your months of preparation made this a splendid moment that
cannot fade. We will cherish it forever.

Love,
Mother and Dad

❑

Dear Rozzy,

I am grateful that Jeff called me. I would have realized, if I had used my
head, that David was the victim and not the perpetrator. I can see Jocelyn in my
mind's eye, luring him out there, climbing over the balcony rail, then pretending she had made a mistake and reaching out, smiling, for him to help her back
in. What trauma he must have endured while she tried to pull him with her—
mocking him by screaming for help—and when she jumped still holding his
hands. Her cruelty is inconceivable. I can see Jeff waking up to her cries,
knowing at once that David would be blamed, giving David money and sending
him down the fire stairs to telephone his parents in the confusion of the streets.
David's grief for Jeff during and after his trial must have been unmanageable
for the whole family, since they all knew the truth. I understand why Jeff felt

that breaking away from his people was the only option to end David's day-to-day suffering. I also understand why Jeff was reluctant to tell you until you really came to love David: he was afraid you would fear him. Jeff wept when he spoke of this. Jocelyn had figured out that attacking David was the most vicious thing she could do to Jeff.

I wish he had shared it with me long ago, but I also admit it is none of my business. I think that what I have always felt about you caused this situation to escalate: you are unnecessarily aloof. There are vast zones of separateness and solitude in you, much larger than they need to be. Quinn and I have felt left out of your life, from childhood. We long for you. We long to be more important to you than your inner realm.

Is it fair that you confided in me more than once about seeking Jeff's past and then did not tell me when David broke his silence? Obviously, you did not intend to relieve my concern. You learned David's secret and verified it with Jeff months ago.

I am to blame, in many ways, for the sorrow we have made but, just once, I would like to hear you say you are also to blame.

Sterling

❏

Dear Sterling,

I am to blame. And that is why I do not want to continue an active relationship with you and Quinn. We came away from our vacation in Florida with a false hope—that fully sharing our thoughts would make us emotionally intimate. But every person has a veil of privacy which should not be removed. Behind it we rest and grow, and design the fabric of our being. It is my source of energy.

You and Quinn have less regard for privacy than I do. Quinn's curiosity overrides her caution, and your need to control overrides yours. You both thrive, to a large extent, in the spheres of others. You find it difficult to accept boundaries. Perhaps this makes you more vital than I, but less serene.

We are personalities that cannot coexist in a reasonable balance. And so, aside from occasions when we must be together for ceremonial purposes, I do not want to see or speak to you and Quinn.

Roz

❏

November 16, 1980

Dearest Sterling,

We just found out none of you girls will be here for Christmas — that you have planned trips elsewhere. Dad and I agree we shouldn't expect to be with you every year. We've decided to stay at home and invite a few folks for Christmas Day dinner. I have to say it won't be the same without our children and grandchildren but we do understand.

Love,
Mother

❑

Scott,

It's not fair to keep you hanging on. I can't come back. I've learned something about myself. I believe I see things clearly but I actually don't. I believe I see myself clearly but I don't. It's like being color blind, I guess.

I am not competent to take care of other people.

Sterling

❑

Rozzy,

Quinn was here. She says she has apologized to you half a dozen times and you forgive her but you won't relent. She and I spent hours at the kitchen table and outside, talking. You are right. We three are incompatible. Husbands and wives can get divorced but blood relatives can't. Sometimes they should. Quinn and I have agreed to let distance come between us.

Out of the best of intentions, we manipulated each other's lives, you and I and Quinn. That can't be undone. Worse, we are likely to do it again. Quinn says not. She says how could we when we see what it brought, when we see how deception has hurt us. But I doubt we could keep the equilibrium that comes so easily to other families.

No one wants to tell Mother. The star in her crown is the harmony among her daughters. Plucking it out will be like plucking out her heart. I offer to be the one — but after Christmas. None of us will be visiting her and Dad — I can't see adding this to that.

Quinn says the three of us are probably better people for what we've been through. I say what does it matter since we won't be using our wisdom to touch each other.

Sterling

❏

December 30, 1980

Dearest Sterling,

What a wonderful Christmas—our three precious daughters arriving Christmas Eve to surprise us, bringing children and husbands and gifts! It was evident you surprised one another, too. You almost seemed disgruntled by the coincidence. But with the heavy snow, I was relieved no one tried for a motel.

It was a blessing we were too crowded to sleep. If we had, we would have missed the magic of sledding on the back hill in the glow from the house—first the kids, then Dad, then the rest of us, joining in one by one, sliding tentatively then jubilantly on flattened cardboard boxes and garbage can lids. To see you and Rosalind and Quinn whispering together, hugging each other, crying and laughing, as the snow sparkled around you, touched me profoundly. I will never be old as long as I can step back into that picture.

To Dad and me, this was the best year ever because of our daughters' steadfast devotion to each other. You are admirable adults who are raising your children in the priceless heritage of family love. It is fitting and right. You girls were always so close.

With abiding affection,
Mother

❏